SINCERELY YOURS

Trevor pulled Joanna toward him by her hand. She didn't resist but stepped closer as he bent to kiss her cheek. He let his lips linger against Joanna's skin. Suddenly he wanted to feel what it was like to hold her in his arms.

He rested his hand against the side of her waist. He meant to lift his mouth away from her face, but found himself brushing his lips closer to Joanna's mouth.

"Trevor," Joanna breathed, suddenly afraid.

But Trevor didn't want to give Joanna the time to change her mind now. He didn't think he'd ever have another chance to get this close to her. He held his mouth a hairsbreadth away above hers, then firmly pressed his lips against her soft mouth. To hell with the consequences.

Joanna forced herself to pull her mouth free. She kept her eyes closed but gently tried to push herself out of his arms.

"I'm not going to say I'm sorry about that," he said with a smile, slow and knowing.

Joanna opened her eyes and glanced at him. "I wasn't going to ask you to."

Sandra Kitt

Sincerely

ARABESQUE
BOOKS

BET Publications, LLC

ARABESQUE BOOKS are published by

BET Publications, LLC
c/o BET BOOKS
One BET Plaza
1900 W Place NE
Washington, D.C. 20018-1211

All Kensington titles, imprints, and distributed lines are available at special quantity discounts for bulk purchases for sales promotions, premiums, fund-raising, and educational or institutional use. Special book excerpts or customized printings can also be created to fit specific needs. For details, write or phone the office of the Kensington special sales manager: Kensington Publishing Corp., 850 Third Avenue, New York, NY 10022, attn: Special Sales Department.

ISBN: 0-7394-1588-3

Printed in the United States of America

*For all the girlfriends, especially Donna,
Sandy, Gwen and Susanne*

Prologue

For a long moment Joanna was mesmerized by the details of the box. It had a high sheen, and the sunlight reflected in long bright streaks on the curved lid. Cherry wood, she would guess. Expensive. The brass fittings were lit like yellow gold, ornate and heavy. It seemed a shame and a waste that such wonderful craftsmanship could not have been for the contents of a dowry, like a hope chest. That, at least, would have indicated a future; instead, the box held the remains of a recent past.

The scene seemed unnatural and poorly planned to Joanna. Though there was a profusion of bright flowers and wreaths, courtesy of a hothouse, all the surrounding trees were stripped bare of leaves. Her own breath vaporized quickly in the cold air. There was nearly six inches of snow in some places—but it was brilliantly sunny. How ironic. Joanna wondered if Sheila would have seen the humor in the circumstances. Sheila used to complain that her timing was bad, that everything about her life was out of sync, although she'd never gone into details. Today just proved it. It was so contradictory for someone of her hot, spirited nature and chaotic temperament to be put to rest on one of the coldest days of the winter.

It also seemed sacrilegious that during one of the most reverent moments of a person's life, that the press was on hand to make a mockery of the ceremony. It didn't matter that for the moment three or four tabloid reporters and a photographer stood at a discreet distance from the proceedings. Their intentions were still to intrude, still to pry out information about the life . . . and death . . . of Sheila James. It wasn't as if Sheila herself was so important or so well known—it was more that she was suspected to be connected to those who were.

Joanna shivered and huddled in her coat. This was ridiculous. She knew that Sheila had somehow gained the attention of several men in the city: politicians and businessmen but not one of them was in attendance. There was just a bunch of indifferent reporters looking to capitalize on the mere hint of scandal. Like . . . were any of these with her when she died?

Joanna tried to keep her attention on the wooden casket, to concentrate on the reverence of the moment. But she felt compelled to look up, to fix her eyes on the tall man standing nearly opposite her. The intensity of his regard seemed inappropriate.

Joanna was cold, but she tried to let the words being spoken drift back into her consciousness. She knew that they were meant to be sincere and comforting but, instead, seemed shallow and contrived. After all, what did the minister know about Sheila? What did *she* know about her? Not much. Except for the unexpected times Sheila would show up at her door, wanting to come in to sit and chat and laugh, as if they were old friends. As if they had something in common. Yet she had never been comfortable with her neighbor; there had always been excitement surrounding the dead woman. Wherever she went, things happened. Good or bad, Sheila had the ability to command attention, to get what she wanted.

As often as she and Sheila had talked—actually, Sheila talked and she listened—Joanna always felt the barrier between them. Their personalities and values were different. And she'd never envied the dead woman's lifestyle.

Ever since Sheila's body had been discovered on New Year's Day, Joanna had felt compelled to be in attendance at the services. She and Sheila were *not* really *friends* . . . but each had been a presence in the other's life. Thinking on it now, Joanna recalled all the times Sheila had tried to broaden their relationship by suggesting they go to the movies, or shopping, or out to dinner. Or asking when Joanna was going to get married. Joanna admitted Sheila had tried to be her friend. And now, she couldn't help wondering if maybe Sheila James *needed* her friendship.

Joanna listened to the minister and knew that this service was in keeping with the occasion, but would have preferred if the eulogy had been given by someone who could speak from personal knowledge. A quick glance around, however, told her that probably no one present would like the honor. That had surprised her almost as much as hearing of Sheila's death. For all of her name-dropping and high profile social life, there was almost no one in attendance to mourn. Conspicuously missing was any family.

It was such a small gathering, which to her seemed a sad commentary on the effect the deceased had had on others. There were just six people—herself and five men—to bid Sheila James a final farewell. Joanna couldn't believe that someone could have lived so long and yet, had touched so few . . .

Joanna recalled, uncomfortably, all the times she'd had uncharitable thoughts about Sheila James. Not mean and catty, but questioning. Her neighbor had been a woman whose existence seemed predicated on having a good time and not taking responsibility for her life. Now that it was, unfortunately, too late, Joanna was more than curious about what had happened between noon on New Year's Eve, and the afternoon of January 1 when Sheila James had been found dead.

As the minister read from rote and with a lack of feeling, Joanna let her gaze stray yet again to the man in the dark suit and trench coat standing to the left of and behind the clergyman. She couldn't help staring at him now, even though she'd been trying not to since arriving at the grave site. He seemed more interested in the mourners and in her than in the deceased. Joanna was glad of her dark glasses, worn against the winter wind and bright sunshine. She could sense his gaze on her throughout the eulogy and prayers. It was unexpected and odd, but she felt slightly breathless by his attention, more than self-conscious, as if the man was examining every facet of her persona. He didn't seem to be there, as some of the others may have been, out of morbid curiosity or false bereavement. Or from a sense of sorrow and responsibility, like herself. The man, with his thoughtful and alert expression, seemed to be in attendance as an observer . . . someone taking notes and gathering information. Like the reporters. Except, Joanna didn't think he was there looking for a story line. He didn't seem impatient, distracted, or embarrassed, but strangely resigned finality.

Joanna assessed the man. He had an athletic frame and erect bearing, a quiet alert way of standing. His face was comfortably handsome. She tried to guess who he was and what kind of background he was from, and how he might have known Sheila. Only one answer actually came to mind and it wasn't especially favorable. She could easily assume he was one of Sheila's former lovers. But why would *he* come to the funeral when so many others had not?

Joanna blinked with mortification when she found the man pointedly returning her steady appraisal. It was as if he were silently asking, *Who are you and what are you doing here?* Joanna didn't know why herself except that it seemed the right thing to do. Maybe deep inside she knew that for all of her former neighbor's gregarious and irreverent personality, for all her acquaintances and dates and hectic social life, Sheila was a lonely person without a grounded life. On the other hand, Sheila had never hurt anyone, as far as Joanna knew, and it seemed cruel and pointless that she would die as she had on New Year's Eve; all dressed up with no place to go.

Joanna's attention surreptitiously strayed again to the man. His probing dark gaze made Joanna feel an odd combination of emotions. Surprise, curiosity, indignation, and guilt. She quickly shifted her gaze to her watch to hide her confusion. This man was so unlike the suave and calculating men to whom she'd seen Sheila attracted.

Someone cleared their throat, distracting Joanna from her thoughts. The service had been unusually long, provided by some unknown benefactor, patron, or sympathizer who was determined that Sheila get a proper send-off. Joanna tried to determine which of the men around her might have put up the money, but she couldn't find a suitable answer. In any case, it was much too late for any answer to matter. Sheila James was beyond caring.

At the funeral home the day before Joanna had sat in the front row of visitors' seats and read the decorative ribbons, with their messages outlined in glitter, that were

attached to the floral arrangements. She'd been unable
to bring herself to look at Sheila laid out. It seemed too
voyeuristic. Linda, her colleague from work, had come
just as an excuse to be away from the office. She hadn't
known Sheila at all, except for the anecdotes Joanna
shared with her about her neighbor's adventures. Like
the time Sheila had crashed a party being held for a
visiting NFL team by the mayor, who was a rabid football fan. She had dated one of the players for almost
the entire season. Two attractive middle-aged men, one
of them white, had come into the viewing salon sepa-
rately, each standing quietly over the open casket before
quickly leaving again. Joanna had not been surprised
when Danny, the maintenance man from their apartment
building, had come. Mr. Tillman, their building landlord,
had been unexpected. He had already complained to the
police about wanting to rent Sheila's apartment as soon
as possible. Danny and Mr. Tillman had brought Mr.
Canin, who lived in the apartment under Sheila; he'd sat
consoling and patting Danny's arm as the young man
had cried openly, surprising everyone with the depths of
his grief. Everyone knew that Danny had been devoted
to Sheila James.

Another man in dark glasses, whom Joanna had not
recognized, had come in, hesitating at the door. He
peered into the open casket and left after only a few
minutes. There had also been Maggie, Sheila's hair-
stylist. And the man. *This* man. He'd stood at Sheila's
coffin longer than anyone, which had drawn Joanna's
attention. When he'd turned away, Linda had poked her
with an elbow and whispered, "Hmm . . ." in approval
of his masculine good looks. But Joanna had ignored
the comment, and the man, until now.

As if sensing the restlessness in the tiny gathering, the minister picked up his pace through the rest of the ceremony. Finally, it was over and time to lower the beautiful box into the earth. Joanna watched for a moment, wondering if there was something else she should do. The last funeral she had attended had been for her grandfather Jack. Then, she didn't have to do anything but grieve and remember how funny and kind Granddaddy Jack had been to her. There had been more than a hundred people at his service; friends, family and even those who disagreed with him but still respected him.

Joanna finally pulled a white rose from an arrangement displayed on an easel, and dropped it on top of the descending box. Then, tightening the scarf around her throat and putting her gloved hands into her pockets, she turned to walk back to her car.

She did not glance again at the intriguing stranger as he waited for the coffin to be lowered. And she didn't cooperate with the none too subtle attempts of the press photographer to get a good picture of her. One reporter quietly called out a question. Joanna ignored them all. She was glad to have this whole unfortunate episode over with so that life could go on. She half-expected him to say something or to follow her, but he didn't. Joanna, nonetheless, sensed that his gaze followed her as she climbed into the driver's seat of her car. She adjusted her dark glasses and let out a deep breath. She began to relax once the door was locked and she'd started the engine. She drove slowly, but was anxious to get back to the world that she knew.

Joanna glanced once in the rearview mirror, and she could see that the man stood alone at the site, watching her departure. As she gave her attention back to her driving, she tried to rid herself of a sudden anxiety.

She'd never known an awful lot about Sheila James, and it was still more than she wanted to know. She'd felt equally bewildered and exasperated by her neighbor. However, Joanna was sincerely sorry for what had happened to her and hoped that Sheila was now at peace.

Sheila's death was still being listed as suspicious, perhaps even a homicide. It made Joanna shiver just to think of her neighbor's helplessness in her last moments of life.

Her anxiety only grew as she thought of that man looking at her. Admittedly he didn't seem the killer type, and he certainly didn't look as if he'd wish Sheila any harm. But that wasn't saying much. The newspapers always said killers were often the people you least suspected. Always someone who seemed perfectly ordinary. But he didn't seem so ordinary, either. And Joanna didn't feel comfortable with his curiosity in *her.* She sighed deeply and turned on the heater.

Well, it didn't matter now, Joanna thought. She was now past the stately entrance of the cemetery and headed toward the main parkway. The surrealism of the past week was finally over. The man at the grave site had been left behind as well.

She would never have to see him again.

One

"Joanna, there's a phone call for you."

"I can't take it right now," Joanna called over her shoulder. Her gold loop earrings swung gently with the turn of her head. "Get a name and number and I'll call them back."

"Right," nodded the blond-haired woman in the doorway before disappearing.

Joanna gave her attention back to the task at hand. She pushed the "rewind" button on the tape deck and glanced at the wall clock. Ten minutes. The mechanism of the unit whizzed smoothly for about fifteen seconds, and then began a rapid clacking noise as the tape fibrillated against the deck heads. The machine suddenly stopped.

"Oh, no . . . not now," Joanna moaned beneath her breath.

For a moment she stood indecisive. She slid her fingers through her short fluffy hair and pressed her scalp as if trying to evoke a solution that would save her from imminent disaster. She pushed the "stop" button, even though the machine was dead silent. Then she pushed "fast forward," "stop," and once more "rewind." The tape started normally again.

"Thank you," she breathed fervently.

A tall skinny young man with a mop of curly light brown hair, dressed in jeans, sweat shirt and ratty running shoes, squeezed into the small sound room next to her. His arms were piled with tapes from the previous day's programs. He dropped them unceremoniously to the cluttered countertop, and six or seven cassettes slid from the pile to the chair and floor.

"I don't get paid enough for this," he said darkly, but without rancor.

"Robby, you have to clean the heads on this thing," Joanna admonished as the machine snapped to an abrupt stop. "It tried to eat my tape." She pushed "eject" and the tape slid out.

"Put it on the list," Robby shot back good-naturedly.

"I'm serious. If I get the clips to the set late, your head is going to roll right along with mine. I'll see to it." Joanna looked at him and decided to appeal to that part of his male ego that needed homage paid. "You're the professional whiz kid around here. You know about these things."

He chortled. "Nice try, Jo, but I'm only an intern. In other words, pond scum—the lowest form of life in the work chain."

Joanna grabbed up her keys, clipboard, and itinerary of the day's shows, and gave him an impatient stare. "Robby . . ." her tone warned softly.

"Okay, okay. I'll get to the heads."

The blonde appeared again in the doorway. "Five minutes, Jo."

Joanna turned to the woman, her ginger-tinted eyes widening in anxiety. "I've got close to seven minutes."

A quick grin spread across the other woman's face.

She pointed to the wall clock. "Wrong. It's slow." Then she was gone again.

Joanna shook her head in exasperation. "It's a wonder this place even functions."

The tape in her hand was suddenly forcibly removed and another thrust into its place. Joanna looked in bewilderment to her assistant. Robert Kincaid grinned and shrugged.

"I knew the deck was a little whacked out, so I copied your material when I got back from lunch. If you'd tried to play the other tape, it probably would have exploded."

Joanna hugged the tape to her chest and backed toward the door. She smiled at Robby in honest gratitude. "Thanks. You're a gem . . . and probably saved my life."

"Right," he drawled dryly. "Tell that to the boss so I can get a raise."

Joanna chuckled, the sound throaty and warm. "You're the boss's nephew. Maybe you can get *me* a raise." She headed out the door but made a graceful one-hundred-and-eighty-degree turn back to the room. "I hope I don't have to remind you not to leave those tapes all over the place. Some of them go back to the tape library. Okay?" She ended on a question to soften her directive.

Robby grunted.

Joanna started out quickly down the narrow corridor. Soon she was moving on the balls of her feet in a gentle run. Every time she was down to the wire for the start of a show, Joanna couldn't help but recall the female character in the movie *Broadcast News* who got the news tape to the control booth on time, by sliding on her knees under a hallway obstruction. The visual image always made Joanna smile. She'd never had to make such a spectacle of herself; the movie exaggerated, but the point was made. Everything at a TV station was managed by the clock. Not in hours, but in minutes and seconds.

Joanna had almost reached the short passageway to the control room when a hand reached out from a doorway and grabbed her arm. She turned to Linda McKenna, and shook her head.

"I can't talk now. I'm late. Catch me in an hour." She tried to move on. Linda's grip was firm.

"You have plenty of time. Four minutes, at least." Linda purposefully pulled Joanna into her office.

Joanna glanced at her watch. Linda was right. She could spare a moment. She sat on the edge of the extra chair. Linda sat at her desk where there were two phone units, one with two blinking red lights from calls on hold. She lifted the receiver and pressed one of the flashing buttons.

"Someone will be right with you," she said pleasantly and put the caller on hold once again. When the second phone began to ring, she answered promptly, "WDRK. Please hold." Another red light went on.

Joanna pursed her mouth and looked at her friend and colleague. Nothing ever hurried Linda, and she broke a sweat for no one. Joanna wondered if she herself was the only person at work who took time seriously and who lived in dread of forgetting or losing her watch.

"You know Stu hates to get the tapes at the last minute."

"I just want to know how things went yesterday," Linda asked as she casually fanned herself with a sheet of pink paper from her desk.

Joanna grimaced. "Oh. You mean with Sheila. You know how those things are. A little strange, a little sad."

"Was that guy there?"

"What guy?"

"The man at the funeral home. You know . . . the one I wanted to jump," Linda replied.

Joanna felt a sudden tension at the reminder of the stranger. She had a clear image of his steady gaze. Even now she wondered what he'd been thinking. "He was there. But he never said anything. No one talked to each other at the site. He was just another mourner."

Linda raised her brows. "I bet he was the cutest."

Joanna shook her head in amusement. She wouldn't have used the word *cute* herself. It somehow didn't seem descriptive enough. "There weren't that many people there."

"What's not many?"

"Only six."

"Embarrassing. I thought you said she was so popular and had all kinds of friends?"

Another line began to ring on the second phone. Joanna frowned. "Don't you think you'd better start taking some of those calls?"

Linda shrugged. "I'm not really here yet. I still have thirty-three minutes before I officially start. So, almost no one was there?"

"I don't think her popularity had anything to do with it. Maybe a lot of people couldn't come. Maybe they didn't want to be seen . . ." Joanna said, looking at her watch nervously. "I better get moving."

"Relax. We haven't missed a start yet."

"What do you mean, *we?* You have the best job here. All you have to do is talk on the phone all day. When you answer the phone, that is."

"Yeah, but to perfect strangers. Girl, you have no idea how hard it is to be nice for hours, talking people into coming on the program, convincing them to tell all the world their business, *and* make them do it for free."

Joanna laughed again. She'd always liked her co-worker's bubbly and irreverent personality. Linda took nothing very seriously, except herself. She had a pretty, round face that was animated and lively. Her hair was a profusion of braided extensions elaborately arranged. Her wardrobe was eccentric and eclectic as well, ranging from stylish suits and designer dresses to Kente cloth skirts and blouses, head wraps, and woven belts. She wore long noisy earrings with beads and coins attached, and had once come to work in harem pants, causing the posting of a polite but official dress code for the entire station staff. And she chewed gum as an alternative to smoking, she said. Better Chiclets than cookies, which would only go right to her hips.

"You could have found out who he was," she said reprovingly.

Joanna raised her brows and chuckled softly. "Sorry. I guess I wasn't thinking. Look, I have to go."

"Who's Trevor Jackson?" Linda interrupted with a puzzled expression.

Joanna's gaze went blank. "Who?"

Linda held up the pink page she'd been fanning herself with, which was from an office memo pad. She tilted her head and read, "Trevor Jackson. Time, 10:28 this morning. 'Would like to get together with you' . . ." Linda arched a brow suggestively. She recited a hotel phone number.

Joanna shrugged, dismissing the information and glancing anxiously at her watch. "I've never heard of him. Maybe he has an idea for a program or he wants to be on one."

"Nope. He wants you. The note is pretty clear if you ask me. Have you been holding out?" Linda asked lightly, her gaze narrowing. She held out the note to Joanna. "He's got a real nice voice. Deep and sexy."

Joanna chuckled as she shook her head and absently stuffed the paper into her pants pocket. She started heading toward the control room. "I don't know who this man is and I'm not interested in finding out."

Linda nodded. "Philip will be happy to hear that, but I think he's too sure of himself where you're concerned. He could use some competition."

Joanna chose not to respond to Linda's comment. It bothered Joanna to know someone was paying so much attention to her relationship with Philip Lee as to have an opinion.

"I'm not interested in trying to make Philip jealous."

"Mind if I call this Trevor back and pretend to be you?"

Joanna cut an amused glower at Linda and turned away. She could hear Linda's laughter behind her. She crossed the corridor and tapped quietly on the door of the control room. Without waiting for an answer, she pulled the door open and stepped inside. The name Trevor Jackson was instantly gone from her mind as a beefy fist reached out and snatched the tape from her.

"Where were you?" the producer asked as the tape was jammed into the VCR unit and fast-forwarded to the first segment.

"There's plenty of time," Joanna said calmly, now that the responsibility no longer rested on her shoulders.

She left the control room and headed toward Stage Set Number Four. She stepped over the fat cables taped or otherwise trailing on the floor. The three cameras were being checked and positioned by the crew, and already the newscaster and his coanchor were putting on mikes and fussing with their clothing and hair. Joanna stood between cameras two and three and followed the routine she'd been part of for nearly seven years, and which she'd grown to love. She watched with interest as the two reporters gathered their script and notes together, and bantered across the news desk with her.

Christopher Todd, the anchor, winked at her.

"Thanks for that bit of information on the civilian review board the police agreed to. How'd you get that, by the way?"

Joanna smiled and shrugged. "You know I can't reveal my sources, but it wasn't privileged information."

"Is it our breaking story?"

She shook her head. "Would you settle for a tie?"

"Absolutely. It keeps us in the running at least. Good work, Jo. We're going to have to give you reporting credit and put you in front of the camera one of these days," Christopher said, and then gave his attention to the coanchor. "I thought you knew people at police headquarters?" he asked.

Ann Marie Lopez only smiled charmingly, but Joanna could detect the shards of ice directed at her from the coanchor's beautiful hazel eyes.

"Okay, one minute," the director called out. He adjusted his headphones and checked the precise time on the studio clock. Except for the bright lights focused on the set and the two reporters, the studio was dark.

"Psssst. Jo!"

Joanna turned around at the urgent whisper and saw one of the assistants from Public Affairs beckoning to her. "What is it?"

The young man handed her two more pink pages, just like the one Linda had given her. "You're very popular today. Someone has been working overtime to reach you."

"Let me see . . ." Joanna said as she took the messages. She frowned when she saw the name Trevor Jackson again. Twelve-fifteen and three forty-seven were the posted times.

"Also, security is holding on the phone," he said.

There was a slight clearing of a throat and Joanna looked up guiltily as the director signaled for silence.

The assistant dropped his tone. "There's someone waiting for you."

"Where's he from? Oh . . . you know, I'm waiting for some materials from the mayor's press office."

"Someone named Jackson," he finished.

Joanna became alert. For just a moment a frisson of apprehension trickled through her body. Maybe I'm just overreacting, she thought. It wasn't as if she was being stalked, after all. This Trevor person had openly left messages in an attempt to reach her. That was no secret. The only major question was why? How did he get her name and phone number?

"Did he say what he wanted?"

"I don't know. Want me to check it out?"

Joanna shook her head. She didn't want to start asking questions and appearing too interested. "No . . . no. But do me a favor. Tell him I'm out of the building doing research . . . and you don't expect me back this afternoon."

"Quiet!" the director hissed. Joanna and the assistant grimaced as he tapped his watch. "Fifteen seconds," he warned softly, giving his attention back to the set. The assistant started to leave.

"Wait a minute," Joanna said in a low voice. "What does this man look like?"

"Got me. I just answered the call from security. Still want me to put him off?"

"Yes, thanks," she nodded absently.

Joanna's frown deepened. She couldn't begin to think who Trevor Jackson was. Had she met him at a professional gathering? At one of the screenings of new films she was often invited to? Was he looking for a job, perhaps recommended by a friend or colleague? Was he a station groupie . . . or some maniac? Joanna was startled out of her considerations at the sound of the director's voice.

"Okay, time. Five . . . four . . . three . . . two . . . one."

"Good evening, I'm Christopher Todd."

"And I'm Ann Marie Lopez. This is the five o'clock evening news."

With her leather tote bag slung on one shoulder and her arms laden with a heavy brown grocery bag, Joanna felt unwieldy and awkward as she left the parking lot. As she pushed through the side door into the lobby of her apartment building, the sudden heat of the hall stung her skin. It was in direct contrast to the below-freezing temperatures outside in this, the end of the first week of January. Joanna sighed in relief and tried to let her body relax. She had managed to elude the persistent and mysterious Trevor Jackson. It was also the first time in a week and a half that there wasn't a reporter with mini-cam and mike, or just curious strangers, trying to question her about Sheila James, her next-door neighbor. Or rather, her *late* next-door neighbor.

Joanna debated stopping to get her mail, but deciding it would only be bills and magazines, she walked on into the center foyer and rang for the elevator. Her mind shifted as she waited, flitting between the phone messages from Trevor Jackson, the research she'd been asked to do by Christopher Todd for a special program on alternative adoptions, to how late a night it would be if she and Philip still went out as planned for dinner. She sighed and shifted her groceries from one arm to the other. So engrossed was she that when the elevator door finally opened and she found a man staring back at her, she gasped. Then she checked herself and chuckled in embarrassment.

"Good gracious, Danny. You nearly scared me to death."

The husky young man looked contrite. He was wearing a heavy down ski jacket and a knit hat. Despite the wet and frozen January weather, he was wearing the same sneakers he wore in the summer. He clutched a shovel in one hand and a pail with a mop protruding from it in the other.

"Sorry, Miz Mitchell."

"Don't worry about it. I just wasn't expecting to meet anyone. Still working?"

They somehow rotated around one another until Joanna stood in the elevator poised to push the fourth floor button and Danny stood outside in the lobby.

"I gotta move the ice off the sidewalk. Mr. Tillman, he don't want no accident. Someone might sue."

"Nice of Mr. Tillman to worry about his tenants'

safety," Joanna murmured sarcastically. She pushed the "door open" button as the maintenance man continued.

"And I gotta mop the lobby. Mr. Tillman—"

"I know. He doesn't want anyone to fall and break a leg."

Danny nodded. Then he blinked. "Ah . . ." His voice was eager and pleased. "I fixed your intercom bell."

Joanna grinned. "Thank you, Danny. I appreciate that." She noticed his inadequately shod feet and frowned at him. "I thought you were going to get some boots. You can't work outdoors all winter in sneakers."

Danny shifted nervously and shrugged. "I don't have any money."

"None? What happened to the Christmas money the tenants gave you?"

Danny shook his head. "It's gone."

"Oh," Joanna said softly, even though she was surprised. Danny could have easily collected close to five hundred dollars. "Did you lose it? Or did someone take it from you?" she ventured, but she could see by his restlessness that he wasn't going to give her a full answer.

"It's gone," he repeated. "I spent it on . . . on stuff."

"All right," Joanna said calmly. "It's not important now. But when you get paid again you get yourself some real boots, okay?"

Danny nodded. "Sure."

Joanna released the button. "Good night, Danny."

The door closed between them, cutting off Danny's mumbled response.

As had been happening since Sheila James was taken away in a body bag, Joanna felt awkward walking past her former neighbor's door. The yellow police ribbon with *crime scene: do not cross* printed on it, originally taped horizontally across the entrance in three places, was now gone. But in its place was a white paper with more official police information. It was glued to the crevice between the door and the door frame. Its message, much to the chagrin of Mr. Tillman, was the same—keep out.

Joanna began to feel much better and safer once she was inside her apartment. After flipping on the light in the hallway, she turned into the kitchen and placed the grocery bag on the counter. She hung up her coat and hat in the hall closet, and left her wet boots on the door-mat.

From the dark of her living room, a tiny red light was flashing rapidly, indicating multiple messages on the answering machine. Joanna walked to the phone but instead of listening to the calls, she lifted the receiver and quickly dialed a number.

"Hi, Preston. I just got home. Is everything okay?" Joanna smiled. "Of course I didn't forget. I'll be down in a minute. See you soon."

She hung up and was about to turn away when she remembered the messages and pushed the playback switch. While she waited, Joanna turned on another lamp and used her toes to search for her slippers under the edge of the sofa.

Beep. "Babe, it's me. Listen, I don't want to go to The Interlude for dinner. The service was terrible the last time we went. I heard of a new place called The Pavilion. The staff of *Preview* magazine hangs out there. I'll pick you up at eight."

Joanna looked at her watch. It was 7:10.

Beep. "Ahhh . . . this is Detective Schultz from the

three O, Miss Mitchell. If you don't mind, I have a few more questions I'd like to ask you. Just some minor details. If you could please call me at the precinct tomorrow, I'd appreciate it. Thanks."

Beep. "This is Angela Lucci at the *Herald*. I'm working on an article about the sudden increase in murders in this area of young single black career women. I would like to interview you. I'll be in my office late. My number is . . ."

Joanna grimaced in distaste. She wasn't sure she'd consider Sheila James a career woman exactly. She pushed her hands into the pockets of her slacks. She encountered a crumbled piece of paper.

Beep. "This is Trevor Jackson . . ." There was a long pause. "Okay, maybe you really aren't home, but I'd like to get together with you. It's about Sheila."

Joanna's stomach lurched. My God, how did he get my home number, she thought, trying not to get upset. The next message was almost over before Joanna realized she'd missed most of it. She replayed it.

"Jo, it's me again. I think I'm going to be a little late. Probably closer to 9:30. Bye."

Beep. The next two callers had hung up without leaving any message. Was that him, too? Was he going to keep trying to reach her the rest of the night? Or had he given up? The last call, and the third from Philip, was anticlimactic.

"I'm sorry, Jo. Can't make it after all. Something's going on at the mayor's office and I'm going over there to find out what. I'll call you tomorrow."

Joanna reset the machine. She stood slightly dazed, in the middle of her living room. She was sorry Philip couldn't keep their date. At least then she wouldn't have been alone. Not that she was suddenly afraid to be by herself, but . . . there was something creepy about someone out there knowing how to find her without her having a clue as to who he was or what he wanted. "It's about Sheila" just didn't cut it, especially since she was dead.

And, Joanna thought as she recovered from the surprise of the calls, she really didn't want to speak to the police anymore about Sheila. There was, however, an urge to call Detective Schultz and tell him about this man who had been pursuing her all day to talk about the dead woman. Well, maybe he wasn't really such a surprise, Joanna considered as she smoothed out the first message she'd gotten from Linda, with Trevor Jackson's hotel and phone number written on it. Sheila had had a slew of male friends although most of them had been covert visitors who preferred anonymity. She hadn't had any female friends, as far as Joanna knew. So, did that mean that Trevor Jackson was a different kind of acquaintance?

Joanna retrieved a video cassette from the top of the grocery bag and left her apartment. She moved quickly past Sheila's locked door, finding the silence from beyond it eery and chilling. It still seemed odd to Joanna that she wouldn't be seeing her neighbor again, with her glamorous allure and seductive smile. With her often open attempt to bridge the differences between them to be girlfriends. As she walked the one flight down to Preston Canin's apartment, Joanna tried to dispel her sense of remorse, as if she had in some way failed Sheila.

"That tape could have waited until tomorrow," Preston said peevishly as he pushed the door closed behind Joanna.

"I'll probably be late tomorrow as well," she said,

standing aside so that Preston could wheel himself into
the living room.

"I figured maybe Philip called and talked you into
going to one of his story things," Preston said, coming
to a stop and turning to face her.

Joanna handed him the tape. "Yes to the first. No to
the second. But I have been running late all day. The
video store promised they'd hold a copy of Patriot
Games for you when it comes in."

"You don't have to do this, you know. I can put up
with that woman from the companion service."

Joanna grimaced at her elderly neighbor. "You don't
like the woman from the home care service. You said
she talks too much and she goes through your closets
and things. You know me, and I'm a lot closer to home."

Preston snorted. "So that's it. I'm just a convenience."

Joanna laughed at him. "Feeling your oats tonight.
Why are you so cantankerous?"

Preston muttered something unintelligible and peered
at her through his glasses. "Getting old is humiliating,
but I can cook my own food and get my own medicine
and still dress myself. What do those damn idiots at the
hospital think I'm going to do? Commit suicide by turning my wheelchair over?"

Joanna sat on the edge of the sofa and raised her
brows at her friend. She didn't comment on the uneven
buttoning of his plaid shirt, visible under the tan cardi-
gan, or the fact that his sparse white hair was uncombed
and standing mostly straight up. She reached out and
put her hand over his. The back of his pale flaccid skin
was covered with liver spots and wiry white hairs. "You
mean you don't want me to come and see you anymore?

Are you bored? Do you have a girlfriend you're hiding from me?" Joanna asked, innocently.

Preston slanted her a crooked glare. He guffawed in a raspy chuckle. "Don't you try that sweet talk on me, young lady. I know reverse psychology when I hear it."

"So. Just feeling sorry for yourself and suffering from cabin fever. Tell you what. If some of the snow melts by Saturday, we'll go down to the courtyard for an hour or so."

Preston pooh-poohed that suggestion. "You'll probably get a better offer before then, you know. What about that guy, what's his name? Trevor something or other."

Joanna blinked rapidly at Preston. She sat back on the sofa, her hands clasped together tightly. "Trevor . . . Jackson?"

"That's him."

"How do you know Trevor Jackson?"

"I met him. He came looking for you this morning while I waited downstairs for the van to pick me up for physical therapy. Do you know that damned fool driver drove too fast and nearly—"

"He was here?"

Preston looked blank. "Who?"

"Trevor Jackson," Joanna enunciated slowly and patiently.

"That's what I said. In the courtyard. Nice man. He knew Sheila. He kept me company, and we had a nice talk until the van came. I had to wait almost twenty—"

"Well, what did he say about Sheila?" Joanna interjected.

Preston scratched his ear and frowned. "Oh . . . that he couldn't understand why anyone would want to kill her. Asked if I knew anything. I couldn't tell him," Preston said, shaking his head in agitation. Then he looked at Joanna. "But don't worry. He'll tell you himself."

Her stomach somersaulted. "What . . . what do you mean?"

"I told him to call you, talk to you. Told him you were a friend of Sheila's, too."

"But I wasn't, Preston. I—"

"He said he'd been trying to get in touch with you but didn't have your number."

Joanna closed her eyes briefly and sighed. "So you gave it to him," she guessed in a monotone.

"Of course I did," Preston confirmed, annoyed. "How else could he reach you?"

"Preston, I haven't the vaguest idea who Trevor Jackson is."

"But I just told you who he is," Preston said, defending himself.

"Why do you believe him? I mean, why is he showing up now? How did he know about Sheila? How do you know he wasn't responsible for her death? How do you know he wasn't just feeling you out to see what *you* knew about the investigation?"

Preston waved the questions aside. "Because he didn't ask a lot of questions about Sheila. Except, you know, about the day she died. He wanted to know about *you.*"

Joanna was again taken aback and stared blankly at the older man. "Me? But, why?"

He smiled at her. "He's a good-looking black man. You're a good-looking black woman. Seems clear to me."

"I don't even know who he is," Joanna said in exasperation.

"Then you have to meet this Trevor and find out for

yourself. He'll tell you," he cackled in glee, and then winked at her.

"I don't think I'm interested in what this man has to say."

"How do you know until he's said it?"

Joanna sighed patiently, shaking her head. "Sometimes, it's very frustrating talking to you."

"Only 'cause I'll say things you don't want to hear. You work in the news business. How come you're not curious?"

"Cataloging tapes and cassettes is *not* quite the same thing as being a reporter."

"Well, you could do that, too. You'd be just as good— better even—as the other women I see every night."

Joanna stood up. "No, I wouldn't."

Preston made an impatient sound. "You don't give yourself nearly enough credit, Jo. You need to stand up for yourself. Don't be so quiet. It's a good thing you have me to keep my one good eye on you." He cackled again.

She smiled fondly at the older man. "You're right. It's a good thing."

Joanna found herself shifting gears from believing Trevor Jackson was potentially dangerous to having a growing curiosity about what he really wanted. She admitted to herself that Preston was right.

"Why don't I set up the VCR for you so you can watch this movie sometime tonight." Joanna walked to the TV. "Sorry there's no popcorn," she quipped.

"Got any beer?" Preston asked, wheeling himself into place in front of the set.

Joanna turned to face him. "I'm not going to contribute to your delinquency when you know you have to stay away from that stuff."

"I'd rather die happy than healthy," Preston said disagreeably as she handed him the remote for the VCR and TV.

"Well, you'll have to be happy with a glass of diet ginger ale. How's that?"

"I'll take it."

Joanna went into the kitchen to fill a glass with ice and to pour the soda. She added a plate of cookies to the tray she prepared. "Sorry I didn't pick up your mail. Hope you weren't looking for that check from Publishers Clearing House," she teased. But there was no response.

When Joanna returned to the living room, she found Preston Canin sitting still with his head slightly bowed. Joanna put the tray on the coffee table next to him and gently shook his bony shoulder.

"Preston? Are you okay?"

Preston suddenly looked up at her, his pale blue eyes watery and oddly blank. "Sheila always brings me the mail," he said absently. "Awfully quiet upstairs. Haven't seen her lately. Suppose she's away or something? She should have told me . . . made some other arrangement."

Joanna gnawed on her lip and bent close to the old man. She touched Preston's arm to get his attention. "Sheila's no longer here, Preston. She's dead. Don't you remember?"

He still looked confused and unfocused. Then he squinted and frowned sadly. He sighed and shook his head. "Too bad. Strange woman, but I liked her. She made me laugh." As if to prove his point, Preston chuckled quietly to himself as if remembering some long-ago incident or visit with his former upstairs neighbor.

Joanna patted his arm. She got up and looked for her apartment keys. "I have to go. I'll pick up the tape in the morning on my way out."

"It wasn't supposed to happen, you know," Preston murmured.

"What wasn't?" Joanna asked absently.

"Sheila dying."

"I know. But I'm sure the police will figure it out."

Preston shook his head. "Naw, they're not going to find nothing. They think they're looking for a killer."

Joanna frowned at the older man. "That's right, they are."

"They'll never find him," Preston said with finality.

"I hope they do. I'll feel a lot safer. If you're all settled for the night, I'm going upstairs."

"Wait a minute. Have something for you." He shifted to the side in order to get his gnarled hand into the pocket of his sweater. He extracted something and handed it to her. "Didn't think I'd forget, did you?"

Joanna smiled as she accepted the two amber-wrapped ovals of butterscotch candy. "Thanks. I'll see you tomorrow morning . . ."

Preston waved grandly as Joanna left his apartment. She pressed for the elevator, musing over Preston's comments about the police investigation. To the detectives at the precinct, it was an open-and-shut case. They had already pegged Sheila James's means of support as shady. Joanna didn't know if they were right or not, although it made sense that one of her many male friends was probably the culprit. Preston Canin, however, had been spouting cockeyed theories that were less than realistic.

The day that the body had been found Preston had told Joanna it had all been a mistake. Then he had said he had known something terrible was going to happen. On the other hand, it was clear to Joanna that, like tonight, Preston frequently forgot that his neighbor had been dead more than a week. When questioned by the police, Preston had rambled nonsensically until the detectives had dismissed him as not having any worthwhile information.

As she waited for the elevator, Joanna recalled a rumor that Sheila's apartment had not appeared to have been ransacked or vandalized, although it was hard to tell if anything was missing. She wondered what Mr. Tillman was going to do with Sheila's belongings once the police removed the access notification from the apartment door.

Joanna decided suddenly that Trevor Jackson was just another reporter looking for a story angle. She remembered, with some annoyance, how Philip had given her the third degree, hoping that some information she had about Sheila James would have given him a head start on all the other stories on the air that night. Joanna had been torn between Philip's lack of sensitivity and the knowledge that the first death in the new year was newsworthy. She also recalled that when she'd first introduced Philip to Sheila he'd seemed uncomfortable around her. But that hadn't stopped Sheila from flirting.

Joanna shook her head and gently yawned as she boarded the elevator. She was thinking it was just as well that she and Philip weren't going out for the evening. It would be nice to just wrap herself in a robe and curl up with a glass of wine and the TV before going to bed. But, Joanna also silently argued, it might have been even nicer if Philip hadn't accepted the late assignment at all. She knew he didn't have to. But she'd learned over the past three years of their relationship that Philip was a real newshound. He might protest the indignities of chasing police officials for statements or interviewing senior citizens scammed out of their life savings, but as a reporter he seemed addicted to human tragedy, compelled to follow sirens, street altercations, courtroom dramas, and people of questionable reputations. That was all fine—as a reporter, Joanna reasoned. She just wished that Philip would sometimes put their relationship first.

The elevator came to a soft stop, and Joanna exited. She turned the corner and pulled up short, her heart lurching suddenly as she saw a man crouched in front of her apartment door.

Trevor Jackson stood across from 311 and stared at the six-story apartment complex. Not five minutes earlier, he'd watched as Joanna Mitchell had arrived home from work. But strangely, after having observed her, he was reluctant to take her by surprise. Trevor was sure now that that approach would not go over big with her. He could see that in her demeanor, which was casual but guarded.

This was enough to make Trevor stay where he was, even though he was becoming damned cold. He'd hoped, of course, that Joanna Mitchell would simply return his calls if he'd left enough messages. Obviously not. But she was careful. He'd probably only annoyed her. It was obvious that she could care less about who he was. He tried to remind himself that if he was in Joanna Mitchell's place, he'd hold himself suspect, too. Trevor knew he'd have to think of something else, a different approach so that she wouldn't shut down and refuse to answer questions. He didn't have any time to waste. And he had few other options.

Trevor then noticed a young man come out the side door of the building. He watched the man walk to the front and, using a snow shovel, begin clearing a wider path through the packed snow. Trevor crossed the street slowly, readjusting his gait and already thinking how he was going to convince the janitor to let him in.

"Excuse me . . ."

The man glanced at him suspiciously and stopped his shoveling. He didn't turn around fully but looked furtively over his shoulder.

"Yeah?"

"Can you tell me if Miss Mitchell has come home yet?"

"Miz Mitchell?"

"Yes. In apartment 4A," Trevor said with as much familiarity as he thought was needed to convince the other man. But he could see caution in the man's gray eyes. "I just missed her at the station where she works, and Preston Canin told me this morning that she's usually home by six." Trevor watched as the man straightened and faced him.

"How come you want to see her?"

Trevor quickly assessed the man, judging him to be in his late twenties. He was strongly built, as if he pumped iron. Trevor held out his hand to him.

"My name is Trevor Jackson."

The man shook it briefly. "I'm Danny. You from the police?"

Trevor pursed his mouth. "No, I'm not."

"How come you want to see Miz Mitchell?"

"I'm a friend of hers," he said easily.

Danny considered him suspiciously. "I never seen you before."

"I've never been here before," Trevor said smoothly. "I'm from out of town."

"Miz Mitchell, she already got a boyfriend. His name is Philip."

Trevor grinned. "I know," he lied. "But I'm just a *friend*. If she's home, I just want to run up and say hello. I'm only going to be in Philadelphia a short time." Trevor gestured toward the entrance. "Is it okay?" he asked with deference.

Danny postured a bit with the authority Trevor had just given him. "Sure, sure. You go ahead."

"Thanks, I appreciate your help," Trevor said, about to walk away.

"She's a nice woman. She never complains to Mr. Tillman when I don't do something. And she doesn't get mad at me."

Trevor took a moment to reconsider the man. He found someone simple and uncomplicated, and of limited scope. He thought about what Danny might or might not know about the tenants of the building.

"Miss Mitchell said there was a recent accident in one of the apartments. Someone died?" Trevor asked with a frown and a slight inflection of horror in his voice.

Absently, Danny used the shovel to chop up and down into a three-inch slab of solid ice at his feet. "Yeah, that's right," he mumbled. He glanced furtively at Trevor. "Nobody heard anything."

"Who was it?" Trevor asked, interested.

Danny gnawed on his lip. "Miz James. She let me call her Sheila."

"That's too bad," Trevor murmured. "So, you were her friend. Did she have a lot of friends?"

"Yeah, I guess so."

"How about a boyfriend?"

"I don't know," Danny shrugged.

Trevor wanted to ask another question but decided to let it go. "Well, thanks again, Danny. Stay warm."

Trevor entered the building and took the staircase to the fourth floor, knowing that it would take less time than the elevator and that he was less likely to encounter one of the other tenants. His observations of the building occupants earlier that morning had indicated an interesting mix of senior citizens, and working men and women on their way to jobs. He hadn't noticed any children but thought that by 9:30 they could already have been in school. He'd also noticed that there were few black tenants, which would certainly make someone like him stand out—especially at night. The neighborhood seemed quiet and entirely residential. A stranger would certainly be noticed.

When he reached the fourth floor, he hesitated for the second time since he'd made the decision to seek out Joanna Mitchell. In fact, at the moment Trevor couldn't even think what he thought he would actually accomplish coming to Philadelphia at all. He was too late to be of any good to Sheila. And she certainly could no longer help him. At least not directly. He glanced around the hallway at the apartment doors.

Four B. This was it. Her apartment.

The sticker on the door made it clear that the police weren't ready yet to let anyone have access to the apartment, but he couldn't help but test the doorknob. He just wanted to be sure.

He walked to the next door and read the name plaque. *J. Mitchell.* He rang the buzzer on apartment 4A and then listened closely for any movement inside, just in case Joanna Mitchell was not answering the door like she wouldn't answer the phone. But it was perfectly quiet. He frowned. She had to be home. He'd seen her come into the building. Nonetheless, there was still no answer when Trevor rang the bell a second time.

It was then that he heard a lock clack open in a door several apartments away. A door opened and a middle-aged woman stepped into the hall dressed in a robe, moccasins, and blue plastic rollers in her dyed blond hair. She gasped in surprise and her eyes grew round.

"Oh!" she said on a high note.

Trevor adjusted quickly and immediately smiled at her. "Sorry if I scared you."

She clutched her bundled newspapers. "I . . . I wasn't expecting to see anyone . . ." Her voice trailed off.

He read the drift of her thoughts and spoke in a low calm voice. "I know. I was hoping Joanna, your neighbor, was home from work by now." The woman visibly relaxed at his familiarity but frowned, the color filling out her pale cheeks.

"Why, she should be home. It's late. I'm sure she'll be along any moment. She's such a lovely young woman," the lady volunteered before walking to deposit her papers in the correct recycling bin near the fire exit. She returned to her door. "Shall I tell her that you came by, Mr. . . . ?"

"Maybe I could just leave a note." Trevor searched for a pen.

"Here. Use this," the woman said helpfully, reaching inside her door and then handing him a small white notepad. He tore off a sheet and gave her back the pad.

"Thanks. I'm Trevor Jackson."

"I'm Mrs. Thatcher." The woman, now reassured, looked upon Trevor with a sly smile. "Are you a boyfriend?" she asked conspiratorially.

Trevor shrugged. "Let's just say I'm interested. We'll see."

"I'll be sure to tell her I saw you. Good night."

When she'd again locked her door, Trevor himself thought that maybe it was time to give up the ghost. At least for the night. He crouched on bended knee to write out the note. He heard the elevator come to a stop and quickly sensed someone behind him. Glancing over his shoulder, he saw Joanna Mitchell.

Her surprise was much greater than his. After all, he'd been trying to catch up to her the whole day. For the merest second her expression was blank, as if she had possibly gotten off on the wrong floor. Her eyes, a light translucent brown, widened in confusion. Trevor even saw her breathing increase, her chest rising and falling under the rust-colored crew neck tunic sweater. It was worn over beige slacks that indicated a slender build, and belted at her narrow waist. Her gold loop earrings caught the light from the hall light as they danced with her movements. Her hair was very short at the nape, and then longer and curlier on top. Her milk chocolate face was oval, and she had a pert nose. The overhead light gave her shine spots on her forehead and chin. Those little details made her seem not so sophisticated, and the realization caught him off guard again.

Trevor saw her expression become cautious and then vaguely annoyed. Even as he silently watched her, his earlier impression about her was confirmed. Joanna Mitchell was a guarded woman. And, he noted, very attractive.

Joanna decided she wasn't going to scream. It was too undignified and wouldn't necessarily bring any help. But she was poised to turn and run. She was literally in a pivoting position when the man stood quickly to his full height and put out a hand in supplication to stop her.

"Wait. Don't run. I was just leaving you a note."

Joanna stopped in surprise at the nonthreatening plea in his voice. She turned back to him, curiosity getting the better of her, but she kept a hand on the wall as if it somehow offered protection. She couldn't see his face fully. It was shadowed and dark, hidden under the beak of his sports cap. He stood still, with his arms and hands out, so that she could see he held nothing more dangerous than a pen and a folded piece of paper.

"I was just going to slip this under the door." He held the folded note out to her but she made no move to take it.

Joanna found her voice. "Let me guess. Trevor Jackson."

"That's right. You're a hard lady to catch," he said lightly, but watched her closely, trying to decide the best approach in gaining her confidence.

Joanna began to relax. Somehow seeing him in the flesh ruined her image of a mysterious man skulking around in the dark trying to accost her. He seemed far less menacing than his many phone calls implied he might be.

"What do you want with me?"

"I just want to talk. Didn't Mr. Canin tell you?"

Joanna pursed her lips. How clever of him to use Preston. But that wasn't enough, given the anxiety she'd been put through all day, wondering who he was and what he was about.

"How did you get into the building?"

Trevor slowly lowered his arms, putting the paper and pen into the pocket of his navy blue anorak. He grinned. "Danny."

"Danny?" she said, astounded. "He knows better. Especially at night. What lie did you tell him?"

"No lie. I said that I'd been trying to reach you all day, that I just wanted to say hello." Trevor shrugged when she remained unconvinced. "I also told him I was an old friend."

"Is that the line you gave Preston to get him to give you my phone number?"

Trevor put his hands into the hugh pockets of his coat and braced his legs slightly apart. *Be careful,* he thought. Joanna Mitchell wasn't naive, either. "No, it wasn't. As a matter of fact, I never asked him for your number. Mr. Canin offered to give it to me . . ."

"After you convinced him that you knew me."

"After I convinced him that I just wanted to talk. What's wrong with that? He trusted me."

Trevor pulled his hand out of the pocket and slowly held up something for her to see. Joanna looked closely. It was a butterscotch candy. Preston only gave them to certain people he liked. And trusted.

"I don't know anything about Sheila. We weren't really friends. I almost never saw her. That's all I have to say," Joanna recited.

He was quiet for a moment, and Joanna knew he was staring at her thoughtfully. "I just had a few questions . . ."

"You're blocking my door," Joanna said with some annoyance.

He shook his head, as if in irony, and stepped to the side. He used a hand to wave her past. "Go ahead. But it would be really stupid to leave my name, hotel, and phone number with so many people if I was planning to hurt you. Right?"

Joanna moved swiftly to the door and fumbled with the key in the lock. She was aware of him standing almost next to her. He was tall. "I don't believe you want to hurt me. But someone killed Sheila. Someone who knew her."

"It wasn't me."

"I don't know that," she said. "I don't know who you are."

"This could have been so easy if you'd answered my calls earlier today. What kind of research did you do this afternoon?"

Joanna's attention was caught by the question. She glanced briefly at him. "I don't know what you mean."

Trevor Jackson chuckled. "I thought so. You were lying. At the station this afternoon the security guard told me you were out of the building doing research."

She got the door open and slipped quickly inside. She turned and faced Trevor. "Maybe you should have taken the hint."

His voice grew urgent as she began to close the door on him. He pulled off the cap. "Hey. You could at least hear me out."

Joanna shook her head, ready to brush aside his argument, when she looked more closely at him in recognition. She stared openly and blinked, her gaze scanning over him rapidly. He was dressed very casually now in heavy boots, which made him even taller, a tan muffler wound rakishly around his neck. His hair was closely cropped. His hands, lightly holding the cap, were large, sinewy, and clean.

Trevor saw the recognition in her eyes and nodded. "Remember me now? I was at the cemetery site. And the funeral home."

Joanna began to feel a bit calmer. She remembered thinking how serious he'd looked that morning of the burial, and how he'd kept staring at her. "Why didn't you say so before," she frowned.

The corner of his mouth quirked up attractively. "I was pretty sure that wouldn't do much for my cause. There were some interesting people at the service, wouldn't you say? Would you trust any of them?"

Joanna couldn't help but appreciate his observation, but she wouldn't let her amusement show. "Are you including yourself?"

"For now, if I have to. But I plan on changing that, if you give me a chance. Why were you there?"

Joanna held onto the door but made no movement to close it or to open it wider. "I . . . I didn't want her to be alone," she found herself saying. It seemed an odd reason, even to her own ears.

"That's what I thought," Trevor nodded. "When I first saw you, you looked like the only person there who might have gotten to really know Sheila."

She raised her brows. "How could you tell? There were only half a dozen people there."

"Yeah, and they were all men," he responded dryly. "I think they knew Sheila in a different way."

She looked at him more carefully. She should have remembered the square face with its prominent jaw line. She recalled thinking, when she'd first seen him, what a strong masculine face he had. His eyes were dark, his skin the color of pecans. His nose was aquiline, and flared at the nostrils. But his mouth was the most noticeable feature. It was wide, and the lower lip was full and beautifully shaped. There was an attractive indentation beneath it.

He didn't shift or move nervously about. He merely waited, giving her all the control. Joanna felt ambivalent. All day long her imagination had filled in the gaps of information about Trevor Jackson and, even now that he'd found her and they faced one another, she still felt vaguely dissatisfied. When she only continued to stare indecisively at him, as if trying to make up her mind, Trevor took a small cautious step forward.

"I still want to talk with you," he said easily, sensing she was on the brink of giving in. Trevor kept his patience, and his easygoing demeanor. He gave her a brief smile, his teeth white and even in his face. "Since you say you know nothing, it shouldn't take very long. But I think you know more than you think you do."

Joanna arched a brow. "That's not for you to say."

"Then give me a chance to find out. All I ask is a little of your time. A few hours." She was about to object and he held up his hand. "Don't say anything tonight. Yes or no. It's late and you probably won't be comfortable letting me in."

"You got that right," she said tartly.

Surprisingly he laughed, the sound rich and amused.

All right, Joanna Mitchell. You're pretty and smart. He carefully replaced his cap and adjusted the beak. He began to peel the cellophane from the candy he held. "Okay. You set the place and time. I'll call you tomorrow, *again* . . ." he said with a raised brow. "Whatever makes you feel safe. Whatever you say."

His face was hidden again. Joanna could only see the jaw and well-formed mouth, which she kept staring at. "I don't know if I want—"

"You're not afraid of me, are you?" he asked, smiling.

That annoyed her. "Please," Joanna drawled, as if the very idea was ridiculous.

"Then are you saying you're not interested or curious about why I want to see you?"

Joanna didn't answer right away because she couldn't deny a growing wonder at all the unanswered questions surrounding Sheila. Trevor Jackson's baiting made her feel indecisive, as though she was passing up an opportunity. More annoying, he made her feel sort of . . . virginal. As if she were amusingly unhip. Nevertheless, Joanna felt an excitement and challenge in his determination. It was as if Trevor Jackson was suggesting that what she might know or not know about Sheila James was important. Joanna suddenly had a feeling of adventure, that something was about to take place that was completely out of the ordinary for her. She discovered that there was a part of her that didn't want to be left out. She wanted to prove that she really wasn't afraid to take a risk.

"All right, I'm slightly interested," she qualified.

"Lunch tomorrow?"

"You can pick me up at the station."

"Good enough," he nodded. Then he popped the candy into his mouth.

Joanna watched in fascination as Trevor sucked on it and then used his tongue to roll it into the side of his mouth. He turned toward the stairwell.

"Wait a minute," Joanna called out after him. He stopped and turned, one foot on the top step and one on the step below. "Just what is your interest in Sheila James? Or can you tell me?"

Trevor stood perfectly still for a long moment, hesitating. When he spoke, his voice was a quiet echo in the empty hall.

"I'm her husband."

Two

Joanna was finding it hard to concentrate.

Detective Leonard Schultz's questions about the death of Sheila James were not nearly as interesting as the announcement Trevor Jackson had made the night before. She could still recall staring at him, dumbfounded, as he'd smiled sardonically at her reaction to his news. She had never recovered enough to voice a response. Trevor had whispered good night and had trotted off down the stairs.

She had closed and locked her apartment door, and then had simply stood in her foyer feeling slightly dazed. It had never occurred to Joanna that Sheila might have been married. The information had kept her awake until well after midnight as her imagination had tried to create a story and history around Trevor and Sheila. Her thoughts raced and swirled and reformed. She tried to see the two of them together, married. In love. Lovers. Much of Joanna's imaging simply didn't work for her. Trevor seemed like a smart man. He was very alert and certainly had his share of confidence. There had been nothing very substantial about Sheila except for her physical looks and the superficial appeal of her personality. Joanna guessed that that alone might have been enough for some men. But Trevor?

Of course, Joanna considered now, as she nodded absently to the detective, that she had no idea what she would have said to Trevor if he hadn't turned away and bounded down the stairs. To have said in astonishment, "you're kidding," struck Joanna as rude and offensive, even if it was how she felt. Certainly there was no reason for anyone to suspect that Sheila was married, given the kind of life she'd led. Frivolous and carefree. Somewhat disconnected from the real world. And she never seemed to have any responsibilities beyond finding other people to take care of her needs. Sheila had once confessed that she didn't know how to cook and she wasn't interested in learning.

Had Sheila run away from a bad marriage? Joanna asked herself. She couldn't help wondering what had gone wrong between her and Trevor Jackson. But as hard as she tried, she couldn't imagine them together. Joanna was also unsettled by a feeling of disappointment. Knowing what little she did of Sheila James, she couldn't shake the intuition that her late neighbor was seriously mismatched with someone like Trevor. Or was it the other way around? Of course, she knew nothing about him either. However, he did appear to be stable and reasonable. Determined. And so . . . so . . .

"Miss Mitchell?"

Joanna blinked and quickly tried to center her attention on the detective. The beefy middle-aged man was waiting patiently.

"I'm sorry," Joanna murmured guiltily.

"I hope you were remembering something."

She shook her head. "Nothing. I think I've described all of the people I've ever seen Sheila with, but I don't know a lot of names."

"Do you happen to recall who she was with on New Year's Eve?"

Joanna sighed and frowned. Her only memory of New Year's Eve a week ago was that she and Philip had gone to New York to attend a private party at the Rainbow Room in Rockefeller Center. She'd spent much of the night annoyed as other women had practically hung all over him. Philip had not exactly been put off by all the admiration.

"I saw her only briefly that day, sometime before noon. I know she had plans to go out that night."

"How do you know that?"

"She showed me the dress she was going to wear."

"The blue one she was wearing when her body was found?"

Joanna tried not to grimace. "Yes, I guess so."

"But she never mentioned her date?"

"Only that he—whoever *he* was—was finally going to take her to some fabulous party and she'd meet a lot of important people. Sheila never really talked to me about her . . . her . . ."

"The men in her life?" the detective supplied helpfully.

Joanna nodded. Sheila certainly had never even hinted at someone like Trevor Jackson. She'd never talked about her past or where she was from. Maybe she and Trevor . . .

"Miss Mitchell?" Detective Schultz said again, patiently.

She chuckled nervously. "I told you I couldn't help with much. Do you have any ideas at all what happened?"

The detective got cagey and sat back in his chair. "Maybe a robbery attempt. Mistaken identity. We're following all the leads . . . making some progress."

Joanna looked interested for the first time since meeting Leonard Schultz and being dragged reluctantly into the investigation. "That sounds like you don't have a clue. Is it still a homicide?"

He raised his brows. *"Possible* homicide. I thought you didn't want to be involved?"

"I said I didn't think I could give you any helpful information. That doesn't mean I don't want to know who killed Sheila. She lived next door to me. It could have been me. I could still be a target."

The detective smiled crookedly. "Maybe. But I can't share any information with you."

"Then I guess we're finished. Oh . . . one person you could try. Why don't you talk to Maggie Bennett."

Detective Schultz glanced through a list of names on a sheet before him. He sat forward and reached for a pen. "Who's Maggie Bennett?"

"The woman who did Sheila's hair."

The detective kept his expression blank. "Her hairdresser? What makes you think she knows anything?"

Joanna shrugged. "Woman tell their hairdressers all kind of things."

"That's very interesting," he murmured.

She knew he was skeptical. "Well, I just thought I'd mention it."

"We'll check it out."

"Can I go now?"

"Just a few more questions."

Joanna looked at her watch. "I'm already late for work . . ."

"There were several messages on Miss James's answering machine," he interrupted, "from someone named Mac. Sound familiar?"

"No, not at all," Joanna said, after a moment of consideration. "I don't suppose he left a phone number?"

"Why make it easy?" he asked dryly. "He used a public phone. Careful man."

"Doesn't mean he has anything to hide," Joanna replied.

"Thanks for your observation," the detective said dismissingly. "Maybe you should be running the investigation."

She stood up, putting on her coat and shouldering her purse. "I'm sorry I don't know more."

"If you remember anything else . . ."

"I'll call. Promise. Bye . . ." Joanna turned to leave the office.

"One more thing. We found a telegram in the victim's apartment. It was sent a few days before she died."

Joanna stopped and faced him again.

"Ever hear of a man named Trevor?"

Joanna's brows were raised in an expression of mild curiosity. She tried not to blink, not to widen her eyes, not to wince as her stomach contracted. Her mind raced with the question. Joanna wondered abstractedly, how much trouble she could get into for willfully thwarting an investigation into a possible murder. Could she later be considered an accessory after the fact, or held as a co-conspirator?

Slowly Joanna shook her head. She shrugged, even as her heart pounded uncomfortably with her spontaneous decision. She didn't know why she was doing this.

"No, I don't know him," she answered clearly.

"So then he said I was the first woman he'd met with a sense of humor. And I said, does that mean you're not going to take me seriously? And then he said—with that kind of sly thing guys do when they're trying to be cute—he says, not at all. He said I had a great laugh and he liked that I was upfront." Linda stopped for a moment, thoughtfully chewing her gum. "He meant that I laughed too loud and I was blunt, didn't he?" she asked. She got no answer and gently nudged Joanna. "Did you hear what I said?"

Joanna came back to the present, trying not to think of Detective Schultz suddenly appearing at her office to take her away in handcuffs. She kept her attention on the labels she was carefully applying to several tape boxes. Quickly she improvised to cover the fact that her mind wasn't on Linda's problems but on the belated possibility that Trevor Jackson may very well have had something to do with his wife's death.

"Every word. So, did he ask you out?"

Linda sighed and gently swiveled back and forth on her stool as she sat next to Joanna in the film and tape library. "He said he would call, but you know how men are. They'll say one thing to your face and trash you behind your back. They can be so insincere."

Joanna smiled. "A minute ago you were telling me how wonderful he was. Honest and charming. Unmarried."

Linda sucked air through her teeth to show impatience. "Well, he probably lied about that, too."

"Does that mean if he calls you're going to turn him down?"

Linda looked at Joanna as if she were demented. "I never said that. I'll send Sean to his father's in a heartbeat."

Joanna glanced thoughtfully at her coworker. "Still scouting out second husband material?"

Linda shrugged. "Every time I have a bad date I

think, who needs this? Maybe I'm better off alone. I don't know. It didn't work the first time, but I'm not ready to give up yet."

"I didn't know you were such a romantic."

"Honey, it's not romantic. It's being practical. Two paychecks are better than one. *You're* the one who day-dreams big time. You keep on waiting for Philip to get serious, and I keep telling you he won't."

"I don't understand why you don't like Philip," Joanna replied.

"Oh, I like him fine," Linda said, but began to squirm restlessly on her seat. "But to me he seems more inter-ested in his career and in being famous than he is in you. Anyway, I'm suspicious of men who are cuter than I am; and know it."

Joanna laughed at the comment, but she understood what Linda meant. She knew from being with Philip that it was frequently disconcerting to be with someone with a high public profile. People openly fawned over him. Not that she wanted to share in the spotlight, Joanna honestly admitted to herself. She just didn't want to be Philip's shadow, either.

There was a knock on the open door, and Robby leaned his lanky frame halfway in. "Hey, Jo? There's some guy waiting downstairs in the lobby for you."

"Thanks," Joanna said and hastened her efforts to fin-ish the tape boxes. Robby left, and a long silence followed.

"What guy?" Linda asked.

Joanna stood up and stacked the tapes. "Trevor Jack-son," she replied smoothly.

"The guy who left you all those messages yesterday?"

"Yes," Joanna nodded.

Linda's mouth stopped working the gum, her gaze

grew incredulous. "You called him back? I thought you
didn't know who he was? I thought you didn't care?"

It was on the tip of Joanna's tongue to explain exactly
who Trevor was, but she quickly changed her mind.
She'd never been a gossip, and somehow it seemed un-
fair to spread it around too lightly about Trevor's connection to Sheila. More than that, Joanna simply
believed that a confidence had been given to her by
Trevor. She didn't want to take advantage of it. The very
fact that Trevor Jackson had sought her out made her
feel that she was in a unique position.

"Well, I don't. But he was the one at the funeral
home." She decided to confide that much.

"That man? How come he wanted to see you?"

"Relax. This isn't personal. He knew Sheila, found
out I was a neighbor, and wants to ask me some questions."

Linda snickered. "Apparently lots of men knew
Sheila. What *else* does he want to know?"

"I'm going to find out," Joanna said stiffly, feeling
unexpectedly defensive. Trevor Jackson didn't strike her
as being anything like the other men in Sheila's life, and
she was reluctant to make a precipitous comparison.
There was something very sturdy and dependable about
Trevor Jackson. Mature in the way of someone who
knew how to take care of himself. Joanna was pretty
sure that *no* one got over on him.

But the other memory that came back to Joanna, the
night before while she lay in bed, was the image of the
way his mouth had played with the butterscotch candy.
It was unexpectedly provocative and she kept coming
back to it.

"I told him I'd meet him for lunch. I'd better go." She gathered her coat and purse.

"Don't forget to tell him you have a terrific friend he should meet. And find out if he's married!" Linda called out as Joanna waved and left the room.

She smiled vaguely at Linda's last command. If Linda only knew . . . On the other hand, Joanna could no more imagine Trevor Jackson with Linda McKenna than she could fathom his connection to Sheila. And she knew she wasn't necessarily going to be accommodating to either Linda or Trevor. She had a few questions of her own to ask. Not the least of which was how did he know Sheila was dead, and how soon did he know it?

Trevor tried not to pace the lobby of WDRK's reception area. As it was, the security guard was carefully watching him with feigned casualness, but alert awareness, as if he expected Trevor to be a terrorist or militant come to bomb the network.

He wondered, now, about the decision to remain casually dressed as he got a sense that no one was taking him seriously. Trevor pursed his mouth wryly. He was also just once again speculating on whether Joanna Mitchell was going to show up or if she had changed her mind. Had he convinced her at all, the night before, that his intentions were—if not totally pure—at least straight up? And if he hadn't convinced her, what was his next move?

He unzipped his parka, his hands pushing into the pockets of his khaki slacks. He continued his thoughtful pacing, his jaw muscles worked reflexively as he quickly tried to process all the information he'd gained since arriving in Philadelphia. The most unexpected so far had been the coroner's report, which he'd spent time reading at the Chief Medical Examiner's office that morning. He'd had no trouble convincing them he was family and therefore had a right to review the report. The details had stated that the cause of death had been due to massive hemorrhaging in the brain, probably caused by a blunt trauma to the side of the head. There was a lesion in the skull. There were no bruises or contusions on the body except around the head area, and so there was no indication of a struggle. The markings also indicated that the body had been moved. Where the victim had been found was not where she'd died. And Sheila had, in effect, bled internally to death. If whoever had moved her had gotten her help instead, she might have lived. The report further stated that she was nearly four months pregnant.

It was a complication Trevor hadn't expected, but in one way it narrowed the possibilities of what might have happened. The question was, who was the man Sheila was involved with? Trevor realized that his plans were being derailed by each new bit of information. Even in death Sheila was giving folks a hard time.

He silently issued a self-deprecating chuckle. He'd thought this was going to be so easy, but it was becoming apparent that he was going to need help to get at what he wanted. It still wasn't clear yet that Joanna Mitchell would really cooperate. But Trevor also realized that Ms. Mitchell was becoming much more than just a means to an end. He hadn't expected to meet anyone quite like her. He'd noticed her right away at the funeral service and assumed that here was a girlfriend, someone who was going to connect him to Sheila's life, someone who would have been a confidante. In other words, she might be a conduit to what he needed to find out. But if Joanna had been a friend to Sheila she was certainly a lot different from anyone in Sheila's life . . . or his own. When he was a young blood, Joanna Mitchell would have been the kind of girl he wouldn't have stood a chance with, and he wouldn't even have tried. He was going to have to change his thinking about how to deal with her.

When the elevator door opened and Joanna stepped out moments later, Trevor felt relief . . . Then something else. Joanna's quiet graceful presence amazed him. He'd noticed a little of it the night before, in the polite but aloof way she'd spoken to him. There was no coyness nor female defensiveness, which he could then counter with masculine aggression. Her demeanor made him feel awkward and crude. He wondered if she could see through him.

For a moment, he even forgot that he had a long list of questions to ask Joanna because, in the light of day, he was really glad to see her again. She came off the elevator bundled up in her winter coat, with a bright scarf wound under the collar and around her neck. She was bareheaded, her short hairdo making her seem serious yet unaffected.

"Not exactly the trusting type," he quipped as an opening.

"You haven't given me reason to trust you," Joanna answered.

Trevor shook his head. "I don't mean you. I mean him," he said, nodding to the security guard.

Joanna glanced around and waved briefly at the man in the gray uniform. "He's not paid to be trusting. Don't worry. I vouched for you."

"I guess that means I have to behave myself."

Joanna wouldn't let herself be drawn into his teasing. "It means you had better not disappoint me," she said tartly.

"That depends on what you're expecting," Trevor said softly, leaning a bit toward her.

Joanna found the movement disconcerting. She was aware, once again, that he exuded a confidence that was somewhat overwhelming. There didn't seem to be anything hesitant about him. It made Joanna feel flushed and nervous. She'd noticed it the night before, in the brief moments outside her apartment. It wasn't exactly that she felt afraid of Trevor Jackson, so much as being aware of his strong masculinity.

He had on the same heavy winter jacket and sporty cap; a black turtleneck sweater hugged his torso. The ensemble only served to make him seem taller and leaner.

"I'm sorry if I kept you waiting," Joanna said, trying to cover her scrutiny of him.

"No problem. I'm glad you could make it."

"I almost never take a full lunch hour," she said, as he lightly touched her elbow and steered her out the revolving door. "I usually order in and eat while I—"

Joanna's words were abruptly cut short as she took several steps and her left foot slid forward on a slick layer of ice. The momentum forced her back as her leg came up. Her hand reached out for something to break her fall.

Trevor's reaction was swift and precise. One arm circled her back as his other hand grabbed hers. He smoothly pushed her upright with the force of his arm, and Joanna found her footing. But adrenaline rushed through her, regardless.

Joanna glanced up at Trevor and found alert concern in his dark eyes. He squeezed her hand briefly and then released it, only to gently take hold of her arm. They were facing each other. He still had his arm loosely around her waist. Joanna didn't look him in the eye again, too embarrassed at her clumsiness and the forced intimacy between them as he'd saved her from falling.

"Okay?" he asked quietly.

Joanna nodded and slowly extracted herself from his arm and hand. But she didn't move any farther away. Trevor turned slightly and held out his bent elbow.

"What were you saying about lunch?"

He asked with such earnestness that Joanna grinned shyly at him, grateful there was no wise remark or stupid joke. She took his arm, feeling the strength of it.

"That I usually eat at my desk as I work."

Trevor sensed immediately that he'd handled the moment smartly. He walked them to the corner, matching his gait easily to her shorter strides. He pursed his lips and shook his head. "Eating at your desk is bad for the digestion."

Joanna grimaced at his diagnosis. "I don't think my bosses are concerned about my digestion."

Trevor arched a brow and glanced down at her as they began to cross the street. His gaze was attentive and probing. "*I* am. You're going to have a decent lunch, and we're going to take our time. The next hour is on me."

"For a price," she responded wryly.

"So you still don't trust me. All I want is to talk to you, ask some questions."

"I warn you. It's going to be a short conversation."

"That doesn't mean we can't enjoy lunch. I plan to."

Trevor was a little amused to see that Joanna Mitchell

didn't have a ready response to his prediction. He liked that she didn't. Somehow, he reasoned, it would have made her seem too clever at flirting, and too ready to do so. He noticed the way she tried not to hold too tightly to his arm.

"There's a Thai restaurant nearby. Is that okay?" she asked.

"Is the food any good?"

She gave him a careful glance. "It's the local hangout for the studio employees."

He nodded knowingly. It was going to be crowded. She'd feel safer there with so many colleagues around. "Then, Thai it is."

The small restaurant was already very busy. As the hostess led them to a table against the wall, Trevor silently followed behind Joanna observing her friendly greetings to several people along the way and their casual appraisal of him. He helped her off with her coat, hanging it and his on a peg. Then he sat opposite her.

Openly gazing at Joanna he would guess she was around thirty years of age. She wasn't wearing much makeup, just some cheek color and a bright red lipstick that drew attention to her pretty face and her pale eyes. She wore a crisp white shirt with a winged collar, a delicate pearl bar pin across the closing at the throat. She was also wearing a toast-colored blazer and black slacks. He knew that she was from a different world and experience than his own. Joanna Mitchell showed a lot of class and style. He was beginning to feel out of his league.

Joanna knew that Trevor Jackson was staring at her, sizing her up. She tried not to be uncomfortable, but she couldn't help feeling on display. She wondered if he might be comparing her to Sheila. She didn't like the idea very much. Joanna used her menu as a shield between them, forcing Trevor to resort to his as well.

"That's a very pretty pin," he commented quietly, opening his menu.

Joanna's fingers brushed across her throat. "Thank you. It was a Christmas present."

Trevor nodded, reading the menu. "Santa was good to you. What's his name?"

Joanna narrowed her eyes at his arch question. "Philip."

Trevor lifted his gaze to stare at her for a moment. He took his time appraising her and was surprised when she stared right back. "He's got good taste," he murmured with practiced ease.

Joanna felt a slow wave of heat warm her cheeks at the compliment. Yet, she wondered if his flattery was sincere or just manipulation.

"We're not here to discuss my jewelry or personal life," she said clearly. He only grinned at her in response.

The waitress appeared to take their order and leave glasses of water. After she'd left them alone, Trevor braced his elbows on the table and leaned toward Joanna.

"Let's cut to the chase then. First of all, I think I'd better explain about my relationship with Sheila."

Joanna fiddled with her place setting. "You said she was your wife."

"That's right. *Was.*"

"Is that *was* as in before or after she died?" she asked quickly.

Trevor raised his brows at her. "Before. Long, long before. I haven't seen Sheila in nearly six years."

Joanna gave up any attempt to hide her curiosity. She again wondered what had brought him and Sheila to-

gether in the first place. The men she'd always seen
Sheila with were slick and stylish. They wore expensive
clothes and were conscious of themselves and their appeal. Trevor Jackson's hair was cut close to his scalp. It
was conservative and severe. His clothes were sturdy
and casual. He dressed for comfort and convenience . . .
not fashion. And there was an orderly masculinity about
him, a kind of natural aura of command that she couldn't
ignore. All in all, Joanna was confused about what she
thought of Trevor Jackson.

"Were you divorced?"

Trevor tilted his head and considered carefully how
to answer. Finally, he shook his head. "Separated. I
couldn't get papers signed for a divorce because I didn't
know how to find her. It was . . . very complicated,"
Trevor murmured thoughtfully.

For the first time, Joanna watched as uncertainty
changed Trevor's countenance to a veiled embarrassment. She felt herself softening toward him. After all,
the man was telling her personal information that might
be painful and none of her business.

"Mr. Jackson . . ." she began awkwardly.

"Trevor," he corrected smoothly.

Joanna averted her gaze and nervously nodded. "All
right. Trevor. How did you find her? Why did it take so
long?"

Trevor hesitated. He spread his hands out and shrugged.
"I didn't know where to begin looking. I don't know a
lot about Sheila's family. She was raised in foster care. I
know she had a grandmother in Tampa. She passed before
Sheila and I . . . got married.

"I never would have found her if it hadn't been for
someone we both knew who happened to see her in New

York back in November. He found out she was living in Philly."

"Why is her last name different?"

Trevor smiled at her quickness and naiveté. "If you didn't want to be found, wouldn't you change your name? James is the name of the family that raised her. Anything else?"

Joanna considered, glancing briefly away for a moment. "The police questioned me again this morning. They asked me if I knew who you were. They found the telegram you sent Sheila."

"Then that should prove I'm not trying to duck them. I wanted her to know I was coming East. She and I had to talk. What did you tell the police?"

"I told them I didn't know you."

Trevor hadn't expected that, and he stared thoughtfully at her. "Why did you do that?"

She shrugged. "Like you said, you weren't trying to hide from them. And I felt you and I should talk first since you were so persistent in tracking me down. You said you wanted to ask some questions."

"I do. I thought if you knew a little more about me and Sheila it might make it easier to be open with me and not hold anything back. But I guess I don't have to worry about that, do I?"

She tilted her head. "You mean, tell the truth?" He merely nodded, his eyes still carefully watching her expression. Joanna shook her head. "I have no reason to lie. There's no one I need to protect."

"Except yourself," he suggested casually.

"I've already told you I don't know anything about Sheila's death," Joanna said in mild annoyance.

"Okay. Let's not talk about her death. Let's talk about what she was like alive."

Joanna airily waved a hand. "You first." Trevor laughed outright. She liked the sound of it. His amusement reached to his dark eyes. Joanna found herself tempted to smile with him but didn't. This was business . . . or something like that.

But Trevor's humor did abate as he thoughtfully pulled on his earlobe. He was *not* going to be able to just roll over Joanna and he gave up any thoughts of attempting to. Besides, Trevor liked her. "She was pretty friendly. Talkative. Drop-dead gorgeous. I'm sure you've noticed."

Joanna gestured silently with lifted brows and a slight roll of her eyes in agreement.

"She was kind of the restless type. You know . . . always looking to get whatever she didn't have at the moment. She could charm the pants off most people. She wanted to be important . . . and rich."

Joanna frowned at Trevor. "You don't sound very upset with her."

He shrugged. "I was always pretty clear about what Sheila was like, and there really wasn't anything wrong with what she wanted out of life. Just how she went about it. Nothing she did really surprised me."

But his comment surprised Joanna. How could he be so cavalier about it? Didn't it bother him at all that his wife was so erratic and unreliable? That there had been so many other men?

"It sounds like you two had an . . . interesting marriage," she couldn't help observing.

Trevor lifted his shoulders in a negligent shrug and shook his head slightly. "There were some problems."

Joanna absently played with the bar pin at her throat.

She looked at Trevor and blinked rapidly. "Were there . . . children?"

Trevor looked carefully at her, hearing expectation in the soft inquiry. That specific question, out of all others she might have asked surprised him. Again Trevor shook his head. "None that I know of," he said cryptically. He saw her appalled expression. "None that were mine. To use a military term, Sheila just up and went AWOL one day."

"But why? There must have been a reason, some sort of warning," she asked, fascinated.

"Maybe she didn't like being married. Or maybe she didn't like being married to me. Maybe she got a better offer. Maybe she just wanted to disappear and start over. Who knows?"

Joanna listened to Trevor's explanation, sensing that while it was probably all true, it also seemed superficial. He spoke of Sheila too casually, as if he'd never loved her nor had asked her to be his wife. "Wouldn't it have been easier and cheaper just to get a divorce?"

"Minor detail. Sheila never bothered with the details. She always took the most direct way out of any problem."

"She's not here to defend herself," she couldn't help reminding Trevor.

He inclined his head. "I'm not here to bad-mouth her." Then he narrowed his eyes as he scanned Joanna's face. "And I have a feeling you know that what I'm telling you is true. I have a feeling you understand what I'm saying."

"What does it matter? It's not going to help her or you, is it?" Joanna asked as their lunch was served.

"It might. Sheila used people. But don't get me wrong; she wasn't mean. She didn't deliberately try to hurt people. She just put her own interest ahead of anything and anyone else."

"So?"

Trevor frowned and paused for a moment as he dished rice onto his plate. "Maybe that had something to do with why she died."

"Then you don't buy the theory that someone may have forced their way into her apartment and killed her during a robbery attempt?"

"Do *you* believe that?"

Joanna shrugged. "I don't know. I haven't really thought about it." She gazed thoughtfully at Trevor while serving herself from a shrimp dish. "You know, you'd probably get a lot more information and help if you talked to the police."

Trevor looked up sharply at her. "On the other hand they could make me a suspect. I don't have time for that."

"But you want me to believe that you're not."

"You know I'm not," Trevor said confidently.

Joanna relaxed a little. It didn't seem likely. Otherwise he wouldn't need to talk to her. "What information do you have about her death?"

Trevor shifted on his chair. "Just what I read in the coroner's report. She was found on New Year's Day. She appeared to have been hit on the head with a heavy object, but they don't know what. She died quickly, and she'd been dead for about fourteen hours.

"No one has come forward to say they saw her or were with her. She was fully clothed . . . but there was a missing shoe . . . and she didn't appear to have been raped."

Joanna listened in rapt attention. Trevor hadn't said anything she didn't know, but it felt eerie and horrible to be casually discussing someone they'd both known, as if Sheila was just a list of characteristics instead of someone who may have been deeply troubled. And it bothered Joanna a little that Trevor was so clinical about the details. Maybe he couldn't be broken up about her death because they hadn't seen each other in years. But his lack of emotion seemed odd and unsettling.

"How do you think she died? Why?" Joanna asked.

"It wasn't random. I'm sure even the police know that much."

"Someone she knew?"

Trevor nodded. "The question is, why?" he prompted.

Joanna shrugged and sighed. "It seemed so senseless."

"That's why I wanted to talk to you. You must have gotten some idea of her life and what she did, the people she knew and hung around with. Who were the people who came to see her? What was she like with people in the building? What did you think of her?"

Joanna shook her head and laughed lightly. "Wait a minute. Hold on. You're going too fast." She didn't know how to start. She fumbled for the right words to express herself. "Look . . . I kind of thought of Sheila as a free bird. She was aimless, didn't seem to have any goals or ambitions beyond living it up royally. She was cheerful and friendly but . . . I also got the sense that while she was living large, there was a lot of desperation under-neath."

Trevor was quiet and observant as she talked, and with just his eyes seemed to agree or understand everything she was saying. "Much larger than she could afford?"

Joanna thought about that. "Yes, exactly. She got along well with people in the building. Especially the men," she said wryly. "She was very kind to Preston Canin and spent time with him. Danny, the maintenance man, would do anything for her. He was really broken up when Sheila died. On the other hand, she was always borrowing money from Preston or stuff from me or asking favors."

"What did she borrow from you?" Trevor asked.

Joanna grimaced. "A few things," she said evasively. Trevor didn't push her.

"After she died the newspapers started speculating on why. There were accounts of big events where she'd been seen. There was talk about the important men she was known to date. If it wasn't for those connections Sheila's death would have ended up somewhere after the sports page and before classified," Joanna mused honestly. "The other possibilities the police threw in were drugs, blackmail, or prostitution . . ."

"Wrong," Trevor said a bit forcefully. He glanced at Joanna's surprised expression and softened his tone. "Wrong. Were those the only reasons they could come up with?"

Joanna frowned. "I know what you're thinking. It wasn't because Sheila was black. I mean—"

"You didn't wonder, even once, if maybe she was involved in any of those things other people thought about?"

Joanna shifted guiltily. "You haven't given me any other reasons."

Trevor nodded. "I know."

"You were married to her but maybe she changed since you last saw her."

"Or maybe she just met the wrong kinds of people."

"But you mean to find out?"

"I hope I can."

"Why? Why is it so important when you said you

haven't seen her in so many years?" Trevor hesitated and Joanna could see his reluctance to answer. "Are you . . . still in love with her?"

Trevor smiled sadly. "I used to be."

His response made Joanna feel strange, as if the idea of Trevor loving someone was too personal a thing to know. The intimacy it implied made her warm all over, and she started to imagine all kinds of things, like, what kind of lover he was.

They stared at each other and Joanna began to feel the subject of Sheila drifting away. In Trevor's eyes she saw something shift. She thought, why would Sheila want to get away from someone like Trevor Jackson?

"Are you in love with someone?" Trevor asked her suddenly.

Joanna self-consciously averted her gaze. She felt an odd little dip of tension in her stomach as Trevor touched on a subject which was fraught with tension and speculations, wishful thinking, and disappointment. "We weren't going to talk about my personal life, remember?"

Trevor chuckled. "I never agreed to that. I've told you an awful lot about me. You know I failed at marriage."

She made a sound of disagreement. "You can't blame yourself entirely for that."

He shrugged. "Things could have ended differently. So, is it Santa Claus? The one named Philip?"

Joanna tried not to but couldn't help laughing. "I thought we were having a serious discussion here about Sheila."

"We are," he said with charm. "Does he know you're out with a man who could be a suspect?"

Joanna looked squarely at Trevor. "If I thought you were a suspect, I'd call the police myself."

Trevor smiled slowly, lifting a corner of his mouth seductively. He certainly couldn't forget that. As much as he had been trying to get next to Joanna, he was taken aback and felt peculiar inside. Shamed. If only she knew . . . He reached across the table and took her hand. "Thanks."

Joanna looked at his hand. It was large and warm and held hers lightly. "Why did you want to talk to me?" she asked softly.

"Because you're a woman. I thought you would have better insights than the police or anyone else who knew Sheila. I knew you'd be honest with me."

She slowly withdrew her hand from his. "You said she used people. How do I know you're not using me?"

"I *am* using you. But I've also told you a lot. I need you to trust me and to help me."

Joanna was mesmerized by the seductive persuasion of his low voice. He flexed his jaw muscles and stared at her, but she no longer felt threatened or vulnerable by his persistence. "It's too late to do anything for Sheila."

Trevor was shaking his head. "No, it's not. I can try and find a reason for her dying. I can put the rumors to rest." Then he averted his gaze briefly. "And I've made a promise that I still mean to keep. I have to take care of the past."

"You mean, like make the final break from being married to her?"

His attention was steadfast on Joanna's face. "That's part of it. I want to move on. I have my own future to think about."

Joanna wondered what that was. What had his life been like during all those years he was separated from

Sheila? Had he found someone else to love? She finished her lunch but didn't ask any of those questions. Despite the fact that she wanted to know, she was afraid to be further drawn into the circle of Trevor Jackson's life.

They stepped out of the restaurant fifteen minutes later, and Trevor automatically held out his arm to her. Joanna took hold, feeling protected. The sensation was pleasant and reassuring.

On the walk back to her office, Joanna couldn't help realizing that nothing had really been accomplished at lunch. Yes, she wanted to know more about the strange marriage of Trevor and Sheila, but there was a very strong sense that he still hadn't told her anything significant. They walked the length of the block from the restaurant. Much to her annoyance, Joanna knew she was intrigued enough by the story Trevor had to tell to want to know more. Not about Sheila, but about him.

"How long are you going to be here?" she asked as they waited for the light to change at the corner.

"About a week," Trevor said. "Depending on what I find out, I may have to return later."

"Return from where?"

"Washington."

"Well, D.C.'s not so far away that you can't . . ." He was chuckling and she turned her head to frown at him.

"Washington, as in the state of," he corrected.

"Oh. Clear across the country. Seattle?"

"Fort Lewis."

"I've never heard of it," she said.

"You never heard of me either, before yesterday. I'm full of surprises," Trevor grinned wickedly.

"That's what I'm afraid of," Joanna muttered.

Hearing a car door slam, Joanna absently glanced around in mild interest. She saw a man and woman hurrying toward her. She saw a camera in the man's hands. Joanna faltered in her steps as the two focused pointedly on her.

"Ms. Mitchell? We're from *Spotlight*. Can we talk to you? Why did the police ask to speak with you again? Does it have anything to do with the death of your neighbor, Sheila James? Are the police sticking to the story of drugs and prostitution?"

Joanna stared, nonplussed. And then she became angry. She felt a strong, firm hand grab her arm as Trevor abruptly pulled her aside, placing himself between her and the reporters.

"She has nothing to say," Trevor stated. He used one hand to keep the two at a distance, and his other to urge Joanna on to the studio building.

"Did you know Ms. James was seen socially with some of the members of the City Council? We just want to verify—"

"Not now," Trevor said with authority, and turned to rush Joanna and himself into the lobby of WDRK. The security guard in the lobby alertly stepped behind them to block the entrance to the aggressive news crew.

"Sorry, I can't let you in," he said, putting a halt to their pursuit. "This is private property."

Trevor and Joanna stepped quickly into an already waiting elevator car.

"What floor?" Trevor asked, hand poised near the indicator panel.

"Nine."

The door eased closed and the commotion near the front door was shut off. The elevator began a smooth ascent. There was silence for a long moment before Trevor turned to Joanna and found her features stiff and guarded. Her unusually light eyes were bright and wide, but her nostrils were flaring and her brows were knit. Trevor watched her for a second. Instincts told him to stay out of it, stay away from her. But after having been in Joanna's company and seeing the kind of woman she was, his inclinations now told him something else.

Carefully, Trevor put his hands on her arms. He could feel her skittishness and expected Joanna to jerk away from him. But instead she looked at him and her expression changed to frustration.

"Are you all right?"

"No, I'm not all right. They won't leave me alone. Everybody thinks I know something. Just because Sheila and I are both black. Just because she lived next to me. Even you," she said accusingly.

Trevor began to gently rub his hands up and down Joanna's arms. He considered her comment silently. "I was thinking maybe you and I could work together. I need to find out what happened. But maybe it's better if I just leave you out of it," he said with deliberate hesitation.

Joanna stared at him thoughtfully. *You and I,* he'd said. Strangely, that calmed her down. If Trevor had said almost anything else she might have sent him packing, not willing to continue being pestered and surprised around every corner. But . . . *you and I* . . . There was something about his believing in her.

"*Spotlight* doesn't necessarily want the truth. It's just a supermarket tabloid. They'll take whatever makes a good story," Joanna murmured, still thinking over Trevor's suggestion.

"We don't have to give them a story," Trevor said smoothly. He let his hands drop from her arms, but stood very close to her in the confines of the elevator.

Joanna didn't look into his face, afraid to see if he was having the same reaction that she was. As if they were cut off from the rest of the world and space had shrunk around them. When Joanna considered the way he'd quickly warded off the reporters on her behalf, she realized that Trevor Jackson no longer felt like a stranger. But still she hesitated.

"I don't know. I . . ."

The elevator came to a stop and the door opened before Joanna could finish her thought. She blinked at Trevor, not really sure what she wanted to say. What she wanted to do. So she quickly stepped past him out of the elevator and turned to face him, taking a deep breath to clear her head of fanciful thoughts.

"Hey . . . where have you been?"

Joanna, startled, pivoted to face the man walking toward her. "Philip." She smiled weakly, feeling disoriented.

The other man, however, tall and slender, gave his attention to Trevor as he continued to address Joanna. "I thought I'd surprise you and take you to lunch. Robby said someone else beat me to it."

Joanna glanced guiltily from Philip to Trevor. She wondered if she was imagining the instant static between the two men, as Philip stood sizing up Trevor in an obvious and rather challenging manner, like . . . *who are you?* She read the dynamics and moved in swiftly with damage control. But before she could say another word Trevor put his hand out, a friendly smile curving his mouth.

"Philip Lee, right?"

Philip hesitated only a second and then took the offered hand. "Right."

"I've been watching your news program at night. You cover some tough stories, man. You have a good delivery. Good style."

The handshake was quick and solid. "Are you in the business?" Philip asked, easily accepting the praise.

Trevor made a self-deprecating chuckle and shook his head. He put his hands into the pockets of his slacks. "Naw. I don't do anything as exciting."

"What do you do?"

Joanna swiveled her head in Trevor's direction. She wanted to know, too.

"I work in a hospital."

"Orderly," Philip declared, with an unmistakable edge of condescension.

"Something like that," Trevor said easily, even as a muscle flexed in his jaw.

Joanna stood listening, but she was fascinated with the subtle change in Trevor which allowed him to deal with Philip. This was another Trevor. Easy and accommodating. But in an interesting male attitude that said, *easy, man; I'm not into your territory.* He set a parameter . . . without giving in an inch to Philip's natural suspiciousness. Even more so than the night before when he'd worked to put her qualms to rest. The thought came to Joanna that Trevor Jackson was a smart man. Streetwise. Maybe a hustler. The two men continued to appraise one another, but Joanna had the strangest feeling that Trevor actually was controlling the situation.

"And you're . . ." Philip coaxed.

"Trevor Jackson."

Joanna looked back and forth between the two men

before entering the conversation. "Trevor is . . . er . . . was a friend of Sheila's." She glanced briefly at Trevor and saw the slight incline of his brows as she altered the information a bit.

"Is that right?" Philip asked, with a marked increase in interest.

Trevor gave him no more with which to speculate. Every fiber of his being, every survival instinct wanted to back this guy up. But Trevor knew it would be a mistake to play that hand in front of Joanna. He was still a long way from having her cooperation. Instead, Trevor kept his voice cool and indifferent, let his body relax and ignored the innate need to square off. He didn't like not being in control, but he'd kill everything if he didn't compromise now.

"Sorry if I ruined your lunch plans. I met Joanna at Sheila's funeral and wanted to ask her some questions. I haven't seen Sheila in years. It was a real blow to learn that she was dead." Trevor sadly shook his head.

"So . . . you knew Sheila," Philip murmured thoughtfully. "How well did you know her?"

Joanna made an impatient sound and frowned at Philip. "Stop that. You're behaving like a reporter. Stop interrogating the man."

"I don't mind," Trevor said good-naturedly. "If I can do the same."

Philip tilted his head and crossed his arms over his chest. "What do you mean?"

"I figure you're used to getting information. You must get tips and inside stuff no one else can. You probably have contacts with the police, whatever. Mind if I ask you some questions?"

"Yeah, I do," Philip said with a short laugh of annoyance.

Trevor's grin was tight and false as he gestured with his hands. "Then I guess we have a standoff."

"Why is everybody standing by the elevator? Are you all coming or going? Philip, Christopher Todd wants to see you before you leave. Hi, I'm Linda McKenna . . ."

All heads had turned at Linda's approach. She was already smiling at Trevor and holding out her hand to him.

"Trevor Jackson. I think I saw you at Sheila's service earlier this week."

Linda beamed. "How nice of you to remember." Then she became more demure. "Wasn't that sad? I didn't really know the woman, but she was a friend of Joanna's. Did you know her very well?"

Joanna shifted uncomfortably.

Trevor smiled slowly, charmingly at Linda. "We go back a ways."

"How interesting . . ." Linda said automatically. "Are you going to be around for a while?"

Trevor looked briefly at Joanna, but her expression was bland. "Unfortunately, a very short while."

"That's too bad," Philip said flatly, his tone indifferent and insincere.

"Yes, it is," Linda crooned. "But maybe we can all get together before you go."

"Maybe," Trevor nodded. He turned to Joanna and held out his hand to her.

For a second, Joanna could only stare at him. She looked at the hand in confusion, remembering the companionable lunch they'd shared, the quiet concern in the elevator. The way he'd broken her near fall on ice. He was now getting ready to leave. She took the hand, but Trevor didn't shake it. He just held it and gently squeezed. Joanna tried to read his expression, tried to figure out the message in his steady gaze, and felt slightly frustrated that she couldn't.

"Thanks for taking the time to talk with me."

She kept watching his face, his brown features still indicating to Joanna a confident and strong man. She felt an odd sensation of being rushed, like there was no real opportunity to say goodbye. Was this goodbye? But she could say no more since Philip looked as though he wished Trevor would hurry and go away, and Linda looked like she was waiting for a proposal. Joanna tried to make the best of the circumstances.

"I'll be happy to answer any other questions you may have before you leave Philadelphia," she said clearly. Once again, Joanna felt the pressure of his fingers around her hand.

"Thanks. I appreciate that," Trevor said with a nod. He released her hand and pushed for the elevator.

"Bye," Linda sang out.

Trevor pointed a finger at Philip. "Keep up the good work."

Philip gave a brief careless wave as Trevor boarded the elevator and the door closed.

Linda again turned to Philip. "Philip . . ."

"Yeah, I know. Do me a favor and tell Chris I'll be there in a minute."

"Sure. I'll talk with you later," Linda said significantly to Joanna in an aside before walking away.

"Huh," Philip uttered skeptically. "I don't trust that dude."

"Really?" Joanna asked with interest, as Philip walked with her to the sound room.

"Come on, Jo," he said with superiority marking his tone. "He shows up *after* Sheila is dead, claiming to be a friend?" He chuckled. "That's lame. And you let him talk you into meeting him? What do you know about him?"

Philip's quick assessment began to play on her. He made sense. He presented the same doubts that she'd had at the beginning. But Joanna still did not have the sense that she had to be careful of Trevor Jackson. She didn't believe he was trying to scam her but she was distracted, nonetheless, by the questions. Joanna removed her coat and hung it up. No. She couldn't have misjudged Trevor.

"Listen, if he tries to contact you again, you let me know. I'll handle it. I don't want you to have anything to do with him."

"Why?" she asked.

"Because I don't trust him, that's why. What did he want to ask you about Sheila? What did you tell him? I thought you didn't even like Sheila all that much."

Joanna sighed. "Philip, stop hounding me as if I were going to be on the news at six."

"I hope you didn't tell him anything important."

"I don't know anything important. I've told you and the police that. I didn't tell Trevor Jackson anything you don't already know."

Philip closed the door to the small room and, taking Joanna's hand, pulled her with sure intention into his arms.

"Philip," she laughed nervously, allowing him to settle her into a loose embrace against his lean body. "Someone could just walk in."

"So what? They'll just see me kissing my woman. I don't mind." He kissed her cheek and ear, hugging her gently.

"I do," Joanna breathed, trying not to let him get carried away. "For someone so careful with his image, you take terrible chances."

Philip smiled charmingly at her, his smoothly handsome face creating a grimace that was meant to be appealing. He kissed her mouth lightly. "Only when I can talk my way out of it."

"You mean, like last night?" Joanna asked wryly as he slowly swayed with her, their hips pressed together.

Philip frowned at her, watching her face. "What?"

"Christopher told me nothing was on at City Hall last night. There was nothing in the news today."

"Checking on me?" Philip asked, a slight peevishness in his voice.

"Do I have to?"

He tucked in his chin. He had a habit of doing that when he was caught between annoyance and not taking something seriously. "I was being briefed on the new city contracts with the police and firefighters' union. Anyway, Christopher Todd doesn't know everything. And he sure doesn't know all the right people. Want to see my notes?" he asked playfully.

Joanna smiled winsomely and eased herself out of his arms. "Just teasing."

"Hey. I'm sorry about last night. Breaking news doesn't wait on romance."

"And I'm sorry about lunch. You should have let me know you were coming."

He leaned to kiss her again, teasing seductively at Joanna's mouth. "When can we get together? Tonight?"

Someone began knocking and pushing on the door.

"Who's in there? It's a fire hazard to have this door closed," the female voice quipped.

Philip stepped back as Linda came in.

"Ooops," she said, without an ounce of regret. "You're still here?"

Philip shrugged as he reached for his coat and prepared to leave. "I'm going. I'll pick you up by about seven." He pecked Joanna quickly on the mouth, stroked her cheek and winked. "I'll call you." He smiled at Linda and left the room.

"I wish you wouldn't bait him like that," Joanna said to her colleague when Philip was out of earshot.

"Did I say something wrong?" Linda asked innocently.

Joanna sighed. "Not really. Probably I did."

"The thing you have to learn, girl, is *never* give a man an option. He'll always take the easy way. Anyway, if you ask me, he only knows one thing . . . how to get what's best for Philip."

"I don't want to hear this, Linda," Joanna said in warning.

But Linda was glancing quickly out the door before closing it. She turned to Joanna with a bright conspiratorial smile. "Well? What was he like?"

Joanna couldn't pretend not to understand. It had been a bit jarring to get off the elevator a while ago and find herself between Philip and Trevor. There had been an immediate visceral difference that had momentarily confused her. "Trevor Jackson? He was okay."

Linda grimaced. "Come on. All men are interesting in the first hour. Did he make a pass at you?"

Joanna gave Linda what she hoped was a disapproving scowl. "He only wanted to talk about Sheila."

"If you believe that, you've been with Philip too long. He saw you at the service, staked you out, and Sheila had nothing to do with it. He could have talked to anybody about her, including the landlord."

Joanna cut an impatient glare at Linda. But her own imagination, her own sudden stimulated sense of possibilities, kept a replay of the time with Trevor fresh in her mind.

"I wish you'd stop trying to make something out of nothing. I'd be surprised if I even hear from him again."

"Do you want to?" Linda pounced.

"No," Joanna said too softly.

Linda shook her head. "An interesting and mysterious black man shows up in your life, and *you* don't sit up and take notice? Honey, don't play dead until you have to," she drawled.

Three

What finally aroused Joanna out of sleep was the smell of fresh-brewed coffee.

The aroma wafted into her nostrils and clear through to her brain. It pulled her from an unsatisfactory dream in which she was pushing against her apartment door to keep Trevor Jackson out. With her eyes closed and her mind starting an ascent into consciousness, Joanna could imagine the rich flavor of Java beans.

It almost made her sick to her stomach.

Her muscles clenched uncomfortably at the very idea of eating or drinking anything, particularly after her experience of the night before when she and Philip had gone out to dinner. Joanna had started to feel sick somewhere between the overspiced baby back ribs and what had passed for blueberry cobbler. She was naturally suspicious anyway of trendy new places with no track record serving down-home foods complicated by sauces and odd additives.

And she would certainly have preferred if Philip had gone home afterward to his own place, instead of watching *Boomerang* on HBO while she lay in bed alone, squirming with cramps.

It was disconcerting also that just as she was finally drifting off to sleep, her mind had caught and fastened onto images of Trevor Jackson. Like the one in which he'd prevented her from slipping on ice, and she'd felt the power in his arms and hand. The other during lunch when he'd centered his attention on her. His gaze hadn't wandered around the crowded restaurant, more interested in the surroundings than in her. And the one where he shielded her from the reporters. In just one hour of his company, Trevor had made himself a presence so strong that she'd dreamt about him during the night.

Now, Joanna could make out the sound of the TV in the living room, as the professional voices of the morning news team on WXIT recited weather, traffic updates, and sports. She rolled from her side onto her back and tried to sit up as Philip appeared in the bedroom doorway. He was dressed in his slacks and socks, his torso bare, and it was evident that he'd showered and shaved. He was munching on an English muffin.

"Hey. I thought I heard you moving around in here. Did I wake you?"

Joanna yawned lazily. She lay propped against the pillows, her knees drawn up and tenting the bedspread.

"No. I could smell the coffee."

"Want some?" he asked innocently.

The sight of him chewing so heartily made Joanna's insides roil. "Please," she moaned, closing her eyes briefly. Philip chuckled. "What time is it?"

"Almost seven."

"Seven? How come you're up so early? I didn't even hear you."

He advanced into the room. "I slept on the sofa. I had other plans for last night and this morning, but one of us got sick as a dog. Making love was probably not on your mind."

She looked at him and frowned. He certainly couldn't be accused of coddling. "That was a good guess. I didn't plan on getting sick, either."

"Just teasing," Philip said, lifting his arm as if to ward off a blow. He finished the rest of the muffin and sat on the side of the bed facing her. "Not feeling any better, eh?"

Joanna sighed. "I guess I do. A little."

"I have a good mind to call the restaurant and lay the manager out. The food wasn't all that hot."

She regarded him through half-closed lids. "Maybe not, but you didn't leave anything on your plate." She reached out and flicked away a crumb that lay on his bottom lip. "What time did you get up?"

"About five-thirty. Your sofa is okay for making out, but not big enough to sleep on. Anyway, I gotta get out of here and to the studio."

"But you don't have to be there until almost noon."

"Babe, there's always something to do. I want to check my e-mail, see if there's anything worthwhile in my in-box. You know how it is," he said, seductively regretful. He leaned forward to give Joanna a brief teasing kiss.

Joanna forgave him instantly.

She reached out and trailed her fingers down his firmly muscled chest. It was smooth and hairless. Philip worked at maintaining a hard body. He had defined pectorals and biceps, a flat stomach. He was never sick. He wouldn't stand for it.

"We haven't seen that much of each other since Christmas. I bet you don't even know how often you've canceled getting together with me."

"Come on. We're together two or three nights a week, Jo," he said.

"It would be nice if we did more than just go out to eat and then come back here or to your place to make love," she complained softly.

Philip sighed and lifted her hand from his chest. A smile framed his handsome mouth as he kissed her knuckles and then her fingertips, nibbling gently. "We do stuff together all the time. How about the premiere before Christmas in New York? And the *Essence* Awards last April. The black journalists network dinner is next week."

"I'm talking about just the two of us, without crowds of people we don't know."

"*I* know them. Anyway, I was here last night. I figure if I go now, you can at least get some rest and I can get some work done."

Joanna narrowed her gaze on him and remained patiently silent. She decided not to forgive him, after all. He kissed her hand again and then stood up.

"Do I have any clean shirts here? I don't want to run over to my place to change. It'll take too long."

Joanna slid down in the bed as she watched Philip open her closet and begin to look through the garments. "There are two on the right-hand side."

"Thanks, babe," Philip said over his shoulder as he pulled out a fresh white shirt and slipped it on. "Why don't you just call in sick today? It's Friday."

"Maybe," Joanna murmured, as Philip finished dressing. She had a peculiar sensation of being rushed again; Philip was blowing off the important point she had brought up.

"I'll call you later, see how you're doing," he said

absently, strapping on his watch and putting his wallet into his pants pocket.

"Why don't you come over after you finish at the studio? I'll make dinner or we'll order in. We can watch the video I gave you for Christmas."

"I don't know," he hedged. "Let's play it by ear."

"Philip," Joanna began. "You know, when people have a relationship, they work at it. They plan things together and then they do them. They don't constantly say 'maybe' or 'we'll see.' "

Philip spread his hands out in supplication. "Come on, Jo. You know what my life is like. We've been through this. I can't help it if I have to cancel seeing you because I have to work."

"You could give unscheduled assignments to someone else. You could sometimes just say no."

"No, I can't. My career would come to a standstill real fast. People would think I couldn't be depended on."

"So it's okay if I can't depend on you, right?"

He made an aggrieved sound. "I have to be ready, willing, and damned good. I don't want to get stuck at the local level forever. I want a network spot, and it won't happen if I constantly have to worry about the relationship and whether or not we watch videos together."

His sarcasm stung. Joanna threw back the bed linens and got swiftly out of the bed to confront Philip. "Then why bother? Why don't you just say that your career is more important, and then go on about your business?"

She stormed past Philip, heading for the bathroom, when he grabbed her hand and abruptly pulled her into his arms.

"Hey, hey, hey . . . take it easy."

Joanna was angry enough to put up a bit of a struggle.

"Don't be like that, Jo. If I can get all my work done, I promise I'll get over here later."

"Don't put yourself out because of me," she said angrily. "Now, let me go."

But Philip only chuckled softly as she squirmed, and he captured her against his body. Her arms were bent and caught between their chests. From beneath the short silk nightshirt she wore, her bare thighs rubbed against his legs. Philip thrust his hips forward and slid a hand down Joanna's back to grab her buttocks. She was bare under the lingerie.

Joanna stopped moving and gasped softly in annoyance when she realized that Philip was becoming aroused. She glanced at his brown face, into eyes that were bright with mischief and confidence. His knowing smile made her feel like she was indeed acting childish. And that slumberous look that now came into his eyes was one Joanna hadn't seen for a while.

"Philip," she murmured. She was not in the mood for making love. She tried to arch her back, to rotate her pelvis so that his hardening body would not be in contact with hers.

"Ummm," Philip uttered in a soft groan. He bent to kiss her as his hand maneuvered further under the edge of her sleepwear.

Joanna wanted to continue her protest, but Philip took advantage of her attempt to speak by covering her open mouth with his. Joanna wanted to be angry at him and his insensitivity, but Philip's embrace gentled and he loosened his arms so that his hands could ride up and down her back, alternately pressing her breasts and thighs against him.

Despite herself Joanna felt the heated magic take hold. She'd always liked the way Philip kissed her. The way he made love to her with a surprising knowledge and expertise that was exhilarating. Philip was the new man who'd learned how to satisfy a woman. He knew which buttons to push. Joanna had never had to give him any signals because what he did had always worked just fine. The physical repletion was wonderful. It was everything else that came with it that gave Joanna problems. Was Philip really fulfilling her needs, or just his own?

He slowly ended the kiss and gazed down into her face. His smile was still in place.

"Maybe I can stay awhile longer . . . if you want me to," he murmured.

Joanna felt the sudden rush of warmth quickly begin to cool. That was his cure-all for her bad mood. She pushed out of Philip's arms and shook her head. "You don't have time. Heaven forbid you should be late because of me."

Philip braced his hands on his hips, looking like he was talking to a difficult child. "Come on, give me a break."

She sighed and stared back at him. She recognized that impatient look. Joanna reached for her kimono robe from just inside the closet door and pulled it on.

"You're right. Maybe it's because I didn't have a good night. I think I will stay home today," she said flatly.

He relaxed. Reaching around Jo, Philip took his suit jacket from the closet and shrugged into it as he stepped into his brown leather loafers.

"Good. This is all just because you don't feel well," Philip conjectured, comfortable with his take on reality.

Joanna crossed her arms and remained silent. She

trailed behind Philip as he went into the living room, picking up his belongings left out the night before. His cellular phone and beeper. His filofax.

He got his overcoat from the hall closet and began putting the accouterment of his job into the pockets. Already Joanna could tell that his mind had jumped to his next destination.

"I have to reach the manager of the Eagles. I hear there's a major trade in the works. I'm trying to set up an interview with Walter Mosely. He's in town to promote his new book . . ."

Joanna opened the door and held it for him.

"Oh . . . and I'm breaking in a new intern. Someone from the graduate program at Temple." Philip stood in front of Joanna, his sunglasses in one hand, his leather gloves in the other. He put an arm around her shoulder and gave her a quick kiss on the cheek. "I'm sorry about this morning," he said smoothly.

"I know you are, Philip. You do sorry very well," she said warily.

He leaned forward, looking earnestly into her eyes. "You're going to be okay." His tone was conciliatory. Understanding. As if with his departure Joanna was going to be adrift for the day. "If you get lonely you can always call that crazy old man who lives downstairs," he chuckled. "I still think he's holding out on what he knows about Sheila. Bye, babe . . ." Philip stepped out the door as he gave Joanna a parting air kiss. "You know I love you, don't you?"

But he didn't wait for a response. He winked at Joanna before waving and heading for the elevator. Their tiff was over. Everything was back to normal. Joanna closed the door, feeling tired and agitated. In the living room the TV was still on, the false cheerfulness of the news team only adding to her general state of frustration.

She picked up the remote, clicked to her own affiliate news station, and lowered the volume.

"You know I love you . . ." Philip had said to her. It was automatic. Routine. The proper thing to say. But Joanna wondered what Philip's definition of love was? Or did he even have one?

Now that she was up she wasn't feeling nearly as bad as she had the night before. But Philip's idea that she stay home for the day was starting to seem like a good one. She made herself a cup of tea and got a container of yogurt from the refrigerator. Curling up on the sofa to eat and listen to the news, she mused about her boyfriend.

Joanna knew that as soon as Philip walked into the studio he'd flirt and joke with the staff and technicians. The rest of his day would be a series of hustles and negotiations for leads, information, follow-ups, and breaking news. He'd pursue a tip or conduct an interview for the twelve o'clock news, and begin immediately to take notes on stories for the four o'clock segment. He'd have lunch at a place where he could be seen, and schmooze with connections to the powerful and the influential in city or national government, in entertainment.

And he'd forget to call her.

Not deliberately. It was never thoughtlessly planned. Philip just assumed that she would understand. She used to.

Joanna finished her breakfast and, pulling the blanket around her which Philip had used during the night, she lay watching the TV. And suddenly wondered what Trevor Jackson was doing just then. What was he going to do today? Would he try to call her again?

Joanna wondered how her parents and her brother would respond to someone like Trevor. Not that it was anything but conjecture, Joanna thought to herself as she began to drift and float toward sleep. Trevor was the kind of man she herself would never go for. With his casual air of command and his persuasiveness. With his urban drawl and the street-smart edge. With his masculinity that was so forceful and in your face. So hard to ignore.

Would her family try to tell her that she was out of her mind for even thinking about someone like that?

No doubt.

But she did anyway.

Joanna heard the familiar sound of the key in the lock and the door being pushed open.

Sheila had finally come back home.

But there was something wrong about the idea, and something wrong about the sounds. Joanna heard men's voices, not Sheila's, and there was tinny applause in the background.

She opened her eyes and frowned. The applause was coming from the TV audience of a popular morning talk show. The men's voices were out in the hallway. The door to Sheila's apartment *was* being unlocked.

Pulling her cramped body into an upright position, Joanna stood up and turned off the TV. She went to her apartment door. She tried to listen through the thick metal but couldn't make out much of anything. For a brief moment, she considered calling the police. Then she quickly reasoned that the men next door might very well be the police.

She unlocked the door and made an opening just big

enough for her head to poke through to see what was happening. In the hallway stood Danny and Mr. Tillman, the owner and manager of the building.

"Don't know why they had to glue the damn thing in place," Mr. Tillman muttered, as he ripped the seal.

"So no one could get in," Danny supplied helpfully.

"I know it's to keep everybody out," Mr. Tillman said patiently. "They could have used tape or something. This will never all come off."

"Use hot water. Or nail polish remover," Joanna suggested softly, making her presence known.

Danny turned quickly to face her, but Mr. Tillman only squinted and scowled.

"Oh, it's you. Thought you'd be at work."

Joanna instinctively pulled back from the man's petulant tone. He'd never been particularly friendly. "I'm not feeling very well. I decided to stay home today. I heard voices."

Mr. Tillman grunted. "Police finally released the apartment. Now I gotta get rid of all this stuff. It's going to take three days to paint in there, and I got someone coming in on the first of the month."

"Oh . . ." Joanna said. The building owner was abrupt and sharp, as if the contents of Sheila's life held no significance to him and interfered with his plans.

"You gonna throw out Miz James's things?" Danny asked.

The manager shrugged. "Nothing but junk." He wagged a threatening finger at his startled employee. "You do like I told you, Danny. Put everything in boxes and out it goes. In the trash. You get rid of all of her things and you can keep whatever you want. Something to remember her by. How's that?" he asked magnanimously.

Danny swallowed hard and moved restlessly from one foot to another. "I . . . I . . ."

"No, you can't do that."

Both men turned to stare at Joanna.

"What do you mean, no?" Mr. Tillman frowned.

"I mean, you just can't throw everything away. You have to give her family a chance to make a claim on her property."

"Oh no I don't," Mr. Tillman snickered. "Anyway, she probably didn't have any family."

"She had a husband," Joanna persisted. And then she wasn't sure she should have said anything. Given the way both Danny and Mr. Tillman stared at her, Joanna also wondered if perhaps she'd been indiscreet. Why hadn't Trevor contacted the landlord first thing?

"I don't believe it," Mr. Tillman scoffed.

Joanna nodded. "I met him yesterday."

"How do you know he was her husband? How come he's just turning up now? What kind of proof does he have?"

Joanna's skin grew warm as she realized that she couldn't answer even one of Mr. Tillman's questions. She began to feel foolish and naive. How could she just have taken Trevor Jackson's word for it?

She took so long to answer that the older man said something impatiently under his breath and turned back to the locked apartment door.

"What if he decides to sue you?" Joanna asked.

Mr. Tillman stopped and faced her once more. "I never wanted to rent to her to begin with. Look what happened? She gets herself killed on *my* property! This is not a welfare hotel."

Joanna stiffened immediately, her jaw tightening. She

spoke very quietly. "Careful, Mr. Tillman. Your prejudice is showing."

Joanna had the satisfaction of watching the man flush as he averted his gaze.

"So, where is this husband of hers?" he asked gruffly.

"I can call him if you like. He's very anxious to get Sheila's affairs settled. He wants to know what happened to her. I'm sure he wants to see her apartment."

"I haven't agreed to that yet," Mr. Tillman said, recouping his disagreeable spirit. "You can call him. If he can get here today . . . well, we'll see." He turned away and headed for the elevator. "Come on, Danny. I got things for you to do."

Danny remained where he stood, staring at Sheila's apartment door. Joanna was struck with how bewildered he seemed. Danny was several years younger than herself or Sheila, and there had always been something innocent and simple about him. His point of view made him sympathetic.

"Danny," she said. She wanted to reassure him that wherever Sheila was she was thinking and remembering him.

"Sheila liked me. She was nice to me," he mumbled, his voice close to tears. "I wish she didn't die. I wish she could come back."

Joanna's heart went out to him with his ingenuous plea.

"Danny!" Mr. Tillman nearly bellowed.

Danny quickly turned to follow the command, and Joanna closed her door.

The first thing she did was to call her office and let them know she wasn't going to be in that day. She offered up the excuse of being afflicted with a twenty-four-hour stomach virus.

The second thing she did was to try and remember the name of the hotel where Trevor Jackson was staying. Unable to do that, Joanna began a frantic fifteen-minute search for the various pink message sheets from the studio, which had Trevor's number on them. Joanna finally located one at the bottom of her tote bag.

She hurried to the phone, aware of her unseemly haste and anxiousness. It crossed Joanna's mind that her behavior was odd. She always did what she was supposed to or what was expected of her. She never made up excuses or bent the rules. But she was inordinately pleased with herself for having found a window of opportunity for Trevor. It was as if she'd also suddenly decided to participate in an elicit, inappropriate affair. This made her hesitate, but then she took a deep breath and began to dial the hotel number.

The operator put through the call. When the phone began to ring in his room, Joanna felt a stab of doubt and apprehension. Why was she withholding information from the police, stalling Mr. Tillman for a man she didn't know, and probably shouldn't? Joanna had no good answer except that she sensed that Trevor was sincere.

What am I doing? she asked herself.

The phone began a third ring. Joanna thought to hang up . . . but, then Trevor answered the phone.

"Yeah?" he opened aggressively.

She was thrown off balance. She started to speak and couldn't. Joanna's hand gripped the phone tighter.

"Yes, hi. It . . . it's Joanna Mitchell." There was only a slight pause but immediately Joanna felt vulnerable again. Too bold. This was the sort of thing Linda did. Not herself. She shouldn't have called.

"Hey," Trevor drawled out slowly.

Joanna felt relief. She liked the sound of surprise in his voice. She thought she could almost see the way he might smile as he said it. "I hope I didn't wake you. It's still early."

"You're probably getting ready to leave for work. I was already up myself."

"I'm not going to work today. I called in sick."

"What's wrong?" he asked at once.

Joanna heard the shift of his tone. From laid back to alert in half a second. "Nothing serious. I went out for dinner last night and ate something that didn't agree with me."

"With what's-his-name?"

"Philip. Yes."

"How are you feeling now?"

"Oh, better."

"Can I do anything for you?"

Joanna felt a strange sensation twist through her stomach. It was like another level of awareness that she wasn't expecting and didn't quite know how to react to. His question sounded so personal. "No, thanks. I'm . . . fine."

"I thought about calling you again," Trevor said quietly. "I was going to call last night."

"Were you? Why did you change your mind?"

Trevor chuckled. "I didn't think Santa would have liked it very much. It was nice getting together for lunch yesterday, but I thought maybe I should just leave you out of this business with Sheila. I know you don't want to get involved. I don't blame you."

Well, that was all true enough, Joanna thought—twenty-four hours ago. But she wasn't so sure anymore. There was something about Trevor's doggedness which had changed her mind, coupled with a sense of being needed.

"You're right. I did feel that way."

"So what changed *your* mind?"

"You did. You sort of shamed me into realizing that someone should care about what happened."

"I didn't mean to dump my business on you. I have my own reasons for wanting to keep on top of this. But it's not your problem."

"Does that mean you don't need my help anymore?" Joanna asked.

"No, that's not it. Maybe you won't like what you find out. Your boyfriend won't like it, either."

Joanna grimaced. "This really has nothing to do with Philip. Besides, he doesn't take you seriously."

"Oh, he doesn't, eh?" Trevor asked smoothly.

"You haven't proven you're who you say you are."

"Do you want me to?"

"Well . . ."

"Is that why you're calling?"

"I don't need you to prove anything," Joanna said confidently.

"You did yesterday. When I first met you, you acted like I was just trying to get over."

She shifted uneasily on the sofa cushions. She felt mildly annoyed with his probing questions. What was he trying to make her say? "Look, in a few days you'll be gone and it won't matter what I thought."

"So why are you calling?"

She hesitated. She didn't have to make it her concern

or become involved. But she already was. "I just thought you'd want to know the police have removed the restrictions on Sheila's apartment. The landlord can do what he wants. He's already leased the apartment and wants to dump Sheila's things out." She was surprised when she heard Trevor utter a quiet oath under his breath. "But I told Mr. Tillman he couldn't just get rid of anything without talking to you first."

"You did?" Trevor seemed startled.

"Well, he would have taken what he wanted, and he may have done that at the beginning anyway . . . and thrown everything else in the garbage. I told him that next of kin had a right to look through the contents first."

"You did?" Trevor repeated. He was less surprised now and more amused.

"And I said, if he doesn't give Sheila's husband a chance, you were going to get a court order or something, or maybe even sue him."

Trevor laughed. "That was quick thinking. I appreciate that."

Joanna sat grinning. "I just thought you'd want to know."

"That was really . . . pretty nice of you, Joanna," Trevor said.

She could detect a little awkwardness in his voice, but the easy familiarity with which he used her first name caught Joanna's attention as well. Trevor had inadvertently removed the last possibility of them continuing to treat one another as strangers. He had brought them closer together. Not exactly friends, but certainly acquaintances. But then, so had she by allowing it.

"You're welcome," Joanna responded. "I'm glad I was able to really help, after all."

A silence dropped between them that was both awkward and expectant. Joanna sensed that Trevor was waiting for her to say something, but she didn't know what. She'd already done more than was characteristic of her.

"What do I have to do now?" Trevor asked.

"You have to get in touch with the landlord as soon as you can."

"Okay."

"And he wants proof that you're who you say you are."

"No problem . . ."

"So that's it."

"Thanks," Trevor said. "Look, I know this is going to sound dumb, but I'm glad you were home sick today."

She shrugged. "Don't worry about it. I know what you mean."

"Then I guess I'd better get myself in gear. Dry off and get some clothes on."

Joanna frowned. "Excuse me?"

"I was just getting out of the shower when I heard the phone. I didn't have time to put anything on."

She stayed silent and stared at nothing in particular. Unexpectedly her imagination conjured up an alarmingly detailed projection of Trevor Jackson stark naked.

In her mind Joanna outlined his chest. It would be broad and firm. She wondered if he'd have skinny legs, or would he have muscled calves and thighs. And then she vividly filled in the rest of what Trevor's body would look like.

Joanna was enthralled with her own depiction.

"Joanna?"

She blinked. She felt embarrassed and breathless. "Yes?"

"What you did was great. Thanks again."

Trevor sounded stiff. Formal. She stood up, restless and anxious to end the call. There was no more to be said between them. He'd gotten what he'd wanted from her.

She felt let down.

"Good luck, Trevor. I hope everything works out."

"Me, too."

"Bye," Joanna said quickly and then hung up.

Trevor listened to the click of the line. Frowning, he, too, hung up. He knew he'd done the right thing. There was no need to continue to try and get next to Joanna Mitchell. Besides, she belonged to someone else. He had been given a bonus opportunity that he could not have gotten on his own. Now it was time to back off and leave her alone.

Trevor absently reached for the towel and slowly began to dry off. All the while, an image of Joanna stayed in his mind with her feminine aloofness. Just like some of the girls he used to know in high school who would have nothing to do with him and who sometimes treated him as if he wasn't good enough. The wrong kind of man. No good. That is, until he'd learned how to do better for himself.

But Joanna was still somehow different. It was true she hadn't trusted him at first, but she hadn't put him down at all. She just wanted him to be accountable. Trevor had been surprised to find out that he might want to. But what good would it do? Maybe he *wasn't* good enough. Maybe it was better to leave her to that dude she was so tight with. Yeah, but he didn't deserve her, either.

Suddenly, Trevor's past seemed to loom over him, huge and out of proportion to his life now. Suddenly, he didn't want Joanna Mitchell to know too much about him. Right now she probably didn't think he was such a bad person. But, if she ever found out the truth . . .

Trevor impatiently tossed the towel aside and began to dress.

Driving his rented car all the way across town to where Joanna lived he kept trying to piece together why she had changed her mind about him. When. Maybe she was trying to just get rid of him. Trevor shrugged impatiently as he huddled in his parka against the cold. What difference did it make? He'd gotten what he wanted. With determination he kept that in mind.

Trevor saw the maintenance man, Danny, but decided to avoid him. He couldn't really be of any help and would only slow him down. He found the management office on the second floor of the building, and the owner, Oscar Tillman. The older man looked him up and down suspiciously, but Trevor was used to that. He didn't like it very much, but he'd learned not to think that every look of distrust was because he was black. He kept himself reserved and returned Mr. Tillman's skepticism with cool indifference.

"You have to be outta there by six o'clock tonight."

"Six o'clock *Sunday* night," Trevor said firmly. He held out his hand for the keys and stared at the man.

"Okay. Sunday, then. But that's it," Mr. Tillman said, dropping the keys in Trevor's palm. He stepped back into his office and abruptly closed the door.

Trevor stared at the closed door and smiled sardonically. He tossed the keys into the air and caught them
again. The first thing he did was to leave the building
and find someplace to have copies made. Twenty minutes later Trevor stood outside of Sheila's apartment. In
just a few hours he could have the answers he needed
and be out of there. By tomorrow he could be out of
Philadelphia and on his way back home. He could go
back to where he came from, back to what he knew.

But then he turned his head to look at the door
marked 4A. Joanna's apartment. He stared at it a long
time, knowing that she was just on the other side. Finally, Trevor slowly approached the other door. He rang
the bell and stood waiting, his hands balled into fists in
his pockets. When the door opened, Trevor knew he was
making a big mistake. But he couldn't seem to stop himself.

Joanna was standing barefoot, dressed in black jeans
that made her seem tiny, and a bright yellow crewneck
sweat shirt. Her hair was combed back from her forehead. Her face was without makeup, and he thought she
really didn't need any. And her expression was so calm,
so open that Trevor had the weird sensation that Joanna
might have been waiting for him.

"Hi," Joanna said quietly, keeping her attention in his
face. She was caught by the uncertainty on Trevor's
sharp brown features. She found it interesting and different and was aware that somehow whatever happened
next between them, was entirely up to her.

Trevor was just going to thank her once again, and
then say goodbye. He was going to look in on Joanna
Mitchell and confirm his belief that she was way out of
his league. But instead, she was looking at him with a

familiarity and acknowledgement that made Trevor feel less awkward and less defensive. He found himself holding up the key ring for her to see. "I have the weekend to look through everything."

Joanna stared at the keys, and then looked at Trevor. She tilted her head. "Do you still want my help?" she asked.

Trevor gave one final thought to doing the right thing. Then he silently nodded.

Four

Joanna and Trevor stood together and looked slowly around the hallway and into the living room. She felt uncomfortable and hugged herself against the chill of the apartment. She had not been in Sheila's apartment more than two or three times, and never for more than a few minutes. So it felt strange to just walk in. Joanna felt as if she were invading someone's privacy, even though now it hardly mattered.

One of the first things to draw Joanna and Trevor's attention, however, was the markings on the beige carpeting that indicated where the body had been found and its position. Joanna just stared at the spot, feeling her stomach tighten. There was almost no blood, just a smear in the carpet where the head had lain. The tape outline otherwise showed that the body was at an awkward haphazard angle.

Joanna couldn't take her eyes off the floor, and she jumped when she felt Trevor's hand on her shoulder. She looked at him, her eyes wide.

"You've never been at a crime scene before." She shook her head silently. "You're lucky." His hand squeezed where it rested. "Want to leave?"

Again Joanna shook her head. "I'm okay."

The apartment was modestly and eclectically furnished. It was as if things had been purchased more on the spur of the moment than with any scheme in mind. There was a general disarray among the contents that suggested someone had been there before them. Certainly the police, looking for clues or information. But Joanna felt peculiar knowing that she was about to sort through the intimate and minute details of someone else's life.

Joanna glanced at Trevor and found him silently frowning at the details of the room. She wondered if he was suddenly feeling sadness or remorse, anger or regret for the way his relationship had gone and ended. She could read nothing in his expression beyond a concentration on his surroundings.

"Where do you want to start?" Joanna asked quietly.

Trevor didn't answer right away as he studied the layout of the furniture, the spaces and corners. He walked to the telephone and lifted the receiver. The line was dead. He checked the tape compartment on the answering machine. The tape was gone.

"I'm not going to bother with the furniture. I don't have the time to sort it all out and get rid of it. Maybe I'll just call someone to come and cart it away. Goodwill or Salvation Army."

"That's very generous," Joanna said somewhat in surprise.

Trevor was shaking his head. "I don't need lamps and chairs. I'm interested in her papers and documents."

"What are you looking for?"

Trevor didn't answer at first as he walked further into the room and glanced around. It would have been too easy if something obvious had stood out at once. The question was, where was Sheila likely to stash important things? Like money. He shrugged. "Letters, receipts, contracts, lease agreements, insurance policies. Anything that suggests a routine or pattern. Things Sheila did all the time. Records of people she knew."

"And then what?"

Trevor sighed. "Then I try to figure out what happened. And why."

"Do you mean last week when she died, or when she left years ago?"

He paused before he spoke. "Maybe both."

"What makes you think you can find out what happened when the police can't?"

Trevor looked at Joanna. "Sheila is just another homicide to them. I bet they deal with several in any given week. But I knew her."

"You mean, she was family," Joanna said.

Trevor stared at her for moment, as though he didn't understand what she was referring to. Then he turned away again. "That's right. She was family," he responded tightly.

"What would you like me to do?"

"I want to look around first. Then let's go through the closets and drawers. Any boxes . . ."

She nodded and shivered. "Maybe I can get Danny to bring up some boxes from the cellar. You can give her clothing to a second-hand store or something."

Slowly, Trevor retraced his steps to where Joanna stood. He noticed how stiffly she held herself. He kept his eyes on her and noticed how uncertain she was. He had a momentary second thought that it would have been better if he'd just come into Sheila's apartment alone. Do what he had to do and leave. But it was for purely selfish reasons that he wanted to see Joanna again, even if it delayed him. Trevor instinctively put his hands on her arms and made a short brisk rubbing movement, up and down. "Are you cold?"

"A little," she murmured. She stared at the front of his sweater, visible through the open parka.

She stood still while he touched her, aware of the way her body suddenly responded to his nearness. Joanna was sensitive to the fact that they were alone together . . . and probably shouldn't be. She looked up into his face and found Trevor watching her intently. His dark eyes seemed to be able to read right into her making her feel so inexperienced. He seemed practiced in taking care of himself by guile and cunning, rather than charm and personality. Unlike Philip. But there was something so exciting about being around Trevor Jackson.

He frowned down at her, his gaze narrowing in consideration. He had second thoughts. "Maybe you'd better not stay. I can do this by myself." He hadn't let go of her arms, and actually, his fingers kneaded into her flesh seductively.

Joanna stared wide-eyed at him. She felt disappointed that Trevor might have changed his mind.

"You're supposed to be home sick, remember?" he said with a shrug.

She smiled. "I only had an upset stomach. I wasn't on my deathbed."

He chuckled silently. "I promise I won't tell anyone. Especially Old St. Nick."

Joanna grimaced and turned to face the room. "I'm staying," she said firmly, putting an end to his quavering on the point.

Trevor had taken off his coat and thrown it over the back of the sofa. There was a wrapped butterscotch candy on the cushion, and another on the end table, near the base of the lamp. Trevor picked them both up and handed one to Joanna. She took it gingerly.

"Sheila was on Preston Canin's candy list, eh?"

"About the only people not on the list were Danny and Mr. Tillman. Sheila had a dish she used to keep filled with butterscotch. Over there." Joanna pointed to an end table.

Trevor saw only an empty space. "It probably got moved during the investigation. I'm going to start in here. Why don't you check out the kitchen or bedroom."

"The kitchen?" she said skeptically.

"Yeah. Maybe she put all her money in a plastic bag in the freezer," he said flippantly.

Joanna had to chortle at the thought. "You watch too many Wesley Snipes movies."

"I like Wesley Snipes," Trevor said lightly, as he began to lift all the cushions on the sofa and side chairs, and search with his hand underneath.

Joanna watched him for an amazed moment. "So do I . . ." she responded absently. She hadn't realized that their search would have to be that thorough, and she still had no idea what Trevor hoped to find that hadn't already come to light by the police. But she left him there and found her way to the small bedroom next to the living room.

There was a queen-sized bed, two small matching bureaus, one on either side of the room. An end table stood next to the bed, and a vanity bench at the foot. The curtains matched the bedspread, and all of it was edged with white eyelet lace. It was fussy and overdone for the size of the room. And Joanna was taken aback by the half dozen or so stuffed animals that were positioned on the pillows.

The presence of the toys seemed so sentimental . . . and adolescent. Joanna never would have suspected it of Sheila.

One bureau top was crowded with a makeup tray, bottles of expensive perfume, and a wooden jewelry chest. One bottle of perfume was spilled, and the smell still lingered gently. The contents of the chest had been emptied on the dresser and spread out. But on closer examination Joanna could see they were all costume pieces.

The bureau contained the usual accessories and underwear. Everything seemed so normal that Joanna wasn't sure she'd recognize if something were different and, therefore, potentially important. She gently rifled through things, nonetheless. Joanna came across three packages of pantyhose. One had been opened but the contents had not been removed. When she hazarded a look into the opening, she noticed that something had been inserted between the nylon and cardboard filler. They were Polaroid snapshots.

Each one showed Sheila at some social function with several other people. There was usually one particular man at her side, and Joanna suspected the pictures may have been taken and kept for that reason. Each man had an air and look of importance and power. All well dressed and urbane. All older. Some of the men were black, some were not. Joanna didn't recognize any of them.

There was one photo in which Sheila's escort obviously didn't want his picture taken. A younger black man, at the last moment, used his outstretched hand to block the camera lens. Only his mouth and chin were clearly seen. She stared at the photo, wondering about someone who wanted to be with Sheila, but didn't want to be seen with her. She squinted, wondering if this was someone she might know.

Joanna put the pictures aside to show Trevor. Realizing now the possibility of things being deliberately hidden in the room, she began to look more thoroughly, feeling as if she'd fallen into the set of a movie. *No one* would believe what she was doing.

A further search unearthed several boxes of new shoes which hadn't been worn. They still had tissue stuffed into the toes, and the bamboo rod for shaping. Continuing with the knowledge that anything was possible, Joanna pulled out the tissue paper in one shoe and found a small zip-locked bag with jewelry. Closer examination showed everything to be real. Diamond ear studs; rubies in a drop setting with French backing; a blue topaz pendant on a thin gold chain.

And she found the diamond drop pendant Philip had given her when she'd been named head of the research department at the station. Joanna gasped slowly as she turned the necklace over in her hand. She was positive it was hers. She remembered Sheila admiring it, referring to the diamond as "precious." Philip had been furious with her when she'd told him she'd lost it. It was about the time Sheila had taken to visiting Joanna occasionally on Sunday morning. Since Sheila had made such an obvious attempt to hide the bag, Joanna wondered whether some of the other jewelry belonged to Sheila . . . or to someone else.

Her question was answered a half-hour later when Joanna was looking through the closet and came across a silk dress she'd lent her neighbor nearly a year ago. But Joanna gasped when she also found a scarf and a sweater that belonged to her which she thought had simply been misplaced quite a while ago.

"How did this . . ." she began in bewilderment, ques-

tioning how her things had come to be in Sheila's posses-
sion. Had Sheila "borrowed" them while visiting her
apartment? Joanna puzzled. What, exactly, had her neighbor been up to?

"Find anything?"

Joanna jumped at the sudden sound of Trevor's voice.
Her hand automatically closed around the necklace. She
stared mutely at him. Should she tell Trevor that his late
wife appeared to have been either a thief or a klepto-
maniac . . . or did he already know that?

"Some photographs. And these." She held up the garments and the plastic bag.

Trevor nodded, but he kept his gaze on her face. He
slowly approached and reached out to take Joanna's
hand, using his thumb to gently pry open her fingers.
He glanced down at the sparkling necklace.

"Where'd you find them?"

"Hidden in things. Her shoes," she whispered, incredulous.

"Are they yours?

Joanna shrugged. "The necklace . . . I think so. I had
one just like it. I thought I'd lost it."

He shook his head and his eyes flashed in sudden
anger. "No. It's probably yours. Take it."

"Trevor, there are other things, too."

The muscles in his jaw tightened. "I bet."

Joanna frowned at him. "You don't seem very surprised."

"I'm not. Nothing surprises me anymore."

Joanna thoughtfully considered the things in her hand.
"Is that a comment on Sheila, or life in general?"

"People always live up to your worst expectations."

"Not mine. Not always," Joanna countered seriously,

trying to read more into Trevor's sudden cynicism. "Just what kind of people have you known?"

He chuckled harshly. "You don't want to know. I'm telling you." He took the photographs from her. "Do you know who these men are?"

"No, I don't," she said, still puzzling over the conversation.

Trevor pointed to the one unclear image. "This one didn't want his picture taken at all."

"What does that mean?"

He pursed his mouth thoughtfully and shook his head as he continued to stare at the photo. "That he didn't want to be seen with Sheila, or he wasn't supposed to be where the picture was taken."

Joanna made a small sound of shock and sat down on the vanity bench. Trevor chuckled again and sat next to her, his arm and thigh pressed against hers. Joanna didn't particularly like what she was doing, snooping through closets and dresser drawers, but she was suddenly glad for Trevor's presence, and she knew this had to be done. He felt so solid and warm next to her. For one thing, he seemed to be a kind of link between the world that she knew and the one that Sheila came from. He was really the only one who could make sense of the kind of life she'd led. Which made Joanna all the more curious about Trevor's background.

She glanced at his profile. "How did you and Sheila meet?"

"At a party," Trevor responded after a moment. "Nothing glamorous or special. Just a bunch of people together trying to have a good time."

Joanna tried to envision them meeting. Were they attracted right away? Did Trevor have to pursue her? Did she come after him? "How long before you decided to get married?"

Trevor stared straight ahead. "A few months. It was fast. Maybe that's why it didn't last." Then he looked at Joanna, his eyes examining her features. "But I got over it."

Joanna cleared her throat. "And what do you think about her now?"

"I think I feel sorry for her. But I'll tell you something. Sheila and I aren't so different."

She blinked at him. "I don't believe that."

He smiled. "That's because you're a nice person."

"You're not anything like her."

Trevor was careful about his response. He continued to look at Joanna, trusting that what he'd learned of her innate character wouldn't mislead him and she wouldn't hold him in contempt. "I used to be, but I was luckier than she was."

Joanna lowered her gaze from the speculation in Trevor's. "I don't know what you're saying. I don't understand."

"I'm only saying that I'm glad I'm getting a chance to know you. You're nothing like Sheila. Or anyone else I've ever met. And you're not . . . afraid of me. I'm saying that Sheila was a long time ago. But now . . ."

Joanna could hear her own heartbeat, could feel the pumping of it in her chest. *What was Trevor trying to say?* "Yes?"

Trevor looked into her pretty face. It would be so easy to take her over, Trevor thought, to sway Joanna now that he'd gotten her to feel comfortable with him. He had a sudden thought that he wanted to know what it was like to make love to someone who wasn't experienced. Someone who didn't play games or have a hidden agenda. Someone who had a family, a background, a past. But Trevor recognized that Joanna Mitchell was the kind of person who would make love with her heart, not just her body, and he didn't want to start something he wasn't sure he would get a chance to finish.

He smiled gently at her, forcing his mind to slide away from an instinct to manipulate the moment. He leaned toward Joanna and kissed her on her temple. He could feel her body stiffen just a bit, but it was more in surprise than rejection. Then Trevor took her hand and threaded his fingers with hers.

"No matter what happens, I want you to know you're one of the nicest things that's ever happened in my life. I'm glad you wanted to help me."

Joanna listened to his words. They surprised and pleased her, but she was also suddenly aware of a kind of dissatisfaction with his confession. She believed Trevor. But she was strangely disappointed that he hadn't said more. Or tried more. Joanna was shocked at the direction of her own thoughts, but Trevor somehow made her feel that she was capable of so much more than others gave her credit for.

"You make it sound like . . . something is going to happen to you. Or to me."

Trevor leaned closer and looked into her eyes. "I'm not going to let anything happen to you . . ."

They were so close that Joanna could detect the faint essence of the butterscotch candy on his breath. She could hear the way his deep voice seemed to come up from the center of his chest. It reminded her again of his mouth. She wondered what it would be like to . . .

"Joanna, I just . . ." Trevor began. He placed his fin-

gertips under her chin. He didn't have to lift Joanna's
chin very much so that his mouth could lightly touch
hers, their lips just barely pressed together.

He expected an outright protest from her, but Joanna
only sat perfectly still. She didn't exactly encourage him,
but she hadn't pulled away from him, either. Trevor decided not to push his luck. He stroked her jaw with his
fingertips and released her mouth.

"I think we'd better get back to work." He stood up.

Joanna's gaze followed him. She sat still, wondering
why she hadn't tried to stop Trevor from kissing her.
Why had it seemed so easy to just sit and let him touch
her? He seemed edgy now, anxious to forget about the
small episode. Should she tell him it was okay? Was it?

He turned in the bedroom door to face her. His expression had closed down. "Let's look for a little while
longer. We're not going to finish today anyway."

"Do you want me to come back tomorrow?"

Trevor stared at her. He was afraid of what would
happen if they were together for another day. He could
see that Joanna had already passed that cautious stage
which had protected her when they'd first met. There
was a growing attraction, and Trevor wasn't sure what
he should do about it, or if he should do anything at all.

"What about Santa Claus?"

Joanna got annoyed. "I'm making the offer, Trevor,
not Philip. He has his own plans for this weekend, and
I'm not responsible for reporting in to him."

"You had a fight," he observed succinctly. "Are you
sure you know what you're doing?"

The question had a gravely warning note to it that
made Joanna's stomach muscles flutter. It almost suggested that Trevor had something specific in mind that

had nothing whatsoever to do with Sheila. "Do you want me to come back tomorrow?" she repeated.

Again, Trevor stared at her. "We'll see," he said, before returning to the living room.

It was a disappointing afternoon. Trevor found one bundle of canceled checks, but it was for an account that had been closed at a bank in another city three years earlier. There was nothing unusual in what the services had been for. Joanna could see Trevor's frustration at not having come across anything of immediate importance.

"Maybe she had a safety deposit box or something."

"I don't think so. That would mean having an account in her name, and leaving identification and a signature. She was too careful for things like that."

"Why?"

"It can be traced."

"Oh . . ." Joanna murmured, not quite making the connection.

But more than that was a dawning sense of Sheila's life as having been one of scams and subterfuge. She looked long and hard at Trevor, wondering just how true his earlier comment was. That he and Sheila were alike.

"I think we should give it up for today. I could use something to eat. Do you feel like going out for dinner?" Trevor asked in an offhand manner.

"Well, I was going to check in on Preston and see if he needs anything."

Trevor shrugged. "How about we invite him to come with us?"

Joanna stared in surprise. She'd suggested that same thing to Philip once or twice, but he'd been adamantly against the idea. And it wasn't that Philip didn't like

Preston; he just didn't want to spend his time with the older man.

"Are you sure? I mean, the wheelchair is awkward and—"

"I know how to deal with a wheelchair."

Joanna nodded, her eyes bright. She was impressed. "I think he'd like that very much. He can't really get out on his own, and the weather is so bad. I was going to take him out tomorrow."

"Is there someplace nearby we can go?"

"There's an Italian bistro a few blocks from here."

Trevor chuckled wryly. "Thai? Italian? I had something else in mind. Don't you have any decent soul food restaurants in this city?"

Joanna laughed lightly. "Not better than my mother's cooking. When I go visit, I get the real thing."

"Does your mom do doggie bags?" he asked.

Joanna found Trevor's response amusing, but when she glanced at him, he seemed serious. There was no chance for her to ask why he wanted to know. They both heard noises outside in the hall, as if something were being dragged across the floor. They exchanged puzzled looks and went to investigate.

Trevor had not locked the apartment door, and when he pulled it open Danny was on the other side. He was clumsily maneuvering several corrugated cardboard boxes.

"Thank you, Danny," Joanna said. "I was going to ask you to bring some boxes up so we could pack things."

Danny stared at Trevor. "How come you're here?"

Joanna frowned and looked back and forth between the two men. "Mr. Jackson is . . ."

"Helping to get rid of the things in the apartment so

you can paint it for the next tenant. Are you here to help, too?"

Danny dropped the boxes and stepped back. "I'm busy. I gotta fix the back door. I . . ."

"You don't have to be afraid to come in. There aren't any ghosts inside," Joanna teased him.

He shook his head. "They found her in there. She was dead."

Abruptly, Danny turned and headed back toward the elevator. Trevor stared after him.

"Is he always that nervous?"

"You have to understand that Danny is sometimes like a little kid. He gets fixated on things. He liked Sheila. All he knows is that she's gone, and he doesn't seem to understand why. Sheila treated him like . . ."

"Like he was important," Trevor said thoughtfully.

"Yes, I think so," Joanna nodded, surprised by his insight.

"Yeah, she was good at making you feel good," he quipped. Trevor touched her arm. "Look, I'll put these boxes inside."

"And I'll call Preston with your invitation."

"Good enough."

Joanna entered her own apartment and saw the flashing light on her answering machine. She hoped that no one from her office had called to check on her. But the first message was from Linda.

"I thought you called in sick? How come you didn't let me know? If you went shopping without me, I'll never forgive you. Talk to you later."

The second message was from Philip.

"Hey, where are you? How come you're not in bed? I told you I'd call. But . . . ah . . . I can't come over tonight. As a matter of fact," there was the sound of a light nervous chuckle, "you probably won't see me at all this weekend. Sorry, babe. I got invited to spend the weekend in D.C. There's a meeting and reception being held by the Congressional Black Caucus. Hope you're feeling better. I'll try to call before leaving tonight."

Joanna didn't feel any surprise. She wasn't even angry. If anything, she felt a little bit of guilt as she remembered that she'd spent the afternoon with another man and had let that man kiss her. A flood of heat over her body made Joanna feel that she was hardly in a position to be indignant by Philip's announcement.

She made a quick call to Preston. When she told her elderly neighbor of Trevor's invitation, he at first declined. He didn't want to ruin their date. Joanna assured Preston that it wasn't a date.

When Trevor arrived for her several minutes later, Joanna was ready, dressed in snow boots and a red jacket. He insisted that she wear a hat.

"I don't wear hats. Messes up my hair," Joanna shrugged.

"You lose body heat through your head. The weather is cold, and you were home sick today."

Joanna sighed in exasperation as she found a knit hat at the top of her closet. "First it's my eating habits, now it's my body heat."

"I might want to check out your sleeping patterns next," Trevor said outrageously.

Joanna took the comment lightly, but her laughter was nervous. It was an incredibly erotic thought, and not an unpleasant one. She stepped out of the apartment and was about to close and lock her door when the telephone began to ring.

"Telephone," Trevor announced unnecessarily as he watched Joanna's hesitation. "Don't you want to get it?"

Joanna shook her head and closed the door. "No. I know who it is," she said quietly.

The last of the dishes had been cleared from the table. Preston pulled the napkin free from where it had been tucked into the throat of his shirt, and wiped his mouth and hands.

"That was good. Sorry I couldn't eat it all."

"Don't worry about it," Trevor said easily. "We'll have them wrap the rest to take home."

"Very thoughtful of you two to include me in your evening." He scrutinized Joanna. "I take it Philip wasn't available?"

Joanna gnawed at her bottom lip and avoided Trevor's silent stare. "He had business to take care of."

"Too bad. But it turned out to be good luck for me," Preston grinned.

"Me, too," Trevor added quietly.

"You two would have had a better time without me." He cackled. "Philip's loss . . ."

"Preston, stop," Joanna said softly, shifting uncomfortably in her chair, aware of the way Trevor was looking at her.

"Trevor would like to be alone with you. Isn't that so?"

Trevor merely grinned in a lazy, unconcerned manner. "I don't think I'll answer that."

Preston laughed. " 'Cause you know I'm right." He shook his head as his humor sobered. "Too bad Sheila couldn't come, too."

Finally Joanna exchanged a silent glance with Trevor but decided against correcting Preston again. It was Trevor who got Preston back on the right track of time and place.

"I guess you miss her."

Preston blinked and looked embarrassed. "Well . . . yeah. Nice woman, but so sad. Her life was just one party after another. I think she didn't like being by herself much. She always wanted me to tell her about when I worked for the city and all the important people I knew in government."

Joanna frowned. "I didn't know that. She was interested in government?"

Preston's laugh was short. "Hell, no. Sheila was interested in who was who. I even got her a job once, working in the press offices of the City Council. Didn't last long."

"How come?" Trevor asked.

"Well, Sheila wasn't really interested in holding a job. She was more interested in opportunities." He frowned and fingered the napkin. "When I see her again, I'll have to tell her to be careful. Those men are sharks. She can't handle them."

"When was the last time you saw Sheila?" Trevor asked, again trying to keep Preston focused.

He squinted and thought hard, rubbing his arthritic hands together. "Why . . . that morning. New Year's Eve. She brought me doughnuts and told me all about this fancy-dancy party she was going to. Then she asked if she could borrow twenty dollars. I gave her fifty."

"Who was she going to the party with?" Trevor asked.

"Mac."

Joanna was very alert. "Mac? The police asked me about someone named Mac."

Preston was shaking his head sadly. "I never saw her alive again."

"Did Mac come to take her to this party? Did you see him?"

Preston continued to slowly shake his head. "He just left her there," he whispered vaguely. "It wasn't supposed to happen."

"Who left her?" Joanna asked, getting confused.

Preston looked momentarily puzzled, and then shrugged and mumbled. "Don't remember."

Joanna felt a little frustrated with Preston, but decided to stop questioning him. When he got tired, he got confused. She stood up. "I think it's time to take you home, Preston."

"Will you watch out for her?" he asked Trevor.

Trevor frowned, not knowing if Preston meant Sheila . . . or Joanna. "I'll try."

"I know you think I'm a foolish old man but you listen to me. It wasn't supposed to happen . . ."

Joanna helped Preston into his coat. "Come on. You're tired. We'll be home soon."

Trevor paid the bill. They left the restaurant and began the short but cold walk back to the building. Preston was silent as he was wheeled along; his head dropped forward and his eyes closed.

"You like him a lot, don't you?" Trevor asked Joanna.

Joanna smiled fondly. "Yes, I do. He's a kind, good man. Preston is a champion of lost causes and the underdog."

"I don't see you as either," Trevor observed.

"Well, I was a young black woman with a new job

in Philadelphia and no place to live. I found out that in this day and age there are still places where it's hard to rent. Mr. Tillman was like that. My credentials sounded good. *I* sounded good over the phone, but when I came to view the apartment, what a surprise to hear it had *just* been leased by someone else."

"So where does Preston Canin come in?"

"Well, I mentioned my problem to someone at work. They thought it was a great human relations-public interest-consumer something story for the news, and did a segment. Preston saw it and called me. He lived in the building and was a retired attorney with ACLU. He said he'd help me file suit. But it never got that far. Mr. Tillman got nervous when the story went public and changed his mind about renting to me.

"Then Preston and his wife Hannah sort of adopted me. Hannah died about three years ago."

"What about Sheila? How did she get an apartment?"

"I don't know. Either Mr. Tillman had learned his lesson, which I doubt, or someone intervened on her behalf."

"Preston?"

"I don't think so. Preston was in the hospital recovering from minor surgery when Sheila moved in."

"Then how did the two of them meet and become so friendly?"

"I had a little birthday party for Preston at my place. I invited Philip and some of the people in the building. Sheila invited herself. She was next door, remember? They hit it off. She made a big fuss over him. Preston loved it.

"Sheila was like that. She was the life of the party.

She even came on to Philip. It didn't matter that he and I were together."

"How did Philip react to that?" Trevor asked.

Joanna wished he hadn't.

She kept her tone indifferent, even though she clearly recalled how Philip had done nothing to discourage Sheila's brazen behavior. "He thought she was just being friendly."

Trevor turned his head to look down at her. "What about you?"

"Like I said, it was a party. Sheila was just being Sheila," Joanna said evenly.

Preston had come awake by the time they reached the building. In his apartment he declared himself perfectly capable of preparing himself for the night. He shook hands with Trevor.

"Thanks for dinner."

"My pleasure . . ."

Preston held onto Trevor's hand and pulled him closer to whisper, "Can you keep a secret?"

"Yeah, sure." Trevor frowned.

"There's something I want you to see. It belonged to Sheila."

Trevor stared at Preston. "What is it?"

Preston looked from him to Joanna. "You have to promise me first that you won't do anything about what I'm going to show you without letting me know. I don't want to do anything to hurt Sheila. But I think she could be in trouble."

"What kind of trouble?" Joanna asked.

Trevor sighed and his expression was knowing. "The shark kind," he murmured.

"I don't get it," Joanna said.

"She was afraid to leave anything in her apartment."

"What did she give you?" Trevor asked.

Preston sighed. "I hope she'll forgive me . . ." He wheeled himself over to a closet and opened the door. He pointed to a brown leather attaché case lying on the floor.

Trevor pulled out the case and took it over to the coffee table. He looked at Joanna as he sat on the edge of Preston's sofa. Snapping the clasp open, he lifted the top and peered inside for a long moment. Then he glanced up at Joanna.

"Bingo."

Trevor sighed as he began to replace the packets of paper back into the case. Joanna had sat next to him in her living room as they'd quickly gone through the contents of the attaché. There were checkbooks, deposit receipts, and two ledgers. There was another little cache of jewelry, letters, and a passport.

"Is that what you were hoping to find?" Joanna asked Trevor as he stood up and lifted the case to the floor.

"It's a very good start. I'll have to sit and go through everything carefully. But I don't think it's everything."

"Well, it's better than we had before."

"Yeah. Thank goodness Preston trusts you," Trevor said with feeling.

"He never mentioned that case to me before. And it's obvious he said nothing to the police about it."

"I wonder why."

"I think he trusts you, Trevor."

Trevor felt uncomfortable with that idea. But he couldn't believe his luck in being able to get ahold of some of Sheila's personal papers. All because they'd taken an elderly man to dinner. "Why would he trust me?"

"Maybe because he believes you can help Sheila. You know. Like clear her name or something like that."

Trevor remained silent and thoughtful as he picked up his coat and put it on. He'd seen his purpose in Philadelphia as being somewhat different. And he certainly didn't think that either Preston Canin or Joanna Mitchell would approve of his intentions. Trevor wondered if they would both change their minds about him if they knew the whole story. For that matter, it could change their entire perspective on Sheila. It wasn't worth taking the chance to find out, he decided. He was close to getting what he'd come to Philadelphia for.

The only factors that had changed since he'd located Sheila and decided to send that telegram, was to discover that she'd died . . . and that he liked Joanna Mitchell. As far as Trevor was concerned, it was Joanna who had the potential for being the bigger problem.

No. He didn't see her as a problem. Just very unexpected. And when he was done with what he had to do concerning Sheila, Trevor wondered, even though he knew he was being stupid, what he was going to do about Joanna.

"Are you going to take that with you?" Joanna asked as they stood by the door of her apartment again.

"I want to go through the papers. Maybe I'll do that tomorrow instead of looking through the apartment again."

"Oh . . ." Joanna nodded, surprised at the disappointment she felt. She stared at Trevor, silently wondering if he remembered what had happened earlier between them in Sheila's bedroom. Had he felt the same confusion and threat as she had, or was she the only one whose imagination had gone into overdrive?

"It's late. I'd better go," Trevor murmured, his expression uncertain.

"Yes," she responded, feeling somewhat shy and awkward under his scrutiny.

"Here . . ." Trevor suddenly said, reaching into his coat pocket and extracting a key ring. He held it out to Joanna. "The keys to Sheila's."

Joanna just stared and frowned at the swaying keys. "I . . . don't think I want to be in her apartment by myself."

"Take them anyway."

Reluctantly, Joanna reached to take the ring. As her fingers closed around the keys, Trevor gently grabbed her wrist. Her attention shifted to his face, and she felt the change between them at once. The danger signal. The sudden heat of anticipation. The curiosity that just wouldn't go away, and which had been tantalizingly close the whole afternoon. She stared into Trevor's eyes and knew exactly what he wanted. He was bold and clear, and Joanna understood the drift of his thoughts. For the life of her she felt no desire to pull away. She experienced a kind of reckless disregard for being sensible and safe.

Joanna sighed inwardly, with the painful realization that Philip didn't seem to factor into her thoughts at that moment. It was frightening to think that their past relationship might not be enough to deter her from the powerful inclination of the moment. Trevor's eyes seemed so dark that she couldn't tell anything from them. His jaw flexed. She could sense his purpose through the warm strength of his hand. It seemed to radiate right into her own body.

"I know I've already said thanks for all you've done . . ." he said softly.

"That's right."

"Then I won't say it again. That's not what I want to do anyway . . ."

Instead Trevor pulled Joanna toward him by her hand. She didn't resist, but stepped closer as he bent to lightly kiss her cheek. That was all he meant to do because he was sure she would not let him do more. He let his lips linger against Joanna's skin. It was incredibly soft and smooth and smelled so sweet that suddenly he wanted to feel what it would be like to hold her in his arms.

When Trevor felt his body begin to tighten at just the thought, he let go of Joanna's hand. He rested his hand against the side of her waist. He meant to lift his mouth away from her face, but found himself brushing his lips closer to Joanna's mouth. He heard the intake of breath.

"Trevor," Joanna whispered, suddenly afraid of her acquiescence. She didn't mind the kiss on the cheek. It had been more affectionate than impertinent.

But Trevor didn't want to give Joanna time to change her mind now. He didn't think he'd have another chance to get this close to her, because convention would get in the way. Or Joanna would realize that he was not the kind of man she should get mixed up with. He held his mouth a hairsbreadth above hers. When Joanna didn't say anything more, Trevor firmly pressed his lips to hers, having decided to hell with the consequences.

Trevor felt swift desire shoot through his groin. Joanna's mouth was not unwilling. Her lips were soft and puckered gently against his. But Trevor wasn't going to accept half measures. He used the pressure of his mouth to force hers open wider, and then let his tongue sweep boldly inside. He felt a reflexive jerk in Joanna's body at the contact. She drew her tongue back out of reach but Trevor quickly caught it, stroking and sucking until Joanna gave in to the erotic dance as their lips fused.

She could hear Trevor's breathing. She could hear her own heartbeat. She could feel the way the tension throbbed in her body. Joanna rested her palms against Trevor's chest, through the opening of his winter jacket. She was afraid of more contact. Their thighs barely touched. His hands rested very lightly around her waist with no attempt to draw her nearer, but his strong fingers squeezed and kneaded into her. Joanna wondered what it would be like to feel his warm hands right on her flesh. The thought made her moan gently, as a quick mental image heightened the fantasy.

Trevor took advantage of the response to deepen the kiss, his tongue relentless in its mating with hers. Joanna's femininity was reflected in the way she kissed him back. Gently. Experimentally. Encouraging.

But for Joanna, Trevor's embrace was like something primal, natural. She had always been aware of the practiced ease that Philip used with her. Like he knew exactly what he was doing and how to get the response and reaction that he thought was right. But Trevor just seemed to let himself go with his instincts. There was not thought as to how he was going to kiss her. He just did. For Joanna, that naturalness made her feel less safe than she did with Philip. Trevor wasn't as predictable. And because he wasn't, she realized that her response could easily escalate out of control.

Joanna forced herself to pull her mouth free from Trevor's. She felt like she had to get a breath of air. Right now, she couldn't even talk. She kept her eyes closed but gently tried to push herself out of his arms.

She waited for Trevor to say something clever and very male. Something that boasted of his sexual ego and intentions. Something like most men would say who are assured of their prowess. But he didn't.

"I'm not going to say I'm sorry about that," he whispered firmly.

Joanna opened her eyes and glanced up at him. His nostrils were still flared and his mouth parted and moist.

"I didn't think you would," she replied. "I wasn't going to ask you to."

"Then you don't mind."

"I guess I don't," she murmured, flustered.

He stroked her cheek. "I'm not going to tell you, Joanna, that I won't try it again."

Joanna stared at him and felt words struggling from her. "Philip and I have been together a long time. My family . . . thinks a lot of him."

Trevor's smile was slow and knowing. He touched his fingertips to Joanna's mouth and stepped back to zipper his coat and put on the brimmed cap.

"Then you don't have anything to worry about," he said smoothly.

Five

Trevor sat on the side of the bed with his elbows braced on his knees, and his hands clasped together. He silently and intently stared at the hotel phone, not sure if he wanted to hear it ring or not. And he didn't know if he felt relief or disappointment when it didn't happen.

Joanna Mitchell could, at that very instant, be calling him one kind of arrogant fool or another, or had made up her mind that what had happened the night before wasn't going to happen again.

Cursing under his breath, Trevor bounced up from the bed and began nervously pacing the room. He wished he hadn't come to Philadelphia in the first place. He should have just let things stay the way they had been for years. He wished he hadn't given up cigarettes. For that matter he could use a stiff drink . . . but not this early in the morning. He wished Joanna Mitchell wasn't who she was. But then, if she had been like women he'd known in the past, or anything like Sheila, he wouldn't even be giving her this much thought.

Trevor had a strong suspicion, if he could judge by his difficulty in getting to sleep the night before and a desire to check out of the hotel and leave the city in the middle of the night, that he was developing a real thing for someone he couldn't have. Someone else's woman.

Hey, it had happened before. That was the name of the game. You see something or someone you want, you go after it. Claim it if you can, walk away if you can't . . . Trevor stopped the restless pacing and stood in front of the mirror. He gazed with curiosity at his face. He wondered how it held up compared to Philip Lee's. *Not even close,* Trevor concluded to himself.

Philip Lee struck him as the kind of black man who had done everything right so that he could be exactly where he was right now. Went to college. Got the right kind of jobs. The right kind of women. He was slick. Turned out. Smart. Knew the rules and how to play them. While *he,* on the other hand, had just been slick.

Trevor frowned at his reflection and nervously began cracking the knuckles in his hands. This whole thing hadn't gone the way he'd planned. Once he'd gotten the information from his friend Bradly that Sheila was on the East Coast, Trevor thought he could straighten out that mess from the past and go on about his business. He hadn't counted on Joanna Mitchell.

One thing, however, was *very* clear to Trevor. He wanted to make love to her. He wanted to be on top of her and feel her arms and legs holding tightly around him. He wanted to hear how she'd sound and how she'd move against him—with him—and know it was because the two of them were together. He wanted to feel that he could take care of her and make her feel good. Maybe Joanna would even . . .

It was never going to happen.

Trevor turned away from the mirror, feeling his gut tighten. "Oh, man . . ." he groaned in frustration.

He had to do something. He had to stop thinking about Joanna Mitchell and how nice she was and how she made him feel. So he had kissed her and she had kissed him back. Forget it, Trevor tried to tell himself, as he'd been doing much of the night. She wasn't about to throw over a man like Philip Lee for the likes of him. So, what *was* he going to do?

He didn't have a clue.

Except, he wasn't going to call Joanna today, and he wasn't going back to Sheila's apartment. He was going to try and locate some of the people whose names he'd gathered while going through those receipts he'd found in the leather case. He was going to try and find out who Mac was, since his name kept appearing on papers belonging to Sheila.

Trevor opened his travel duffle and took out fresh underwear and a clean shirt. On Monday he'd try to see what the bank would tell him about the two account books he'd also found. He'd try to see if he could get the money. That's all he really wanted anyway.

But just for the moment, Trevor decided as he headed for the bathroom, he was going to take the proverbial cold shower.

Joanna also wasn't going to think about why Trevor hadn't called her yet. She didn't want to analyze why it even concerned her except for the fact they had kissed. Joanna admitted to herself, with some embarrassment and defiance, that she was glad she'd had her curiosity satisfied. She had expected something very physical and expressive. And it was. It had been powerful. It had been . . . wonderful. So, she should have been grateful that the break in communication had given her some time to come to her senses. Philip had called from D.C., and that was like a dash of cold reality. She couldn't get involved with Trevor Jackson. It was out of the question.

Who was he, anyway?

But that question hadn't occurred until sometime on Saturday afternoon. In between had been a lot of erotic daydreams. Joanna was appalled by her attitude and behavior. Linda would laugh at her. Her parents would be scandalized and disappointed. And Philip? She didn't want to think about Philip. That's when Joanna realized that she was in deep trouble.

Linda had called early in the day.

"How come you weren't home when I called you yesterday?" she asked.

"Maybe I was in the shower," Joanna lied uncomfortably. "Later I spent some time with Preston. You know, my downstairs neighbor. I didn't bother listening to my phone messages until last night."

"Were you really sick or just faking it?"

"I think it was something I ate the night before last."

"Or maybe it was Philip."

"I wish you'd leave the man alone," Joanna sighed patiently.

"Sorry. I forget that you think he's wonderful. He just cleans up good and speaks well. Trevor is more my type."

"Just what type is that?" Joanna asked in amusement.

"Earthy," Linda said without hesitation. "No pretense, nothing phony. He's just out there."

"Linda, all you did was say hello to the man. How would you know what he's like?"

"I just know," Linda said with superiority. "And if you can't tell that he might be on to you, I wish you'd give him *my* number. I'd know what to do with him."

Joanna sucked her teeth. "You're impossible. You didn't call to see if I'm feeling better. You wanted to pump me for information."

"I thought I'd come over for a while since Philip's away and Sean's with his grandmother for the weekend . . ."

"And maybe Trevor will show up to talk about Sheila."

Linda laughed outright. "I swear I'll be good."

"I think you're going to be disappointed, but come on over . . ."

They went to see a movie in the afternoon, and gossiped over lunch about everyone at work. And then a little after eight, Linda left. Joanna thought she could feel righteous, knowing she'd done nothing to ruin her friend's chances of meeting Trevor Jackson again. But by the end of the day, Joanna had been given yet another opportunity to see him herself. She had discovered more boxes of personal items belonging to Sheila James.

She was down in the laundry room of the basement when it came to Joanna that, as Trevor had observed, there was nothing stored in the apartment. No boxes, no bicycles, or skis . . . no luggage. But everybody owned luggage. Joanna wondered if Sheila had left some of her things in the basement of the apartment building. It didn't matter that keeping packed cartons was a fire hazard and illegal in Philadelphia. Joanna knew that if Sheila had asked Danny to keep things for her, he would have done it.

Joanna got her wash started and cautiously began to explore the basement complex of corridors and rooms. The level under the first floor was a kind of netherworld. No one took it seriously because no one ever went down

there, except for the laundry room. No one saw it as a
place where Danny, the maintenance man, also lived. No
one saw him as an independent man with viable needs.
He was just someone who was a bit dull and slow, who
had suffered a serious head injury as a teenager. He was
just someone who fixed toilets and helped move heavy
furniture. Joanna admitted to herself that that was how
she'd always seen Danny. But now she was curious. And
she had an ulterior motive.

The door to Danny's apartment, three rooms next to
the elevator shaft, was locked and he was nowhere
around. The basement was a kind of creepy place. There
were no windows to the outside world. It also housed
the motor for the elevator and the oil burners for heat.
All the mechanisms were going at once for a continuous
background of noise that sounded like a factory. The
basement had the kind of shadowy dimness that made
Joanna feel as if someone was going to jump out of
hiding any moment.

There was the room where recycled garbage was
bagged or tied for pickup. There was the supply room
where extra cans of paint, tools, light bulbs, ladders, and
leaf-blowers were kept. And the storage room which
wasn't supposed to be a storage room.

Joanna hesitated outside the darkened room and decided that there was no way she was going to rummage
around in there by herself. But the door was wide open,
and there didn't seem to be a lot of things inside. If she
went in quickly now, no one need ever know she'd been
there. Her only other concern was vermin crawling
about.

She shuddered, but reached into the storage room and
let her hand wave blindly about in the dark until she

found the cord for the ceiling light. She yanked and a single bulb went on. Joanna blinked rapidly against the glare and quickly established that the room was smaller than she'd imagined, square with most of it closed off but visible behind wire fencing. There were just a few cartons, a dozen or so suitcases, an oversized steamer trunk which was probably a real antique and worth money, and a long-forgotten baby carriage.

Joanna tried the gate to the cordoned off space and found it unlocked. It opened with a little bit of squeaking, and she stepped inside the cage to try and read the labeling or identification on the suitcases. It didn't take long for her to find two cases marked, not with Sheila's name but with the apartment number, 4B.

Joanna felt excited, the way she had the morning before when she'd convinced Mr. Tillman to let Trevor into Sheila's apartment. The way she had when Preston had given them the attaché. This was another breakthrough.

She lifted the larger of the two cases, but it was so light that she knew it was empty and didn't see any point in opening or moving it. The other definitely had something stored inside. Now what to do? She stood there thinking.

"How come you're in here, Miz Mitchell?"

Danny's voice made Joanna start violently. She let go of the handle abruptly and the case tottered back and forth before falling over and slamming flat on the cement floor. A light layer of dust billowed up from the edges. Joanna jumped again.

"Hi . . . D . . . Danny," she stammered. "I . . . I'm helping to . . . eh . . . clear out Sheila's apartment. I was just checking to see if she had things down here."

Danny stared wide-eyed at her. So long, in fact, that

Joanna frowned. She chuckled nervously, stepping back from the case. "I should have asked you first, but I . . . eh . . . couldn't find you. I didn't think . . ."

Danny suddenly stepped forward. "Don't tell Mr. Tillman. He'll get real mad at me."

"I won't," she promised with a surprised shake of her head.

"She was gonna move them. She said she could take them someplace else."

Joanna walked to the entrance of the gate. "That's okay, then. I can move the suitcases. I'll take them upstairs before Mr. Tillman finds out."

"But . . . they don't belong to you."

"It doesn't matter, Danny. You don't want Mr. Tillman to know, right? I'll put them in Sheila's apartment, and he'll never know. Then you won't have to worry. Okay?"

He nodded rapidly. "Okay."

Joanna let out the breath she was holding. She didn't want Mr. Tillman to find out, either. She wanted to get the cases upstairs so Trevor could see them. "Come on," she said urgently to Danny, tugging briefly on his sleeve. "Hurry."

Joanna let Danny retrieve the two cases and carry them out into the corridor. He set them down near the elevator. Joanna frowned at him. "Aren't you going to come with me?"

He blinked at her. "To . . . to her apartment?"

Joanna could see he was about to protest. She touched his shoulder. "I'll put them in the apartment. You just help me get them upstairs. Now, is this everything? Try to remember, Danny. Did Sheila leave anything else with you?"

Danny visibly twitched and stared blankly at Joanna

for a moment. His eyes shifted left and right, and he finally shook his head. "No, no. That's everything," he said quickly, pointing to the two cases.

Joanna frowned at his response but didn't want to waste any more time questioning him. He helped her up to the fourth floor, but did not stay. Joanna unlocked the door with the keys Trevor had given her. She felt her heartbeat quicken. She knew she was behaving as childishly as Danny, but Joanna didn't want to be in Sheila's apartment alone, either. She slid the cases just inside the door and quickly retreated. She wasn't going to go back unless Trevor was with her.

Joanna looked out the window again. There was a soft blanket of snow covering the backyard, making white monsters out of bushes and shrubbery, and the canvas-covered summer furniture. The giant sun umbrella, under which she'd spent quiet afternoons in shorts and sunglasses, reading romantic paperback novels, was closed and looked like a new species of tree under the layer of snow.

"Tsk . . . look at that. I just knew you should have stayed home today," Evelyn Mitchell sighed as she stood next to her daughter and frowningly gazed out her kitchen window.

"When I left Philly this morning, it wasn't snowing," Joanna reminded her mother. "As a matter of fact, this wasn't predicted to start until tomorrow morning."

"Well, your forecasters were wrong," Mrs. Mitchell said succinctly. "Getting paid all that money and they can't even get the weather right."

Joanna smiled absently. She wasn't about to worry her

parents unnecessarily, but she was concerned about the quickly accumulating snow on the ground. It had started out as flurries just after she'd arrived in Somerville, but had gotten an inch deeper just in the last hour.

"We're not in charge, Mom. Mother Nature is still calling all the shots."

Joanna turned away from the window with a sigh of tension, a slight frown creasing her forehead. For the moment she wasn't even thinking about her own circumstances. She'd been wondering, off and on, what Trevor Jackson was doing on a day like this. Even now that it was too late to do anything, she wished she'd called and invited him to meet her parents and have Sunday dinner with her family. But what kind of signal would that have sent? What would her parents have thought? The fact that she'd concerned herself at all was enough to make Joanna feel peculiar, as if she'd stepped outside of her skin. Why should she give any thought to a stranger? Except that that stranger had managed to touch a side of her persona that she hadn't realized existed. The part that was spontaneous. The part that wasn't always the obedient daughter, reliable employee, predictable lover. She had let this stranger kiss her passionately. And she had enjoyed it.

Joanna could still feel the full and thorough way Trevor had kissed her, but she also remembered the restrained way in which he hadn't taken further advantage. That had been even more thrilling because it had left her wanting. Joanna had not expected that. And perhaps that bothered her more than anything. She felt, in a way, unfulfilled.

"I'm not blaming anyone," Mrs. Mitchell defended herself. "If it comes to that, I trust the good Lord to take care of things. But I'm worried about you being on the road alone in this weather, especially at night. It's going to be dark by the time you leave," she speculated as she fussed with dinner preparations.

Joanna returned to the stove. She removed a pair of oven mitts from a hook under a cabinet and, putting them on, reached inside the oven to remove the macaroni and cheese casserole.

"There's almost nothing on the ground," she said, trying to reassure her mother. "It could stop before we've even finished with dinner."

"Maybe you should think about staying the night, Jo," Samuel Mitchell said, standing quietly in the kitchen doorway. He exchanged glances with his petite wife.

"I'd feel much better if you did," her mother added.

Joanna smiled regretfully at her parents. "I can't stay. I really have to get into the studio in the morning."

"Then call in sick," her father suggested. "It makes more sense to be careful and safe."

Joanna decided it was best not to mention that she'd called in sick on the previous Friday.

"Daddy, there's less than two inches on the ground."

"And before you know it, it will be six or eight inches," Mr. Mitchell complained, stepping aside as Joanna passed him with the hot casserole on her way to the dining room.

"Well, maybe your brother will drive you back. You could put him up on your sofa. He doesn't have to return to Princeton for another week."

Joanna turned to relieve her mother of a bowl of lima beans and the platter of sliced pork loin. "I can't leave my car here." She faced her parents, her hands held out helplessly. It was very nice that they worried so much about her safety, but it was too much in Joanna's eyes. Her parents sometimes forgot that she was an adult capable of making adult decisions for herself. "Look . . . I'll start back home as soon as we're done with dinner, okay? You can get Sonny to help with the cleanup."

Evelyn Mitchell rolled her eyes and chortled in amusement. Samuel Mitchell shook his head.

"Your brother will come up with some lame excuse and your mama will let him get away with it. She's spoiled you kids rotten," Joanna's father scoffed, as he turned off the TV set where a Sunday football game was in halftime.

"Listen to him," Mrs. Mitchell said, bringing in gravy and a dish of warmed applesauce. "As if he had no hand or say in how his children turned out."

"I didn't mean to start a fight," Joanna laughed as she stood behind her chair at the dining table. This was her place, and no one else's. This was the spot she'd occupied at family meals since she was five years old. At her father's right hand. "I promise to drive very slowly. I'll call you as soon as I get home. And I promise you, Jameson *will* help Mom with the kitchen cleanup."

"How are you planning on doing that?" Mrs. Mitchell asked with cheerful skepticism.

"Bribery."

Mr. Mitchell looked as doubtful as his wife. "Whatever it is, he won't go for it."

"I told that boy we were going to sit down promptly at three," Mrs. Mitchell fretted under her breath.

"There's still five more minutes," Joanna said wryly.

"So what is this bribe?" Mr. Mitchell held out the chairs for his wife and his daughter as they sat down.

"Two tickets to next week's playoff games with the Eagles."

Mrs. Mitchell shook her head, her eyes bright behind her glasses. "Sonny just might sell his soul for that."

"I don't want his soul," Joanna said, turning her head at the sound of the front door opening. "Just an hour of his time."

"Wash your hands before coming to the table. And don't track snow all over my floors!"

"Yes, ma'am!" Jameson Mitchell laughed deeply from the hallway.

It never failed to amuse or amaze Joanna that her younger brother, her *baby* brother, even though he was almost twenty-one, had such a commanding voice, and had grown to just over six feet tall. Even more outrageous was that he treated her as if *she* were the baby in the family.

"Jameson!" Mrs. Mitchell called out as they all waited.

The whole scene made Joanna smile. It made her feel comfortable, and threw her back into a childhood and adolescence with similar exchanges. She would ask her father a million questions, because of course he knew everything. And her mother would try to curb Jameson's antics, but without any censure or real criticism. There was just an awful lot of love.

For whatever reason, just then, Joanna also remembered how taken Trevor had been with the information that she frequently visited her parents. As if it was a novelty. Joanna suddenly wondered if he wasn't used to being in a family, or to home-cooked meals. Did Trevor Jackson have a family with traditions and history like her own? She frowned as the observations she made about him began to come together like pieces of a puzzle, and made up the picture of a man more interesting than she'd first believed.

Joanna spread her napkin over her lap and watched her brother stroll into the dining room and immediately grab everyone's attention. The good son. His mother's pride and joy. It had always been that way. *Women raised their daughters, but they loved their sons* . . . went through Joanna's mind. Jameson kissed his mother's cheek and then hers, calling Joanna by the current nickname of "Little Jo." Then he nodded to his father and took his place at the table, opposite his sister. They all silently folded their hands and waited for Mr. Mitchell to begin grace.

"I'm so sorry Philip couldn't make it this time," Mrs. Mitchell lamented halfway through dinner.

Joanna didn't respond right away, aware that she really wasn't sorry herself. The thought surprised her and made her feel guilty. It wasn't Philip who'd been on her mind all afternoon. "He had to go to D.C. for the weekend."

"Well, I sure miss not seeing him. He's been so busy lately. When do you two have time for each other?"

"It's a matter of priorities," Joanna said stiffly. She regretted the remark as soon as she saw the glance her parents exchanged.

"Oooops," Jameson chuckled, eating heartily. "Sounds like trouble in paradise."

"Sounds like you're eating with your mouth full," Joanna said slyly. Jameson shrugged good-naturedly.

"I thought you two were serious?" Mr. Mitchell probed none too subtly.

Joanna shifted in her chair, thinking frantically for a way to get off the topic of their relationship. "Serious about what?" Joanna asked, knowing that neither her mother nor her father would openly voice their hopes and concerns. But again they exchanged looks.

"Sam, don't ask her that. I'm sure when the two of them decide to make plans about their future, we'll be the first to know. Right, dear?"

Jameson shook his head sagely. "I wouldn't bet on it. Jo might not marry at all. Or she might even marry someone else, just to throw you off the scent."

Mrs. Mitchell gave her son a quelling stare. "What is that supposed to mean?"

"It means, lighten up. Can't you tell Jo doesn't want to discuss her personal life? Maybe Philip Lee isn't the man of her dreams."

"Well, *I* want to know if something is going on," Mrs. Mitchell insisted. "He's such a fine young man. What's the problem?"

"Yeah, my man Phil is pretty cool," Jameson added. "Not like some of those other dudes Jo used to bring home. Remember that artist?"

Joanna's parents laughed lightly, despite themselves.

Joanna calmly continued to eat. She was reviewing her history with Philip Lee and a hope that she couldn't deny she'd felt when they'd met and started to date. For a time it had been serious dating. And then it had seemed to stall. Functioning at a level that was comfortable and stable . . . but didn't seem to be going anywhere. The initial passion had become warm desire. The imagined great love was now just great affection. She'd never noticed before that it was changing. She'd never honestly looked at what she felt for Philip. But being the object of this impromptu dinner discussion allowed Joanna to clearly, and for the first time, look at what she *didn't* feel.

It made her feel a little empty. And very confused.

The dinner conversation finally got off Philip and herself when she refused to respond and be drawn into the speculation by her family. But Joanna had a sense that she was somehow letting them all down. When she'd first brought Philip home to meet her parents, to have a traditional Sunday afternoon supper just like this one, her parents had responded as if they'd died and gone to heaven.

Philip's behavior fulfilled all of her parents' fantasies of a decent and worthy black man with honorable designs on their daughter. He impressed her parents with his good manners and bearing. With his family background and education. He was everything that was right and expected. He was everything she should want in a man. A prospective husband and mate. But he wasn't anything like . . .

"Is everybody ready for dessert?" Mrs. Mitchell asked, getting up and beginning to gather the used dishes.

"I don't think I'd better," Joanna said, grateful for the interruption. "I'm going to start back now."

"Well, let me pack up some of this extra food, and you can take it with you."

Joanna chuckled as she helped to clear the table. "You don't have to. I'm not returning to a college dorm, you know. I do have a kitchen and I can cook for myself."

"Yeah, omelets and pasta salads." Jameson wrinkled up his nose. "The girl forgets where she came from."

"The girl is watching her weight," Joanna said, grinning at her brother and following her mother into the kitchen.

"Well, nonetheless, it won't hurt to have a little something you just have to heat up. You and Philip can share it. He said he liked my macaroni and cheese. And I'll wrap up some of the apple cake . . ."

"Mom, don't worry about it," Joanna said, but knew her words fell on deaf ears. Already her mother was hunting for the plastic wrap. Joanna sighed in resignation. Philip would *never* eat any of it. He hated leftover foods. And he had inadvertently declared one time, after they'd visited, that macaroni and cheese was so country.

Fifteen minutes later Joanna stood by the front door to the house, surrounded by her parents as they saw her off. Everyone seemed to be talking at once, offering advice and extracting promises that she should call them the minute she walked into her apartment. The door opened and Jameson stepped in, along with a rush of cold air and the smell of winter. He stomped his boots on the mat.

"Thanks for brushing the snow off my car," Joanna said, reaching to kiss his cheek.

"Hey, thank Philip for the tickets. I owe him."

She kissed her mother and father and quickly left.

Joanna had been on the road nearly an hour when she admitted to herself her parents had been right. She should have stayed the night. Her speed had been reduced to just thirty-five miles an hour . . . and was going down, along with the outside temperature. The now heavily falling snow was like a veiled curtain in front of her windshield, and Joanna couldn't see more than a hundred feet ahead. Her car had already stalled once, and she'd slid and swerved on packed-down snow which was starting to turn to ice.

Beginning to feel more than just a little bit nervous, Joanna knew that under the current circumstances, it would take her hours to get back into Philadelphia. Or to return to her parents' house. She decided to keep going forward. But after twenty minutes in which she'd gone barely five more miles, she didn't have an option either way. The windshield wipers stopped moving, and the car stalled again. She got it started once more but was afraid she wasn't going to get very far before the car shut down again. The number of cars pulled over on the side of the road and abandoned, increased her anxiety. Was this to be her fate for the night?

Joanna continued to sit for several moments more, trying to make a decision, preferably one that would correct the foolishness of leaving her parents' home in the first place. Putting her hazard lights on, Joanna started slowly forward. Nearly a mile later she saw an exit sign. She was just outside of Lawrenceville. Already Joanna felt relief. Wherever there was an exit, there was often a service station. And telephones.

The service station she located was closed for the night. But the public telephones were available on the side of the station house. Joanna got out of her car and was stunned to see just how deep the snow actually was. The thought came to her that she could end up sleeping in her car all night.

Using her calling card, Joanna dialed her parents' house. Jameson would come and get her, and she'd just have to be late for work the next day or not go in at all. But the line was busy.

"I'm going to kill you, Sonny," Joanna muttered in

frustration under her breath, automatically assuming her popular and handsome brother was on the line with one of his girlfriends.

Joanna leaned back against the side of the building, out of the swirling wind. Her feet were very cold, and she wiggled and flexed her toes in her boots, trying to keep the circulation going. She kept her gloved hands inside her pockets and tried to pay no attention to the tingling sensation in her exposed ears or the settling of snow on her hair.

She waited nearly ten minutes and tried her parents' number again. Still busy. She began to feel annoyed. Not at Jameson, but at herself. Joanna knew she couldn't continue to stay where she was, but her alternatives were few. She stood pensively considering each one.

Finally, searching through her purse, Joanna located the now tattered and soiled pink sheet with Trevor's hotel number. She dialed it and then silently prayed that he'd be in his room. The operator put the call through and when the line was picked up on the second ring, Joanna sighed deeply.

"Yeah," Trevor answered in a comfortable voice.

Joanna turned her back to the wind. "Trevor, hi. It . . . it's Joanna."

"Joanna . . ."

He sounded surprised to her. And pleased. "Hi. I'm sorry to bother you, but . . ."

"What's the matter? Where are you?" he asked alertly.

His quick attention already made Joanna feel better. She sighed. "I'm on the road. Well, not exactly. I had to pull off of US 206 outside of Lawrenceville, New Jersey. I . . . I don't think I can make it back to Philadelphia."

Trevor heard anxiety in her voice. "Are you by yourself?"

"Yes. I was at my parents'. I guess I should have stayed there, but . . ."

"I'll come and get you."

"I'm so embarrassed to be calling, but . . . could you?"

"I'm on my way. Tell me exactly where you are."

Joanna did, recommending to Trevor that he take Route 95 north, since it was an interstate and more likely to have been plowed during the day. Then she gave him some landmarks to help locate her car off the exit.

"I want you to get back to your car and lock yourself in. Leave your blinkers on and run the engine if you can to keep warm."

"Okay."

"And don't let anyone offer to help unless it's the highway patrol or from a state road service crew. Understood?"

"Okay," Joanna nodded. She was beginning to shiver.

"You'll be fine. I'll get there as fast as I can."

Joanna chuckled lightly. "Well, you be careful, too. The roads are really bad."

"I'll find you. Don't worry," Trevor said firmly.

Joanna believed him. She hung up, reluctant to break the connection between them. She was back to being alone again, at a closed service station with nothing else around, and no traffic on the road. Joanna carefully made her way back to her car and followed Trevor's instructions. She felt better for having made a decision to call him. She felt better knowing that he was on his way.

Joanna settled in to wait, watching anxiously through

the windshield as her car was quickly covered with
snow . . .

It was clear to Trevor that no cars had been on this
road in at least a half-hour. The last car tracks had already been filled in with snow. But he could see the
neon light of the service station and hoped that this was
the one from which Joanna had placed her call.

He was still trying to process his feelings upon hearing her voice on the phone a little over an hour ago. It
wasn't the anxiety in her voice which had grabbed
Trevor's attention. It was the need. Joanna was by herself
in an unexpected storm, and she was a little scared. But
she had acted quickly to get help. She had called *him*.

Trevor was a bit stunned. He couldn't remember the
last time anything so simple had made him feel so good.
A phone call. He didn't doubt that Joanna knew a dozen
people she might have called, including her boyfriend.
Trevor had spent the entire time on the road trying to
figure out what her call meant. He quickly cursed himself for a fool for thinking it could possibly mean anything.

Then he saw the Honda Civic with the flashing caution lights, sitting deserted and nearly buried under snow.
Trevor pulled up slowly behind it and put his car into
neutral. As he opened his door to get out, Trevor stub-
bornly stuck to his own version of the facts. Joanna had
probably called him because she didn't want to trouble
anyone else. He was unwilling to admit he was afraid
to believe anything else.

Joanna heard the car door slam, and her heart lurched
in her chest. She swiveled her head and could only see

the blur of the headlights reflected through the snow-covered rear window. She jumped when someone slapped their hand on the roof of her car. Joanna sat still for a second longer, and then rolled down her window a fraction of an inch. She saw Trevor squinting against the snow at her, his face hidden and protected by the beak of his cap. Tension discharged and flowed quickly out of her.

"Trevor," she murmured in relief.

She hastily got the car door open and stepped out into a drift of snow almost to her knees. But Joanna only looked at Trevor, as if he were an apparition.

She tried to step toward him. He reached out to aid her as she stumbled forward. Joanna grinned at Trevor, but his expression seemed tight and closed. His hands closed around her arms. When Joanna looked into his face, a surge of warmth flowed through her. He was so sturdy and his presence seemed so invincible that she felt immediately safe.

But there was something else as well. A sense of letting go of her breath. Of letting go of speculation. Of questions answered that hadn't even been voiced. Trevor gently hauled her toward him and closed his arms about Joanna. She hugged him in return, and it seemed so easy and felt so natural. Just for a brief few moments. Silently.

Joanna stepped back first, feeling embarrassed and disoriented.

Trevor felt disconcerted. He had been taken totally off guard.

"Where's your hat?" he asked briskly.

Joanna blinked at him and sighed. She was glad that Trevor wasn't going to make a comment about the way they'd greeted each other. "I didn't wear one. I was in the car, and . . ."

He pulled off his cap, slapped it against his thigh to shake off the snow, and placed it on Joanna's head. It was, of course, too big for her and made her look like a child wearing a grown-up's hat. The brim made it difficult for Joanna to properly see Trevor, and she had to tilt her face up in order to see under the rim.

Trevor chuckled silently at her. "You look like a little bird," he said.

Joanna didn't say anything, but she liked the sound of warmth and affection in his voice.

"Come on," Trevor said. He reached for her hand and helped Joanna through the snow to his car. She climbed into the passenger's seat and Trevor closed the door for her.

Then he returned to her car, searching through the glove compartment for something to write with. On a paper napkin from Big Boy, Trevor wrote that the owner would call the station house in the morning and he left her name. He removed Joanna's tote and packages from the back seat and locked the car.

Trevor got back into his rented car and shifted into drive. All his attention became focused on his driving. It was the safest thing to do. But it felt peculiar having Joanna seated right next to him. It had a certain kind of coziness that he wasn't used to. Her depending on him felt odd, too. Trevor liked to keep things simple. He liked being in control. He wasn't comfortable with surprises because they almost never worked in his favor. So he was going to have to be very careful *not* to let Joanna get to him or change his mind about anything.

He'd decided that morning that not seeing Joanna on

Saturday had been the smart thing to do. Except that the abstinence of Saturday hadn't helped at all. It had only increased his desire to have her.

Trevor glanced at Joanna as she sat huddled in her seat. "You'll get warm in a minute."

She silently nodded, afraid to say anything that would be a reminder of the incredible tension between them. They drove in relative silence for a number of miles.

"Tomorrow, you should call Triple A and have them tow your car."

Again, Joanna only nodded. His formality was daunting. She wished she hadn't practically thrown herself at him. They were moving past Trenton.

"You probably would have done better if you'd gotten on the turnpike," Trevor said officiously. He ground his teeth. He sounded like Philip Lee. But Joanna didn't respond. She was staring thoughtfully out the window. What had he said to offend her? "I guess you don't feel much like talking."

Slowly Joanna turned her head and stared for a long time at Trevor's profile. She didn't understand the sudden distance between them. He was cool and impersonal.

"I'm really sorry I had to bother you. I guess I should have called a tow service in the first place. I didn't think it was going to start snowing so early. I didn't want to stay at my parents' house, but my mother tried to tell me that—"

"Dammit!" Trevor suddenly gritted softly through his teeth.

Joanna stared in further confusion at him.

Suddenly Trevor put on the signal light and slowly pulled the car onto the service shoulder of the highway. He put it into park. He turned to Joanna and let his gaze travel thoroughly over her features. She was confused and apprehensive now. Well, so was he. And he needed to do something about it.

Joanna sat watching as Trevor slowly reached over and pulled his cap from her head. He efficiently snapped open the top fastening on her parka and, locating the zipper, pulled it down. Then Trevor snaked his hand into the opening and around Joanna's waist. He heard her gasp quietly, but she didn't resist as he bent forward to capture her mouth under his.

Joanna was stunned. She simply closed her eyes, opened her mouth and let Trevor assuage himself. She quickly felt herself sinking into an abyss of heat and desire, and let the heady stimulation of Trevor's invasion turn her body to soft malleable need. She no longer even felt cold. It happened so fast she felt dizzy.

Joanna didn't think she'd ever been kissed so that she felt as though nothing else mattered. The joining of their mouths, their dancing tongues, was an unimaginable delight. It made her feel weak and silly. It made her aware of being female next to Trevor's utter maleness, and she felt cocooned in his arms and the bulkiness of his coat. It made Joanna wish they could somehow get closer to each other. But a part of her mind, aware of their circumstances, their location, was relieved that they couldn't. She was afraid to consider what might happen if she and Trevor were truly alone. She didn't know if she was ready for that. But the mere idea of intimacy between them was enough to release a sudden rush of giddiness.

Trevor's hand pressed against her side, then rode up over the wool of her sweater until the heel of his hand rested just under her breast. Joanna gasped into his mouth, suddenly holding her breath as she waited for his hand to cover her breast. She wanted to know what that would feel like and her body began to tremble just from anticipation. But in the meantime . . .

In the meantime Joanna just enjoyed the way Trevor's mouth pressed and manipulated and moved across hers. He was slowly deepening the kiss but maintaining a control that was erotic in its slow intensity. The thrusting of his tongue reminded Joanna of another action, and her arm curved around Trevor's neck, her fingers stroking his nape. Trevor forced himself not to let his hand explore any farther up Joanna's body, although the temptation was killing him. He let himself imagine, instead, what her breast would feel like under his palm, his fingers. Without the sweater in the way. Trevor allowed himself another fantasy, one that was much more intimate . . . and then he let it go.

Before Joanna knew it, before she was ready, Trevor was slowly ending the shattering embrace. She was awkwardly resting against his shoulder, her breathing chaotic. She was afraid to open her eyes, but when she did, Joanna found Trevor regarding her with a slumberous gaze and tensing jaw muscles. He lowered his head to pull another very brief kiss from her lips.

"Did Santa Claus ever make you feel like this?" his voice whispered over her skin.

It was like a caress, and the sensation was sending eddies of warmth rippling down her spine, twisting her stomach muscles into a knot. "Don't . . . don't call him Santa Claus," Joanna said quietly.

Trevor brushed his lips against hers once more. His tongue moistened her lips. "Okay. Philip. Did he ever make you feel this way?"

The question made Joanna even more conscious of what she and Trevor were doing. She felt guilty and awful. She couldn't speak, so limp did she feel in Trevor's arms. But slowly she shook her head. "No . . ."

Trevor stared down at her. His inclination was to continue kissing her. But for sure that would lead to something else. It was exactly what he wanted. Trevor didn't feel particularly noble when he forced himself to sit back and release Joanna. She sat silently staring as he rezipped her coat and he turned back to the steering wheel.

"You'll be back home soon," Trevor murmured, reminding Joanna Mitchell that she had one. That she had a routine and a life and people who cared about her; he couldn't be part of that.

Joanna sat and huddled in her seat again. Her senses were still swirling, and her mouth could still feel the firmness of Trevor's. She was bemused and couldn't seem to focus on a coherent meaningful thought.

"Trevor? What . . . are you doing? Why are you doing this to me?"

He could hear the confusion and hurt in her tone and realized that he'd already gone too far. He *knew* he should have stayed away from her. He *knew* it was just going to create problems he couldn't deal with.

Trevor sighed but it was filled with annoyance. "I'm not trying to do anything. I kissed you. I liked kissing you. No big deal."

"That's it?" Joanna asked in a small, stunned voice.

Trevor's hands gripped the steering wheel. He clenched his teeth so tightly that his jaw ached and his muscles felt like they were going to cramp. "That's it." He glanced briefly at the way she stared wide-eyed at him. Not accusingly. Just bewildered. He cursed again, silently to himself. "Hey. You're very sweet, Joanna. I don't want to hurt you. I told you I wouldn't apologize," Trevor said easily.

She shook her head. "You're . . . confusing me. I thought . . ."

His hands tightened around the steering wheel. "You have to understand something. I'm not like Philip or any of those nice guys you're used to. If I take you to bed and make love to you, I can walk away afterward. Do you understand?"

She flushed at the blunt confession, and the rest of her ardor quickly cooled off. It was too late. He *did* hurt her with his attitude. Joanna had no idea what was happening with her and Philip. Perhaps they'd just gotten off on the wrong track because they'd fallen into too much of a predictable routine. Perhaps she'd become attracted to Trevor because he was so different from Philip, and because he'd been bold and upfront and had kissed her like he had on Friday . . . like he had just then . . . just because he wanted to. She liked feeling wanted and desired. She'd finally admitted to liking it from Trevor Jackson. The trip home took them through part of Fairmont Park. Joanna concentrated on the beautiful landscape outside her window. She wished they could keep riding through the park until Trevor changed his mind about how he felt. Or she did.

Joanna realized that she was probably not like women he was used to knowing. But did that mean there was something wrong with her? Was she not enough woman for either Philip or Trevor?

"I understand perfectly," she whispered in as calm a voice as she could manage.

She and Trevor had no more conversation until they

got into the city and she gave directions to her apartment building. Her intentions were to thank him quickly, gather her things, and get out of the car.

His intentions had been pretty much the same thing. But with the engine turned off, with the quiet of the storm continuing outside, and the two of them together in the confines of the car which held so much strain and wariness, neither seemed able to move or say anything.

"I appreciate you coming to rescue me," Joanna said quietly.

Trevor wondered if her choice of words was deliberate. "No problem."

"I hope I wasn't—"

Trevor sighed and turned to her. "Joanna . . ." He shook his head. "You weren't interrupting anything."

She blinked at him. "I thought you'd call and come by yesterday."

"Why?" he asked sharply.

"Because of Sheila's apartment. We didn't finish on Friday."

He averted his gaze. "I was busy. I made a list of some of the names on the papers and receipts I got from the case Preston was holding."

"Any luck?" Joanna asked, glad for the distraction and a chance to gather her wits.

He shrugged. "There were a couple of videotapes, but I don't have anything to play them on. Someone named Mac kept turning up. There were a lot of notes to Sheila from him on printed note paper. Initials NAM. I haven't been able to find a full name, yet."

"Well, maybe there will be something in the other cases."

Trevor's attention focused on her. "What other cases?"

"I found two more cases in the basement yesterday. We're not supposed to put personal things in the storage room, but Sheila never paid much attention to the rules. I thought maybe she left something down there. She had."

Trevor was staring at her in amazement and slowly started to smile.

"Danny helped me bring them upstairs. I put them in Sheila's apartment, but I didn't open anything."

"Why didn't you?"

She looked at him. "I was waiting for you."

Trevor shook his head again and reached out to stroke her cheek. Joanna let him, but turned her head away in confusion.

"You're better at getting things done than I am," he murmured wryly.

Joanna didn't respond to his comment. She was just aware of the warmth of his strong fingers against her skin. "I . . . don't understand you," she whispered.

"I know."

"You make me feel so . . ."

"I know. That's why I don't think you should have anything to do with me."

"Well, what about you?"

"You don't know anything about me. I told you, I'm a lot like Sheila."

"And I said I don't believe that. What has that got to do with the way . . . *we're* feeling?"

"How do you know what I'm feeling?" Trevor asked brusquely.

Joanna arched a brow and her smile was superior and sure. "By the way you kiss me."

"I confuse you, Joanna. You don't know what you're feeling. You have Philip, remember? You're not the type of woman who does things like this."

"What?"

"Fool around."

Joanna cringed. It sounded so crude and ugly.

"Before last Wednesday night you didn't know who I was and could care less. Don't ruin your future because of me. In a few days I'll be gone. Like you said, then it won't matter."

"Maybe you're right. But we still have a few more days. You have two more cases to look through. If you give me the videotapes, I can play them at work, see what I can find out."

"I've taken up enough of your time," Trevor said.

"It's my time," Joanna said formally, gathering her things together, giving Trevor back his hat. He stared at it but didn't put it back on.

"I'm sorry, Joanna. For getting you mixed up in this. With me."

"You can drop off the tapes at the studio in the morning."

"Okay. I have some other things to take care of first, but I'll check out those suitcases in the afternoon. That is, if your landlord doesn't kick me out. I was supposed to be finished by this evening."

"I wouldn't worry about it. Mr. Tillman lives outside of Philadelphia. I don't think he'll bother trying to get to the building tomorrow because of the storm. You still have time."

"That's good to know," Trevor nodded thoughtfully.

"Joanna . . ." he said, reaching out to grab her arm as she started to get out of the car. "What happened wasn't your fault."

"Yes, it was. And it was yours, too. But you know what I think? I think you're afraid of me."

Trevor couldn't even answer. He watched as she closed the door behind her and hurried into her building, bent against the wind. The way his stomach churned let Trevor know that Joanna wasn't too far wrong. But he couldn't let her know that.

Joanna stood at her door fumbling with the key, pensively trying to figure out what was going on with her, and with her and Trevor. She was so deep in her thoughts that at first she didn't hear the door opening down the hall until a head cautiously peeked out. It was Mrs. Thatcher, her hair twisted up in her usual blue rollers. Absently, Joanna wondered if the woman ever combed her hair out or left her apartment.

"Oh, it's you, Joanna," Mrs. Thatcher tittered.

"Good evening," Joanna nodded, pushing her door open and heading inside.

"I don't suppose you found out what was going on this afternoon?"

Joanna frowned. "I don't know what you mean."

"Well, there was the most terrible sound. At first I thought Danny was moving things out or changing the locks next door."

Joanna thought of Trevor attempting to get into Sheila's apartment the next day, and unable to. "Did he?" she asked.

"No. He was too busy mopping the hallway and keeping the sidewalk clear in front of the house."

"So what was going on next door?" Joanna asked with a sense of foreboding.

"Someone tried to break into that woman's apartment," Mrs. Thatcher announced dramatically.

Six

Joanna stared into the screen and tried to keep the smile fixed on her face. She suspected that she looked dazed and spaced out, but hoped that no one else would notice. She also hoped that no one could tell that the muscles in her jaw and around her mouth were beginning to quiver from the strain of looking poised and alert.

The studio lights were overly bright in her face, and she wondered if her nose and forehead were shiny, despite the application of makeup. More than anything, however, Joanna wondered if she came across as professional and adult. Or had the sound system picked up the thunderous pounding of her heart?

"Well, that's it for now. We'll keep you informed as the reports and weather conditions continue to come in during this snow emergency. Stay tuned for the national news. I'm Christopher Todd . . ."

"And I'm Joanna Mitchell, sitting in for Ann Marie Lopez. Have a safe day."

The director signaled for the set mikes to be turned off. Christopher turned to Joanna as the cameras pulled back, and the ending credits and music were played for the TV audience at home. His smile was practiced and theatrical. A pro who knew what to do in front of a camera. But there was also warmth and understanding. Admiration brightened his eyes as he leaned toward her.

"Well done! You did a great job."

Joanna gnawed her lower lip and blinked at the anchor. "I tripped over a few lines," she murmured apologetically.

"Hey, you're not used to reading from a prompter. You did a first-rate job. Besides, we're lucky you were here to step in for Ann Marie."

"You can tell her her job is safe," Joanna said lightly as the mike was removed from the neckline of her blouse. "I was scared out of my mind."

"We all feel that way at first. You'll get the hang of it. By the noon broadcast, you'll be an old pro . . ."

Christopher was distracted by the news director, and Joanna got up from her chair. She felt that she was still suffering the sensation of having been suspended and was only now slowly settling back down to earth. And that is exactly what had happened to her.

First had been a restless night thinking about Trevor Jackson, while at the same time anticipating that at any moment, Philip would show up at her door, wanting to stay the rest of the night. She wasn't sure which thought made her most anxious. Joanna had tried to concoct several reasonable excuses to put Philip off if he'd come to her, but in the end she didn't have to use any of them. Philip had called to say he was stuck in D.C. because of the storm and couldn't get back into Philly until Monday morning. Joanna had been sympathetic but grateful. And then worry and guilt had set in.

This morning when the phone woke her up, she was sure it was Philip calling to let her know he was back. Joanna really had hoped, however, that it was Trevor calling to say that they needed to have a talk about what was happening between them. Instead, it was the news director from work.

She had been made an impromptu TV anchor, plucking her from relative obscurity as head of research behind the scenes to instant recognition on local news. The last thing Joanna had expected was to be recruited to replace Ann Marie, who hadn't made it into the station because of the weather. There had been no time to protest or to show panic. Joanna had been rushed to makeup, given the copy for the half-hour news format, and hastily instructed by Christopher what she would be covering. And now that it was all over, she couldn't remember a thing she'd said on air.

Joanna left the sheets of copy on the desk and only then fully realized that her hands were trembling. Her knees felt wobbly, attesting to her nervousness. She made her way from the set and, as she stepped past the cameras, a small gathering of people broke out into applause. She stopped and smiled uncertainly, staring into the dark gathering, trying to see who her audience was.

"That was pretty cool, Jo."

Joanna recognized Robby's voice. His lanky frame and the fall of his curly light brown hair were silhouetted against the back of the studio.

"Girl, you were great. Ann Marie better watch out." That was Linda.

"Thanks," Joanna grinned.

"No need to be so surprised. Joanna is very special." Joanna blinked into the darkness. That was Trevor.

But she had no more time to react, as the news director and much of the crew surrounded her with more congratulations. And all the time that she smiled and graciously accepted their comments, Joanna was acutely aware that Trevor was present. Her physical response made that perfectly clear.

"Hey, you know . . . I think I like you better on the set with Christopher. Ann Marie always looks like she's auditioning for a Hollywood lead," Robby boldly declared.

"Come on, be nice," Joanna admonished as Robby gave her a final thumbs-up and loped off in the direction of their office.

"He's right," Linda chortled. "All she's doing is reading the monitor. This isn't Shakespeare."

"Well, that's all I did for the last half-hour," Joanna said.

"But you were really into it," Trevor said smoothly, stepping forward from the back row. "I was watching your face. You were there with each story, and your response to each story was genuine. *That's* real. That was you."

Joanna took a deep breath before she looked into his face. She hoped that she appeared calm and indifferent. But it didn't work. As soon as her gaze connected with Trevor's, she experienced the now-familiar fluttering of her stomach. The attraction was so tangible it felt like an ache deep inside. It was not going to go away, but instead seemed to have escalated from just the night before, when he'd dropped her off after rescuing her. Joanna wondered if Trevor felt it, too.

"It's very nice of you to say that, but it only proves that I don't belong on the set. I'm not supposed to react to the news. I'm only supposed to report it."

"Actually, I think it was pretty effective to see you respond the way you did, Joanna," the news director interjected. "It makes the news seem less cold and remote. I think the audience can relate to that. You done good," he added with a wink before turning to a waiting assistant.

"Thanks," Joanna repeated and then, taking another deep breath, she turned to Linda and Trevor.

"I guess this means you and your fiancé will be a two-anchor family," Trevor speculated quietly, staring at her.

Joanna swallowed at the reminder of Philip's presence in her life. She shook her head. "No one's made any offers, yet," she said carefully.

"I know which one *I'd* accept," Linda chuckled.

She was smiling happily and chewing her ever-present gum as she linked her arm through Trevor's. He was standing with his jacket unzipped, his hands deep in his trouser pockets. His casual dress made him seem so rugged and physical, and when Joanna caught his gaze it was to find that he was staring at her with equal interest and intensity. But Joanna remembered that he'd made himself perfectly clear the night before, and she had no intention of doing anything to further embarrass herself.

"Look what I found," Linda said cheerfully, hugging Trevor's arm possessively, as if they'd known each other for years, rather than a few days.

Trevor smiled down at Linda, patiently indulgent. "Sorry. I wasn't lost. Joanna knew I was coming by this morning."

Linda shrugged. "Maybe. But I got to you first."

Trevor lifted a hand, forcing Linda to let go of his arm, and reached into an inside pocket of the winter coat. He pulled out two video boxes and handed them to Joanna. "You said it was okay to drop these off with you. Are you sure you can do this?"

Joanna took the tapes, avoiding contact with his hand. "It's no problem. But I probably can't get to them right away. It's very busy here right now because of the weather . . ."

"I understand. Whenever. Should I call later and maybe come by about five or so?"

"Well . . ."

"Tonight's the association dinner. You have to get home to change," Linda said. At Trevor's puzzled expression she turned to him. "The local chapter of the National Association of Blacks in Journalism is holding its annual dinner tonight. At the African-American Historical and Cultural Museum. Would you like to come?"

Joanna gasped softly in surprise and stared at her colleague and friend. "Linda . . ."

Linda looked innocent. "Well, what difference does it make? He could come as a guest. You're going with Philip, right? I don't have an escort."

Linda glanced guilelessly at Trevor and did everything to look appealing, short of batting her lashes.

He laughed in amusement. "Are you asking me to be your date?"

"Unless you have other plans for the evening . . ."

Trevor looked briefly at Joanna, and for a moment she imagined she saw doubt and determination in his dark eyes. Trevor dropped his gaze first, but Joanna continued to watch and gauge him, wondering if he was going to make it easy for both of them.

"I have some things to take care of this afternoon, but I'm free this evening. Sure. I'll take you to this dinner if you want."

"Terrific," Linda enthused.

Joanna felt a strange sinking in the pit of her stomach. She concentrated on the way her body and senses were responding to the announcement, and momentarily tuned out of Linda and Trevor's discussion of arrangements. Joanna tried to tell herself that of course it made sense and it was okay that Trevor had agreed to escort Linda that evening. Why should she care? And, after all, she had Philip. But the knowledge only made Joanna feel edgy and unexplainably annoyed.

Joanna clutched the tapes. "I have to go. I have a lot of work to . . ."

"Yeah, that's right. My phones are probably on overload at this very instant," Linda said. She reached out and touched Trevor's arm as she began backing away. "Come on to my office. I'll give you my address and phone . . ."

Joanna watched as Linda hurried away, but she and Trevor didn't move. Once again they faced each other. Awareness and frustration were wedged between them, keeping them at an emotional distance. Safe and manageable.

"That was very nice of you to agree to take Linda tonight."

"I don't know that I really had a choice," Trevor remarked dryly.

"I'm sorry," she murmured awkwardly.

"So am I," Trevor answered, his tone suddenly deep with disappointment.

Joanna put a hand out toward him, and then quickly drew it back. "No. I mean, I'm sorry if Linda put you on the spot."

He watched her, his eyes probing and intense. "And I mean I'm sorry things didn't work out."

Joanna felt a rush of warmth to her face and was powerless to respond. There was nothing she could say that she knew in her heart wouldn't be a lie.

She looked at the tapes in her hand, wanting a distraction. "What . . . what do you think is on these?"

"I don't know. There's no labeling. They could just be copies of films. Or home movies . . ."

The possibilities suddenly made Joanna widen her eyes.

"Look, maybe I shouldn't let you see these. Just in case . . ."

"No, it's okay. I can handle it, even if it's blue." She laughed nervously again as the conversation lapsed. And then she couldn't help herself. She looked at Trevor, into his steady, considering gaze. "Why did you agree to go tonight? You don't know Linda. You don't know anyone in this industry."

Trevor's smile was slow and seemed ironic. "I know you. This could be my last chance to see you. I want to be there," he said quietly.

Joanna clutched the tapes. She lowered her gaze and shook her head. "Don't. We covered this last night, remember?"

Trevor shrugged. "I think it had to be said. I'm not the kind of person you think I am, Joanna." He straightened his shoulders, and when he spoke again, his voice was calm; he was in control. "I'm going to check out Sheila's bank account today. If there's any money in it, I'll probably use it to pay off one or two of her debts. I have a few more people to talk to. By Wednesday or

Thursday, I'm out of here. I have to get back to Washington."

Joanna gnawed on her lip and averted her eyes briefly. She decided not to comment on that issue. "What about the cases in Sheila's apartment?"

"I don't think the contents will tell us much more, but I'll get to them. It'll have to be tomorrow. And I need to do it before your landlord has me thrown off the premises or changes the locks," he said.

Joanna nodded, already experiencing an indefinable reaction to the fact that Trevor would be leaving Philadelphia before the week was out. She couldn't decide if she was relieved at the news or disappointed.

"I better go. I have tapes to process and another airing to get ready for. And Linda is waiting for you."

"Then I guess we'll see each other later," Trevor murmured, his gaze traveling over her as if committing the details to memory.

"Yes," Joanna acknowledged a bit breathlessly.

After a long moment of regarding her, Trevor inclined his head and then turned to walk away.

The paunchy and graying manager folded the official-looking paper and handed it back to Trevor.

"Well, the certificate seems to be in order. Your ID checks out. I'm sorry to hear about the death in your family."

"Thanks," Trevor said, putting the paper away.

The manager sighed sympathetically. "Horrible thing, finding someone dead like that. I'm sure the police will solve the case soon."

"Yeah, I'm sure," Trevor said flatly.

"I'll okay a withdrawal or transfer of the remaining funds in the account. Whichever you prefer."

"A bank check is good."

"Fine," the manager nodded, opening his file drawer and searching through several folders before extracting a multipaged document. "This should finally put everything in order for you. The money will clear up that other problem, and hopefully put an end to the open case. Will you be staying in Philadelphia very long?"

Trevor stared absently as the bank manager filled out the form and added a seal and his signature to the bottom. "Just a few more days."

"So, what did you think of our city while you were here?"

A smile began to curve Trevor's mouth as he remained silent and grew reflective. He had no idea what he thought of Philadelphia. He hadn't seen anything of the city, and hadn't expected to. Of course, he also hadn't expected to meet someone like Joanna who, in just under a week, had him reevaluating certain beliefs he'd held for a long time. For the better, Trevor would say, although it wasn't going to do him any good.

"I don't know. Most of it was under snow for the time I was here."

The manager chuckled. "Yeah, I guess I should apologize for that. Your visit here wasn't exactly a vacation in any case. Right? Under the circumstances, you're probably happy to be leaving soon."

Trevor lifted a corner of his mouth. "There's little to keep me here."

"Well, take my word for it, we have a lot to offer. Come back sometime when the weather is better. Who knows? You could find a reason for staying permanently." He folded the document, placed it in an envelope, and handed it to Trevor with a pleasant smile.

He accepted it, knowing that if things had gone the way he'd wanted, he could have been in and out of Philadelphia and never have noticed a thing. And now, he was always going to wonder just what he had missed.

"Yeah. Who knows," he said. But Trevor didn't hold out much hope that it mattered.

Joanna stared out the windshield, letting herself become hypnotized by the repetitive motion of the wiper blades on the glass. But it wasn't distracting enough to block out Philip's voice. More than his voice, which was really a wonderful modulated tenor, but his tone. Right now it was lecturing and superior. And it was getting on her nerves.

Philip's car was moving very slowly. The precipitation right now wasn't more snow, but rain. The last bit of the snowfall from the night before was turning to slush in the streets and on the sidewalks. And the slush was quickly turning to ice.

Joanna's feet were cold. She hadn't worn boots, which would have made more sense, given the weather, because they would have clashed with her evening wear. So she kept wiggling and flexing her toes in the thin suede pumps, once again remembering how Trevor Jackson had saved her from falling on the ice the day he'd taken her to lunch and had solicitously protected her from it happening again. Remembering how Trevor had come to find her in the storm and gotten her back home, safe and warm. Remembering that Trevor had congratulated her on doing a good job as

temporary anchor that morning. And all Philip had
done so far was to patronize and criticize.

"The thing is, babe, not everyone can be an anchor.
You have to know how to play to the camera. You have
to be someone the public trusts with giving them information. You have to understand the politics of what goes
on the air and what doesn't."

Joanna sighed. "Yes, I understand all of that. I told
you I didn't expect it to happen."

"Well, maybe you just should have said no. Why
make yourself look foolish before the whole city?"

Joanna made an impatient sound through her teeth
and cut Philip a glaring look. "I did not look foolish.
Everyone at the station thought I did a good job."

"Yeah, it was probably okay. But you're not cut out
to be an anchor, Jo."

"If I didn't know you better, I'd say you're jealous,"
Joanna threw at Philip.

He laughed. "Yeah, right." He gave her a brief glance,
his smile magnanimous and amused. "I've been at this
a lot longer than you have. It takes a certain kind of
personality. You have to be tough. You have to know
people."

"You mean, cutthroat."

"That's right. The black reporters have a hard enough
time as it is in this business. Black women have it even
harder. And they just don't know how to deal."

"Well, let me put your mind at rest. The station has
no plans to replace Ann Marie Lopez with me. I'm still
just a researcher, and I *like* working in the tape library."

"Good," Philip approved with a nod.

But Joanna didn't tell him, as she'd wanted to at first,
that she'd been called into the news director's office after

the noon telecast and complimented again on her professional handling of the situation she'd been thrust into. And he'd indicated that the news staff had been impressed enough to consider training her formally to be a substitute on the air, with every opportunity to move up to coanchor.

Joanna had been pleased and flattered. But she wasn't sure that that was what she wanted to do. She was told to think about it, but felt certain what her response was going to be. She'd been planning to let Philip know, as well. But she'd never had a chance. Almost as soon as he'd shown up to get her for the drive to the museum, he'd been treating her like an adolescent.

"How was Washington?" she asked, as a way of getting off the subject of her TV appearance that morning.

"Washington?" Philip repeated blankly.

Joanna frowned and turned to look at him. "You said you were going down for something with the Black Congressional Caucus."

"Yeah. They had a reception for Colin Powell. Everyone wants to know if he's planning to run for office now that he's retired, and everyone's trying to get on his good side just in case he does."

"Well, it sounds like it was interesting," Joanna murmured, turning her attention once again to the traffic and weather. Philip hadn't asked how her weekend had been.

There were over three hundred people attending the dinner. As she and Philip entered and checked their coats, Joanna's apprehension began to rise as she wondered if Trevor had already arrived with Linda. She'd tried to block out the idea of them being companions for the evening, even though she knew it was a convenient and innocent arrangement Joanna had had fantasies of what it might have been like to come with Trevor.

Joanna never particularly enjoyed going to these big special interest kind of events. She never knew enough people to be comfortable. And she never knew enough of the inside stories and politics to contribute much to the polite gossip. The chattiness was friendly but super-ficial. And there was always a fair amount of covert watching and whispering about who was with whom, and who was wearing what. Already she was wishing the night over.

Trevor saw her first.

But then, he'd been looking to spot her. He'd been hoping to just watch her from a distance and absorb a visual memory of her that he could recall later when he was back at Fort Lewis. Trevor swiveled in his chair toward Linda as she sat exchanging industry information with a couple seated across the table. But his gaze wandered past her, scanning the room for just one person in particular. When he finally did see Joanna, Trevor felt his gut tighten and his jaw tense. His gaze narrowed as Philip was almost immediately swallowed in a circle of cronies and Joanna stood quiet and self-contained, wait-ing through Philip's audience with his friends. Trevor just stared at her.

She was wearing a winter-white pantsuit ensemble, the jacket beaded along the lapels and around the cuffs with pearls. There was no chemise or top under the jacket, providing Trevor with an enticing view of décolletage that had him vividly imagining what lay un-derneath. The milk and coffee tone of her skin contrasted beautifully with the suit, and Joanna stood out dramati-cally from the other women dressed in darker evening

colors. Her short hair was curled, with wispy bangs adding a waiflike delicacy to her face. And looking at her,
Trevor knew that his decision to leave Joanna Mitchell
alone had been the right one.

Joanna let her attention roam as she waited patiently
for Philip, trying not to show too much curiosity about
the other guests. Then she, too, saw Trevor and her attention was riveted. He wasn't dressed in formal evening
wear or a dark business suit. He was wearing a high-
necked black cashmere turtleneck under a charcoal gray
worsted wool jacket. His slacks were also black. He
seemed unimaginably masculine and virile, and unique
against the background of tuxedoed men and sequined
women. Joanna couldn't take her eyes from him.

"What's he doing here?" Philip asked in annoyance
as he took Joanna's arm to steer her into the crowd and
toward their table.

"Why don't you ask him?" she responded tartly.

Philip frowned at her. "Look, that guy is bad news.
You don't know anything about him."

"Well, neither do you," Joanna defended.

"That's where you're wrong. I've found out quite a
lot about him."

Joanna faltered and blinked at Philip. "What do you
mean?" she asked, puzzled.

But already they were at the table and Philip had put
on his celebrity face, smiling good-naturedly, shaking
hands with the men, air-kissing or lightly hugging the
women. When it came to Trevor, however, Philip merely
nodded and looked him over with obvious disapproval.

"Looks like you've wandered into the wrong party."

"No, he didn't," Linda immediately piped up.
"Trevor's here at my invitation."

Philip smirked. "You're a little underdressed."

Trevor shrugged and raised his brows. "You're the only one who's said so. I like your Kente cloth bowtie. That's sharp. And politically correct."

Linda cackled. Joanna glanced covertly at Philip to see how he'd taken Trevor's remark. His grin was forced and tight.

"Thanks," Philip finally answered.

Trevor turned his attention to Joanna, and the admiration was evident in the bright sparkle of his dark eyes. They also held a certain sensual regard that Joanna hoped was not noticed by anyone else. She smiled tentatively at him.

"Good evening," she murmured, somewhat shyly.

"Good evening, Joanna."

Joanna knew instinctively that he wasn't going to comment on her outfit, although she could tell he liked it.

Linda had chosen to pull her extensions back and wrap a glittery gold lamé scarf around her hair. She wore a gold-toned tunic with dolman sleeves over a cocktail-length black crepe de Chine skirt.

The seats Joanna and Philip took placed them opposite Trevor and Linda. Joanna couldn't decide which was worse: sitting so close to him and feeling his heat and sensuality, or being across the table from each other where eye contact was unavoidable.

Joanna tried to keep up polite conversation but didn't enjoy the food, because her stomach roiled from the unbearable tension. She knew that Trevor's gaze was on her, calm and steady, and was annoyed that she seemed to be the only one having trouble getting through the night. After dinner the lights went down in the hall as statements and speeches were made and awards given. To make matters even worse, Philip kept getting up to table-hop around the room, visiting with professional friends or encouraging new ones. At one point, Joanna couldn't see him at all. And when she did finally, he was sitting in conversation with a few people she recognized and a tall, attractive young woman who was nodding at everything Philip was saying.

Joanna turned her attention back to her own table only to discover that Trevor was once again watching her closely. Joanna flushed uncomfortably and tried to concentrate on the speaker at the dais. Linda got up to go to the ladies' room, but Joanna declined to accompany her. As soon as Linda was gone, Trevor changed seats and took the vacant chair next to Joanna.

She didn't acknowledge his presence. But his leg brushed against hers under the table, and he rested his arm along the back of her chair.

"You're not having a good time, either," he said in her ear.

She couldn't help it. A tiny smile of awareness touched her lips. She shook her head almost imperceptively.

"That's a great outfit on you."

"Thank you," she whispered, pleased despite herself.

"It's a great preview," Trevor said slowly.

She frowned. "To what?"

"On how you'd look on your wedding day, dressed in white."

Joanna clutched her hands together, his breath whispering over her ear and cheek. "Preston said the same thing. I went downstairs to see how he was doing."

"Preston is a very wise man." Trevor sighed and

glanced around the darkened room impatiently. "Do you know all these people? Are they your friends?"

She turned her head, realized how close he was next to her, and faced forward again. "N-no. I . . . I know a few people. Philip knows everyone."

"Yeah, so I noticed," Trevor drawled, glancing off briefly in Philip's direction. He leaned closer. "Jo, are you serious about Santa?"

Joanna couldn't even answer. She almost instantly forgot the question. Trevor had called her Jo. It seemed so insignificant, but it was the shortening into a nickname, an endearment that made Joanna not only catch her breath, but feel a sudden emotional swelling inside. He'd made her special again.

"I . . . I . . ." she fumbled. "How can you ask me that?"

"Easy. I have nothing to lose. I'm leaving, remember? No, I take that back. I *do* have something to lose." His voice dropped to a husky urgency. He cursed softly under his breath. "I'm going to lose the chance to find out what we could have been like. I'm never going to get a chance to make love to you."

Joanna felt like she couldn't breathe. And oddly, she felt like she was going to cry at any moment. "Trevor, I . . ." but she couldn't finish. Joanna scrambled quickly out of her chair, excusing herself, and hurried off in the direction of the ladies' room.

She'd never felt so confused in her life.

She and Philip had made no plans for the future. They hadn't even discussed it. Joanna just assumed, as her parents and brother assumed, that somehow it would work out between the two of them. Their occasional arguments and difficulties notwithstanding, Philip was the kind of man she'd always imagined marrying. But suddenly the thought that they might indeed one day marry made Joanna feel . . . frightened. And unsure.

And what were her options? That she'd met an intriguing man who stirred her senses and who made her feel desired and feminine? Joanna didn't even want to think about what it might be like to have Trevor make love to her. The thought was so provocative that it made her feel giddy. But Trevor was right. He wasn't the kind of man she should be involved with.

Joanna reached the restroom just as Linda was coming out. Linda frowned at her.

"Hey, are you all right?"

Joanna grimaced and lied. "The speeches are boring."

Linda laughed shortly. "Well, I don't come for the speeches anyway. I just want to check out the landscape, if you know what I mean. Trevor is the most interesting man here tonight."

Joanna grinned but didn't say anything.

"But it's only for tonight."

"What do you mean?"

Linda sighed. "No chemistry. No sparks. Don't get me wrong—Trevor has been real nice to me. But I don't think he's going to ask to come in for coffee when he takes me home."

"Well, you could be wrong."

"But I'm not. Look, if it weren't for Philip, I bet he'd go for you."

Joanna opened her mouth to deny it but couldn't. Then the bathroom door opened and another woman came out, passing between them, and ending the speculation.

"He's mine for part of the night, anyway. So I might

as well go back and enjoy it." With a cheerful shrug Linda headed back to the banquet hall.

When Joanna came out of the ladies' room herself ten minutes later, she found herself reluctant to return to the table. She was afraid to face both Philip and Trevor. She wandered about the exhibition area, blindly looking at the current display on the history of African-Americans in the Philadelphia area more than a hundred years ago. Joanna turned around to slowly retrace her steps. When she came almost to the entrance of the exhibit hall, she spotted Philip in conversation with the striking young woman whose table he'd visited earlier.

She was not surprised. When she'd first started dating Philip she'd been jealous and concerned with the number of women who'd boldly try to gain his attention. But Joanna had realized that Philip wasn't going to risk his reputation and future for a brief stroking of his ego.

He seemed to be having a serious talk with the young woman, who stood listening quietly. Eventually, Philip took her arm and they headed back into the program.

Joanna wished she could just stay in the corridor until everything was over. She wished she could just go home. But she knew that sooner or later someone would come looking for her.

She returned calmly to the table five minutes later and took her seat. Philip had also returned.

"Where were you?" he asked a bit sharply.

Joanna didn't look at him. "I went to the ladies' room. Where were you?"

Philip sat back in his chair and didn't answer.

Joanna assiduously avoided Trevor's gaze, giving her attention to the next speaker.

But Joanna was hardly expecting that the next an-

nouncer would point out her unexpected appearance before TV cameras that morning. The speaker spoke in
glowing terms and congratulated Joanna on handling it
so well. The audience began applauding, and she was
forced to stand up and be acknowledged. She smiled
and nodded and quickly sat again. As the applause died
down, Joanna stole a quick look in Trevor's direction.
He winked at her.

Finally, it was over. Joanna breathed a sigh of relief
as people began getting up, saying good night to one
another, and heading for the exits. She'd developed a
headache and was anxious to leave and get home. Several people stopped by the table to add even more congratulations to what had already been said and done. She
began to feel embarrassed and overwhelmed.

"Look, I'm going to get our coats before it gets too
crowded. Meet me by the door," Philip instructed impe-
riously as he walked away.

"I think you're stealing his thunder," Linda commented as she accompanied Joanna out with Trevor behind them.

"I don't want his thunder," Joanna said impatiently.
"This morning was a one-time deal. I wish everyone
would stop making such a fuss about it."

"Is that how you really feel, or you just don't want
Philip to get upset?" Trevor offered.

Joanna turned her head to look at him, but said nothing.

The exodus to the door was slow as people continued
to mill about, wait for coats, make last-minute trips to
the restrooms. A producer from Philip's station came
over to say a belated greeting. Behind him Joanna saw
the young woman again and asked him who she was.

"Oh, Keisha Mallory. She's our new intern this year."

"She's very pretty. I suppose she wants to be an anchor," Joanna commented.

The producer laughed. "I think that'll do for starters. She has her sights set a bit higher."

"Well, I wish her luck."

The producer shook his head. "I don't think she's going to need it. Some of her attributes are pretty obvious. They sent her down to D.C. recently to see if she could handle a story."

"And?"

He pursed his mouth. "She did a good job. But then, she had a lot of help. Philip supervised her through it."

Joanna nodded and smiled calmly, but felt a twinge of unease at the revelation. But it wasn't as if this was new. Philip had worked closely with interns each year for the past three years. Joanna whispered goodbye absently as the producer said good night.

"You handle it very well," Trevor said quietly behind her.

Joanna took a deep breath and turned to him. "Handle what?"

"Fame."

Joanna shook her head wryly. "I'd rather just have the money. You can keep the fame."

Trevor laughed. Then his humor slowly faded. He gazed steadily at her. "Jo, despite everything, I'm glad I came tonight. I'm glad we met."

"Yeah, well, I don't think it's such a good thing."

"Philip," Joanna frowned at him, as he approached with their coats over his arm.

"Hey, it's okay," Trevor said, placatingly. "My man here and I got off on the wrong foot. I'm sorry about that."

"I don't believe you," Philip said in a controlled but challenging tone. "I thought there was something funny about you the first time I saw you. All that business about Sheila and wanting information and just finding out she was dead."

"Philip, what is the matter with you?" Joanna asked, stunned.

"Come on, guys," Linda said impatiently. "You're both too old to be facing off. Besides, it's embarrassing. And one of you could get hurt."

"It's not going to come to that. Let's go, Linda," Trevor said smoothly, helping Linda into her coat. "I'll call to say goodbye when I'm leaving, Jo."

She stood apprehensively, not at all sure that Philip wouldn't try something now that he was so angry and worked up.

"Who told you you could call her Jo? I wasn't going to say anything, but I don't like you. You had no business being here tonight. I don't know what kind of story you've been handing out, but I'm telling you, stay away from Joanna."

"All right, that's enough!" Joanna stepped in. They were beginning to attract curious attention, and she certainly didn't want any more of that. "What is going on? Why are you being so rude?" she asked Philip.

Philip did face off in front of Trevor, stepping up close to him and staring contemptuously at him. "I had our man here checked out. I called up a few people and ran his story past them. It's full of holes. I wasn't going to say anything, but I don't like the way he hangs around you."

"Just back off," Trevor said quietly, but in a firm warning voice.

"Did he tell you he's not from Washington, but from Detroit? Did you know he has a criminal record?"

Joanna's eyes widened, and her gaze turned sharply on Trevor. But his attention was solely on Philip, his eyes alert and watchful, his mouth a grim and angry scowl.

"Go on," Trevor encouraged.

Linda sucked her teeth. "Philip, leave the man alone. How do we know *you* don't have a criminal record? Ever do something you weren't supposed to?"

"Did he tell you that Sheila was his wife? Well, she wasn't."

Joanna gasped softly and her mouth dropped open.

"Go on, ask him," Philip urged.

Trevor slowly turned his attention to Joanna. He tried desperately to convey his innermost thoughts to her with just his eyes. He hoped she could see both the excuses and apologies, and maybe figure out the reasons for both. He wanted her to see that she hadn't been wrong to trust him. But Trevor also knew he was asking way too much. So he just waited for her to make the first move, ask the inevitable.

"Is . . . is that true?"

Trevor nodded. "Yes, it's true."

Joanna swallowed. "All of it?" Her voice was barely above a whisper.

"Yes . . . all of it," Trevor responded, almost in defeat.

Seven

Joanna stood in front of the mirror and absently attached the gold loop earrings to her pierced lobes. Then she applied a light smear of lipstick to her mouth and a little blusher to her cheeks. She decided that the overall effect was good. She looked pulled together and ready to face the world again. Except for her eyes. Her eyes somehow seemed different this morning and told a different story from the rest of her appearance. She adjusted the neckline of her sweater, and turned resolutely from her image. Makeup and accessories weren't going to disguise the way she was feeling inside.

Shrugging into her blazer and grabbing her purse, Joanna headed for the living room. She picked up her half-finished cup of hot chocolate from the coffee table and headed for the kitchen to pour the rest of it down the sink. The telephone started to ring.

She stopped in her tracks as the shrill sound startled her, and she stared at the phone. It was now on the third ring. If she let it continue, the answering machine would take the call. But then, she'd only have to replay the message later. No matter who it was. Reluctantly, Joanna put the cup down and picked up the receiver.

"Hello," she answered with trepidation.

"I hope you're feeling better this morning," Philip said petulantly.

Joanna sighed at the opening. "Yes, thanks."

"I wanted to stay last night, you know."

"But I didn't want you to. I told you, Philip, it was late and my day had been a lot more hectic than I'm used to. I just wanted to get some sleep, that's all."

"It's more than that. I don't know why you're mad at me because of what I found out about Trevor Jackson."

"I'm not mad," Joanna claimed weakly.

"Well, it sure felt like it," Philip said bitingly.

"Well, I'm sorry."

"Look, Jo. The guy is a loser. He's a criminal and he's a liar. God only knows what his relationship was to Sheila. I know you thought you were helping him or something," he chuckled lightly, "but you can be so naive. He handed you a line, that's all."

Joanna began to feel agitated. She didn't want to discuss Trevor Jackson with Philip. She didn't understand how she was feeling. Or why. "Philip, it's getting late. I have to go."

"I thought I'd meet you and we could have breakfast first."

"I've already had breakfast," Joanna said.

"Jo . . ." he said patiently. "Okay, so you've had breakfast. I was really talking about us just spending some time together. Why don't I pick you up for lunch?"

"I . . . I don't know. I'm really backed up with work because of yesterday. I thought I'd skip lunch today."

"So when are we going to get together?"

Joanna sighed anxiously. "I don't know. Why is that so important this morning? I've been trying to tell you for weeks that we don't spend enough time together, and suddenly it has to be today, now, because you want it?"

"Hey, all right . . . so I've been busy. I realize that maybe I haven't been around very much. But we do have a relationship."

"Do we? If it weren't for my telephone and answering machine, I'm not sure that we would."

"Come on, Jo . . ."

"Philip, I have to go. We'll discuss this later."

"Babe . . ." Philip took a deep breath. "All right. I'll call you later."

Joanna shook her head wryly. "Right," she said softly and hung up.

Joanna hurriedly got the rest of her things together, feeling annoyed with Philip and his phone call. He was right, of course. The information he'd confronted Trevor with had been a total surprise and not a particularly pleasant one for her. She recalled how stunned she'd felt. How upset. How disappointed. But the thing was, she didn't know if she was more angry at Philip for finding it necessary to play investigative reporter or at Trevor for having lied. Both, Joanna decided. But there was no question in her mind that after the initial shock of the information, the balance of her letdown seemed to have shifted uncomfortably more to one side than the other. Joanna didn't want to examine yet which side and in whose favor.

She just remembered the way Trevor had stared down at her, denying nothing, his dark eyes sharp and intense as if he were willing her to see more in them than just his admission of guilt. Joanna wanted to. She thought she'd seen regret but also a stubborn determination in Trevor's gaze which made her waver just a moment before she silently let Philip lead her away. And when

Philip had churlishly whispered, "I told you so," Joanna's inclination had been to tell him to shut up.

She shuddered. Why couldn't Trevor Jackson tell her the truth from the beginning, especially after going to so much trouble to single her out? Especially after that searing kiss they'd shared. Or had that been part of the scam? What *was* the truth?

Then Linda had telephoned her close to midnight to find out what was going on. Joanna didn't have to pretend not to know, because she didn't.

"Well, what was it he told you?" Linda insisted.

Given that most of it seemed to have been a lie, Joanna told her about Trevor contacting her, claiming to be Sheila's husband.

Linda scoffed. "I wouldn't have believed that for a minute."

"Why?"

"Because from everything you've told me about this woman, Trevor isn't anything like what she'd go for. Sheila sounded like the kind of person who attached herself to other people who could do things for her. What could Trevor do for her?"

Joanna felt an odd sensation of falling sweep over her. She'd slid down farther into her bed linens and whispered, "Love her."

"Please. To quote someone who ought to know, 'What's love got to do with it?' "

"I . . . don't suppose Trevor said anything to you after Philip and I left."

"No. He apologized, but when I asked a few questions, he just said he couldn't talk about it. Then he took me home and that was it."

"What do you mean?"

Linda groaned. "He was a real gentleman, which wasn't exactly what I was hoping for. He kissed me good night . . . on the cheek. And he said I was a lot of fun to be with. You know what *that* means. I'm cute but he's not interested. So that means we both struck out."

"We?"

"Well, I always thought he was seriously interested in you. If Philip wasn't in the way, I bet Trevor would try and make a play for you."

Joanna didn't confide in her friend that Trevor had already done that. "I don't think I'd want to get involved with someone who tells lies and could be a criminal."

"You've spent time with him. Do you think Trevor was scamming you?"

Joanna couldn't really answer that. It hadn't felt like Trevor was. He hadn't kissed her and then tried to be careful as if he had a different agenda. But Joanna only told Linda that she was too tired to think any more about it, and soon got off the phone. The questions, however, stayed with her well into the night, into her dreams, and resurrected themselves in the morning. Joanna's instincts told her one thing. Her head told her something else. She didn't know which to believe.

She left her apartment and walked the one flight down to Preston's. The older man was in a bathrobe, his shock of white hair standing on end. From the woodsy smell upon entering the apartment, Joanna would guess that he'd made his coffee too strong and had burnt his toast.

"How are you making out?"

"Nice of you not to say, 'You burnt your food, Preston,' " he grumbled.

Joanna grinned at him. "It's only eight o'clock and

already you're in a bad mood. Didn't sleep well last night?"

Preston turned his wheelchair and headed back to the living room and the tray which held his half-eaten breakfast. Joanna put her things down and helped him place the tray across his lap once more. She glanced briefly into the kitchen to make sure that all the burners were turned off and the coffee maker had been unplugged.

"Well, there was all that noise upstairs. Sheila must have had company again."

Joanna sighed and shook her head. She wondered if the time was fast approaching when she'd have to contact Preston's son in Arizona and suggest he consider some sort of in-house care for his father. Joanna knew that Preston wouldn't like the idea.

"Preston, there couldn't have been any noise—you know that. Unless it was Danny or Mr. Tillman."

"Naw, it wasn't Tillman. He's not going to come out in this weather unless the rent is due."

"Well, what kind of sound was it?" Joanna asked, sitting on the edge of a chair.

"Oh . . ." Preston began on a sigh, frowning as he tried to concentrate. "Something on the floor. It was heavy. It was dropped on the floor or fell over."

"Then it must have been Danny. He's supposed to start moving stuff out of the apartment. It's rented, you know."

Preston was shaking his head. "He wouldn't go back in there by himself. Not after what happened."

"Mrs. Thatcher said someone tried to break in upstairs. Maybe that's what you heard and you're getting confused. Maybe it wasn't last night at all." Joanna got up and removed the tray, taking it into the kitchen. "I just came to see if you wanted me to get a new film for you this afternoon?"

"No, I don't think so. Don't feel much like TV. But I saw you yesterday," Preston cackled. "You were good."

"My one and only claim to fame," Joanna smiled.

"How was the thing last night?"

Joanna sobered and grimaced. "It was okay. Long speeches, terrible food."

"Why did you go?"

"You know why. Because Philip likes these things, and everyone gets to see everyone else, and you get real dressed up and give each other awards. And I'd already gotten my ticket."

"Well, you probably would have had a better time if you'd just gone out with Trevor. I bet he doesn't go for all of that fussy stuff."

Joanna sighed. She bet he didn't either. But it no longer mattered. He'd lied to her. She didn't know what Trevor Jackson liked or believed in, and she wasn't likely to find out. "You haven't known him any longer than I have. How would you know what he's like?"

"Because I know. The man's a straight shooter. He's the kind of man you should be with and not that—"

"I thought you liked Philip," Joanna said in some surprise.

"He's okay. Good-looking and smart as they come. But he's not right for you. He's too . . . calculating. Now Trevor's a man's man. You get him on your side and he'll be loyal and true."

Joanna felt besieged. "You don't know anything about him, Preston."

"I know what I need to know."

Joanna decided it was a conspiracy.

Were Linda and Preston seeing something that she couldn't see? Or was her vision being confused and clouded by a history with Philip and her parents' expectations? Joanna wondered, as she finally got on her way to work, why she couldn't just trust her heart and feelings.

"Are we having fun yet?" Robby muttered, snatching another tape from the deck and wearily shelving it on a metal book cart along with dozens of others for transport back to the film library.

"Depends on your idea of fun," Joanna murmured absently, applying a label to a cassette holder and marking it on a ledger of dates and programs.

"Not watching bad segments of unused news clips for one thing. 'Jeopardy' would be better than this stuff."

"Well, we're almost done. In fact, I can finish up. You can go home if you like."

"I owe you," Robby said, eagerly accepting the offer of freedom.

"How are you going to pay me back?" Joanna grinned at him as he pulled on his leather biker jacket and swung a knapsack over his shoulder.

"How about I buy you lunch tomorrow?"

"You owe me a lunch from last week."

"Oh."

"I'm just teasing. Aren't you glad you asked your uncle if you could work here during your holiday break?"

"Let's just say I can't wait to get back to school," Robby quipped. "Don't tell my mom I said that." Joanna laughed. "Hey, but it was great working with you. You were real nice to me, Jo."

"Well, that's nice of you to say so."

"And I plan on putting in a good word for you with the old man."

"Good. I'd like a raise, a new car, or a three-week cruise," Joanna chuckled.

"It's after six. Why don't you split and get out of here? What doesn't get done tonight won't matter, right?"

"I suppose."

"See you tomorrow."

" 'Night," Joanna said absently, rubbing at her tired eyes.

Robby was right. What tapes remained could be taken care of the next day. Joanna began to clear her work area. She felt lethargic and numb, even though she'd worked pretty steadily all day long to catch up on her own work. Her mind had been a jumble of confused thoughts and consideration. Not the least of which was what she was going to do about Philip. And what she really thought about Trevor Jackson.

Joanna lifted her purse and tote out of the bottom drawer of her desk and saw two tapes. For a moment she frowned at them, wondering how they had gotten there and what could be on them. Then she remembered the tapes Trevor had brought by the studio the morning before. The very first thought that went through Joanna's mind was that if she viewed them as she'd offered to do, she would have to contact Trevor to let him know what she'd found. On the other hand, she could just send them back by messenger to his hotel.

Not taking any time to examine her decision, Joanna quickly removed the tapes from the drawer, opened the first one, and placed it in the VCR unit. She didn't give herself time to ponder anything. She just did it. The first thing that became apparent was that the footage was from the previous summer. It had been shot mostly around the time of the last mayoral campaign. The tape was a hodgepodge of events, speeches, and receptions at which various candidates were appearing.

Joanna couldn't figure out any particular significance to the tape until she realized that one or two people were appearing more than others. And there was one very handsome black man who seemed to be at the center of most of the occasions. He looked familiar to Joanna, although she didn't know his name. But she was sure she'd seen his face either in the newspaper or on TV.

Finally, Joanna viewed one section in which the man was being addressed as Nat or Nathan. A few moments later at a function he was being introduced directly as Nathan A. MacCauley. Joanna fast-forwarded through the tape, stopping occasionally, recognizing one important figure or another from city government. It was only near the end that she suddenly came across a frame that had Sheila standing in a gathering with Mr. MacCauley. He had his arm around her waist, talking intimately to her. And it seemed pretty clear to Joanna that he was not aware that he was being taped.

Joanna had no idea how Sheila knew someone like MacCauley, but it certainly seemed as if their relationship was more than just casual. And now that she'd seen them together, there was something else about him that seemed very familiar, but more recently than the filming date of the tape. She stopped the tape, not seeing any point in watching the rest, and hit the rewind button. She was not at all anxious to sit through another tape of the same type of scenes, but decided it was already so late that another fifteen minutes of her time wasn't going to matter. Joanna exchanged tapes in the machine and began to play the second one.

It was very specific. It was some sort of convention, a gathering of black professionals in and around a hotel setting. But then Joanna realized that it was really more like a college reunion. She frowned, wondering why Sheila would have tapes of someone's reunion.

There was a dance, and the dimly lit room made it a little difficult to make out many details, but the photographer was scanning the crowd, the tape catching people's spontaneous reaction, most of it cheerful. Then Joanna caught sight of Sheila. She was dancing with a man whose back was to the camera, but she was smiling over his shoulder into the lens, waving a hand airily. The man made a half-turn with his head, but when he realized a camera was pointed at them, he danced himself and Sheila in the other direction until she could no longer be seen and they blended in with the other dancers.

Joanna sat forward in her chair. She took the remote and pressed reverse. The tape screeched backward, and she stopped it at the first sight of Sheila. Joanna watched the scene again. She stared hard at Sheila and her partner, concentrating on every detail. She played the scene over and over again but was not having her curiosity satisfied. Joanna became very alert, her exhaustion vanishing.

There was a sensation of daring and mystery. And one of intuition that made Joanna's heart begin to beat a little faster. She wondered if she had stumbled on a secret. Now she was looking for just one thing to be clarified by the remaining tape. One silent question to be answered. She found it five minutes later.

The scene was a softball game in a park. The diamond was surrounded by picnic areas and trees. The camera was recording the activities of those in attendance. Many of the faces she recognized from the earlier dance sequence. The cameraperson began to walk through the gathering, shooting left and right and wide angle, passing to the edge of the group where there were fewer people and it was more quiet. The camera slowly and quietly approached a London Plain tree, where it was clear that someone was standing on the far side of the trunk. As the image became sharper, Joanna could see a woman's elbow, bent as she had her arms up and around someone's neck and shoulders. The man's arms were braced on the side of the tree as he held himself tightly against the woman, pressing her into the trunk. The undulating movements of their hips indicating a restless rising desire that apparently they were trying to satisfy. Joanna was embarrassed watching but felt compelled to let the tape run. The camera picked up sounds. The murmuring of passion could be heard with the couple's breathing and the moist kissing of their lips. The camera moved to the right, bringing the intertwined pair into full view. Startled, their mouths separated as they both turned their heads to the camera. Joanna gasped. "Oh my God . . ."

It was Sheila. And Philip.

She'd sat silent and stunned for a long time afterward. She didn't even bother watching the rest of the tape. She'd gotten the idea. But Joanna found it more telling that her response had been so calm after the initial shock of seeing Sheila James and Philip. She felt no betrayal, no anger. She had no idea how Sheila and Philip had gotten together, unless it had been at that party she'd had for Preston. She had no idea when their interest in one another had begun or how long it had been going on. This was confirmation of many hints and clues over the past year or two. She'd always suspected that Philip was capable of infidelity, but she'd always hoped to be proved wrong.

Joanna walked slowly into the entrance of her apartment building, deep in thought. Distracted, she got her mail, pushed for the elevator, and reached into her purse for her keys. She was on automatic pilot. Joanna was also still trying to understand why what she'd found out about Philip seemed to have so little effect on her. Less than the information she'd found out the night before about Trevor. The first thing she'd done after reboxing the videotapes was *not* call Philip for a showdown. Instead, Joanna had called Trevor's hotel to let him know she had information about the tapes. He wasn't in, so she'd left a message. And then she'd come home. When she finally reached him, she would tell Trevor about MacCauley. But she wasn't going to say anything to him about Philip.

As Joanna approached her apartment, keys ready to be inserted into the locks, she was aware of sounds from inside Sheila's apartment. For a moment she felt spooked, knowing that there shouldn't be anyone inside. But of course, any one of three people had access. Joanna considered that perhaps Trevor had received her message and gotten to the building ahead of her. Maybe he'd decided to check out the two cases found in the basement.

Joanna tapped lightly on the door and turned the knob. The door was unlocked. She pushed it open slowly and peered around the edge of the door into the apartment. All the lights were out except for the one in the bed-room, at the back of the apartment. That was where the sounds were coming from.

"Trevor?" she called out quietly. There was no imme-diate answer, and the movements and sounds continued, like someone searching through things.

Joanna let the door swing closed behind her. It shut with a soft click. She walked toward the light source. She tried the wall switch just outside the living-room door. It didn't work.

"Trevor, it's Joanna . . ."

She got no further. A terrible fear gripped Joanna when the noise coming from the bedroom abruptly stopped. And then the light went out. She was plunged into sudden darkness. Her vision had no time to adjust, and the quickly rising terror in her demanded that she not wait. Joanna pivoted and tried to rush to the door but couldn't see a thing. In a panic she crashed into the living-room door frame with her shoulder and arm. The impact knocked her off balance, and she cried out shortly as she tried to catch herself and keep moving. Now there was movement behind Joanna. Someone was leaving the bedroom and coming after her.

She put a hand out, blindly trying to touch anything to get her bearing, but hoping that she was at the door. Her boot stubbed against something hard that didn't move, and she yelped again as she tripped and fell for-ward over the obstacle. Joanna landed clumsily on a knee and elbow, and her head grazed the edge of what she knew was the coffee table. A sharp tingling pain spiraled in her head. She could sense someone moving swiftly toward her in the dark. Some unknown spirit or monster. Joanna grew hot with fright.

"No . . . no," she began moaning. Her own voice became louder as she felt a scream ready to burst from her throat. A dark shadow suddenly loomed over her, reaching out for her.

"Shut up! Shut up!" a male voice ground out harshly.

Joanna felt herself grabbed and brutally hauled upward. Still unable to see anything, her arms flayed out wildly and she got tangled in the long strap of her purse. She dropped her mail and her keys. "Please . . ." she could barely whisper.

A large hand abruptly covered her mouth and nose. Joanna grabbed at it because she couldn't breathe. Her chest heaved as she tried to take in air. She was shaken, and she tried to stop the low moan that was coming from deep in the back of her throat. Her knee throbbed from where she'd landed on it. She didn't want this man to do anything else to her.

"I said shut up."

Except for her trembling Joanna tried to stop moving. The man was in back of her and she could feel his hot breath against her cheek as he bent closer to talk to her.

"I'm not going to hurt you."

There was a knock on the door.

"What's going on in there? Who's in there?" came a strident female voice.

Joanna recognized Mrs. Thatcher. The man stood perfectly still at the sound of the voice outside the door. Joanna still concentrated on trying to breathe. Then the man moved backward into the narrow hallway just inside the door. He dragged Joanna with him, his hand still covering her mouth. She could hear his ragged breathing and realized that he was scared, too. It didn't make her feel any better.

The door slowly opened, and the sudden bright light from the hallway silhouetted Mrs. Thatcher against the beige wall in the corridor.

"Is . . . somebody in here?" she asked timidly.

The man holding Joanna abruptly released her, shoving her violently away from him. Then he ran for the open door. He rushed past a startled Mrs. Thatcher, pushing her aside as he made his escape. The older woman gave a startled cry of fright and turned and hurried back to her apartment. Joanna heard her neighbor's door slam and lock.

Joanna had been thrown right into the wall, and her forehead and nose collided with the hard surface. She felt the immediate trickle of blood from her nostril. She slid to the floor, unable to stand. Her legs felt like rubber, and every part of her was shaking. She sat cupping both hands to her nose, trying to catch her breath and calm down. But her chin began to quiver, and finally tears started to roll down her cheeks.

The apartment door was still open. Someone else suddenly appeared.

"Sheila?" she heard Danny's voice call out incredulously into the apartment. "Is . . . that you?"

Joanna turned a tear-streaked face to him. "Danny . . ." she whimpered from the dark interior.

Danny's mouth dropped open. He shook his head and backed away. "No . . . no . . ." He turned and disappeared, too.

Joanna was sobbing openly now. When she again

heard sounds in the hallway, she didn't even bother to move. She didn't even look up. She felt totally done in.

"Joanna?"

She heard her name and recognized the voice, and felt relief flood through her. She tried to say Trevor's name, but couldn't. He rushed into the door toward her. She could hear the concern and anger in the oath he uttered.

"Joanna . . ."

She felt his hands take hold of her, haul her into his arms and against his chest. Joanna cried even harder, unable to stop because the low soothing murmuring of Trevor's voice made her feel safe.

And she was right where she wanted to be.

Joanna sat curled in a corner of her sofa, hugging herself tightly. She'd taken off her coat and sat shivering occasionally, despite the fact that the apartment was well heated. The cold damp washcloth which she held pressed to her face dulled the ache around her nose, and the bleeding had stopped. But the fright lingered, and each time Joanna relived that moment of having been grabbed in the dark from behind, a pain tightened the muscles in her chest and she experienced the fear all over again.

She laid her head back against the cushions of the sofa, her eyes closed. The blare of one uniformed officer's walkie-talkie was a reminder that she was now safe, but it was opening her eyes and seeing Trevor across the room that made Joanna believe it. His tall, sturdy presence made her feel she could rely on his strength. He glanced in her direction as if sensing her regard. Trevor gave her a long steady look of reassurance and a slight nod. Joanna sighed and closed her eyes again.

She recalled Trevor holding her as she sat cowering on the floor of Sheila's apartment. Trevor had repeatedly asked if she were hurt, but Joanna had been unable to utter a single word. She could only demonstrate her relief in the way she'd pressed her body into his and cried. Trevor had finally helped her to stand up and had guided her out into the lit hall. He saw the blood on her face and hands, and again cursed. He gently tried to examine where the damage was, and Joanna had gasped in consternation as she realized her blood was on his jacket.

"Look what I did. I'm . . . sorry," she choked out.

Trevor had pressed his hand to the back of her head and bent to kiss her forehead. "Don't worry about it."

When Joanna didn't have the keys to her apartment, Trevor returned next door to search in the dark on the floor until he'd found them. Once inside, he'd further surprised her by immediately calling the police. After the call, Trevor had made her lie flat on the sofa. He'd gotten the washcloth and gently cleaned the blood from her face. He then examined it, touching the darkening abrasion and the one developing on her temple. Joanna lay complacent and still, comfortable in the knowledge that Trevor was taking care of her. He had sat on the edge of the sofa next to her, placing his hand against the side of her face and stroking her cheek with his thumb. Joanna could sense his muscles bunching in anger, and his jaw was tight with worry.

Now, Joanna opened her eyes slightly and saw Trevor standing in conversation with the uniformed cop, who was taking notes, and Detective Schultz. They'd arrived only ten minutes before, with her purse, tote, and her mail. The detective had looked at Joanna and quickly suggested an ambulance to get her to the hospital, but she had adamantly refused, and Trevor had assured the officers that she was okay. And then Trevor had taken over, explaining to the detective and the officer, and taking them next door to figure out what had gone on.

They had just returned. The officer finished his note-taking and was sent next door again to continue his investigation. Trevor and Detective Schultz approached Joanna, the detective sitting in one of her side chairs, and Trevor taking up a position close to her on the sofa. Joanna drew strength and comfort from his presence.

"Are you sure you're okay?" the detective asked.

"I'm fine," Joanna whispered.

The detective glanced at his notes. "I thought you said you didn't know Trevor Jackson?"

Joanna swallowed and hazarded a wide-eyed stare at Trevor. "I . . . I didn't know him," Joanna responded carefully.

"But you *had* heard his name?"

She nodded guiltily. "Yes," Joanna murmured.

The detective looked at her. "It's a good thing he isn't dangerous. Mr. Jackson came to see me himself."

Again Joanna looked at Trevor. "You did?"

Schultz nodded. "It was smart of him to come in."

"It saved time," Trevor said, knowing it forestalled the police digging further into his own history.

"He found some letters and papers that suggest a possible suspect."

"Nathan MacCauley," Joanna blurted out.

Both men exchanged surprised glances before looking at her. The detective narrowed his gaze. "Why do you say that?"

"Well . . . I'm not saying he had anything to do with Sheila's death, but . . . I think they were having an affair. There was a videotape I viewed that showed them together and . . . and showed that there might have been something going on."

"Are we talking *the* Nathan MacCauley? City Council member?"

"Yes," Joanna nodded.

"I'd like to see that tape."

Joanna hesitated, aware of Trevor's eyes on her. Nonetheless she stood up and got her tote from the other chair where it had been placed by the uniformed cop. Nervously she opened it and reached inside. She was happy that she'd taken the time to mark the two boxes so she could identify one from the other. Joanna retrieved the one tape, not even mentioning the second one, and handed it to the detective.

"Where did you find this?"

"The same place I found the letters and some of the jewelry," Trevor volunteered. "I didn't have a way of looking at it, and Joanna offered to take a look for me. Sheila is the only person I would have recognized in any case."

"Why didn't you turn it over to me?" Detective Schultz asked.

Trevor glanced briefly at Joanna, watching the way she averted her gaze and blushed. "I didn't think of it," he responded smoothly.

"Do you think Nathan MacCauley was involved?" Joanna asked the detective.

"With the deceased? Yeah. With her death? I can't speculate on that. There are letters; now there's this tape . . . and the dead woman was four months pregnant."

Joanna visibly stiffened. "I didn't know that."

The detective shrugged. "It was in the coroner's report."

Joanna looked quickly at Trevor. His jaw tensed reflexively. She was trying to gauge his reaction when they all heard voices raised outside the apartment door. Joanna jumped, her nerves already on edge. The door opened and Philip came rushing in as the officer tried to block his way.

"Jo, what's going on?" Philip's attention quickly took in everyone in the room. When he spotted Trevor, annoyance twisted his mouth. He jabbed a finger in Trevor's direction. "What's *he* doing here?"

"Who are you?" Detective Schultz asked coldly, waving the officer back outside the door.

"This is Philip Lee," Joanna introduced quickly, stepping forward. "Philip, this is Detective Schultz."

"What happened?" He frowned. "Christ, there's blood all over you. What did he do?" Philip glared at Trevor.

"I'm okay."

"Excuse me, *I'm* asking the questions," the detective reminded Philip. "How do you know Miss Mitchell? What are you doing here?"

"She's my fiancée," Philip said possessively.

Joanna stared at him. "No, I'm *not*," she countered quietly. For a moment there was dead silence in the room.

"Jo . . ." Philip began.

"All right, all right, hold it. I'm not interested if she is or isn't. What brought you here now?"

"I wanted to make sure that *he* stays away from her. I don't know who he is, but he showed up last week with some phony story about Sheila James."

Detective Schultz looked at Philip. "Did you know Miss James?"

Joanna carefully looked at Philip as well. She watched the way he rubbed his hands together and licked his lips. He did a combination shrug and hesitant shake of his head, as if he couldn't make up his mind what his answer should be. "Well . . . I'd met her once or twice, sure. She was right next door to Joanna. But I didn't really know her."

Joanna briefly closed her eyes, a chill rolling through her. She could also sense Trevor's eyes on her across the room, and when she glanced furtively at him, she found his eyes intense and probing.

The officer stuck his head in the door again.

"We're all finished, Lieutenant."

"Thanks. You guys can leave."

Joanna stood silently, aware that Trevor and Philip were staring at one another. Aware that she stood between them. Aware that after tonight, nothing was ever going to be the same between any of them. Joanna looked at the detective as he faced them again.

"I'll take it from here," the detective said, preparing to leave. He looked sternly at both Trevor and Joanna. "Stay out of the apartment. I want my men to have a look through all of that stuff that was in the case. And I want to see if we can find anything that would lead to the man who accosted Ms. Mitchell in the apartment."

"Someone attacked you?" Philip asked, incredulous. "Why?"

The detective cleared his throat. "I may still need information from you," he said to Trevor.

Trevor nodded. "You know where to find me."

"I appreciate your help. Both of you. But anything

else you do I'll take as interference. We're still not sure
what we're dealing with here."

Joanna accompanied the officer to the door. Once the
door was closed behind him, the air became instantly
tense. Joanna turned reluctantly back to her living room.
Trevor was now standing and leaning negligently against
the bookcase, and Philip stood in the middle of the living
room. They just stared silently at each other, although
Joanna could see nothing but calm from Trevor, which
was in direct contrast to the blustery impatience coming
from Philip.

When Joanna looked at Philip, she no longer saw the
Philip she'd always known. He was still lively, handsome, impeccably dressed. Yet he seemed a stranger.
Both men had secrets. But Philip's seemed the most
damaging in light of the past she had shared with him.

"So what went on in Sheila's apartment?" Philip
asked.

The question irritated Joanna. He wasn't asking to
find out why she'd been attacked. He never even asked
if she was hurt. He was asking because he sensed more
information. A revelation.

"I'm not the detective. I don't have to answer your
questions," Trevor said smoothly.

Joanna spoke up directly to Philip, "I surprised someone. A man. He was looking for something." Joanna
walked to Philip and stared at him. "I'd offered to help
Trevor clear out Sheila's things so the landlord could
have the apartment to rent. There were letters. And
videotapes."

Philip put his hands in his pockets and stared blankly
at her. "Videotapes? Of what?"

"We both know what was on the tapes, Philip," she said softly.

"I'll wait outside," Trevor said, pushing away from the unit.

"Why don't you just leave? This isn't any of your business," Philip said in annoyance.

"No, don't," Joanna said quickly, looking plaintively at Trevor.

"I don't want him in on my business."

"It's my business, too," she said.

"I can't believe you want anything to do with someone like him."

Someone like him . . . Joanna thought as she watched Trevor walk to the door and out into the hallway. Someone who had always been there when she needed it. Someone who had been protective . . . and shown the ability to be loving. Someone who had been all the things she'd wanted from Philip . . . and had not gotten.

"I didn't tell Detective Schultz about the tape with you and Sheila together."

"Look, whatever was on that tape doesn't prove anything."

"It proves that you were seeing Sheila behind my back."

"We ran into each other at a couple of things . . ."

"She was pregnant," Joanna said flatly, and watched the blank look spread across Philip's face.

He smiled easily and shook his head at her. "No . . . it wasn't me."

"Are you sure?" she asked simply.

Philip got angry. "Do you think I'd do something so stupid to ruin my career?"

The words hit Joanna hard, and she could feel the

impact in her chest. Not of hurt and outrage, but of disbelief. He hadn't denied an involvement. "No, you wouldn't. But you obviously never gave a thought as to how it could affect our relationship."

"Sheila is dead. I don't care about her," he said dismissingly.

Joanna slowly shook her head. "You don't really care about me, either. I'm not what you want. Last summer it was Sheila. Last weekend it was Keisha Mallory. She went with you to D.C., didn't she?"

Philip started to protest and then stopped. "Babe, it was . . . business. Yeah, we spent a lot of time together. What else do you want me to say?"

Joanna looked at Philip for a long time but felt nothing more than sadness and an odd relief. "How about goodbye?" she said. She turned and walked to the door.

"Are you sure you want to do this?" Philip asked.

Joanna smiled at his arrogance. She pulled the door open. "I'm sure."

Philip straightened his shoulders and put on his leather gloves as he slowly approached her. "You're making a mistake. I don't know what Jackson's been telling you, but this is a big mistake." He was at the door when he turned back to her, a look of righteousness transforming his features. "What are you going to tell your parents?"

She'd already considered that. They were going to be disappointed. "I'll tell them the truth." Philip looked startled. "You and I weren't suited to each other."

His mouth tightened and, without another word, Philip walked through the door and out of her life.

As soon as he was gone, Joanna felt her emotions loosening. She hadn't realized how much she'd been holding herself in control. Her hands began to tremble. Not because Philip had gone and she was going to miss him. She knew she wouldn't. But because everything about her life was changing, and she wasn't sure how things were going to end. She only knew for sure that there was no future for her and Philip together.

"Jo?"

Joanna started and turned swiftly around. It was half a statement, half a question. It held concern. Trevor stood there staring at her. His dark features were composed and still. Only his eyes were watchful and seemed filled with uncertainty. Joanna had never seen Trevor unsure of himself before. But Joanna was also surprised at the degree of comfort she took from Trevor just being there. He came to stand in front of her, and she felt his warmth and his solid ruggedness, which made her feel safe.

"Are you okay?" He touched her arm.

She nodded.

"I saw Philip leave."

"It's over between us."

"I'm sorry."

She stared up at him. "Are you?"

Trevor arched a brow and chuckled silently. "No, not really."

"Why?" she persisted softly.

Trevor's gaze traveled slowly over her face, noting the eyes with their questioning brightness, the slightly parted mouth . . . waiting. Joanna seemed small and fragile, but ever since he'd met her, she'd proved him wrong. About a lot of things.

"He messed up. If you were my woman, I'd never let you go," he said, his voice rich and deep. His head was inclined toward her, his mouth pursed and his nostrils flaring gently. "If we were together, I'd only want your love. Your loyalty. If I had you to believe in me . . . I'd think I was pretty damned lucky."

Joanna felt her chin starting to quiver with emotion, and she bit her lip gently to control it. "You . . . you've thought a lot about this."

"Yes."

"So, what do we do now?" she asked in a whisper, keeping her eyes on his face, his mouth. Watching the tightening of his jaw muscles. Sensing the way Trevor was holding himself in check.

Trevor looked at her for a long moment as if trying to remember every detail and imprint it on his memory. "I'm leaving. Tomorrow I fly back to Washington. You'll go back to doing whatever you were doing before last week. Before you met me. Pretend it never happened, Joanna."

Joanna slowly shook her head. "I can't."

"You have to," Trevor said, stepping back from her. "I will. Goodbye, Joanna Mitchell."

With that Trevor turned and headed with determined strides toward the door. Joanna couldn't believe he was just going to leave. Just like that. In that moment she knew that she didn't want him to. She had no idea of his background. She didn't know the severity of his criminal past or what he did for a living. But she did know that he had more integrity than anyone else she'd met in a long time. That had to be worth something. She had only known Trevor's sincerity, his earnestness. And he'd always kept his word. That was all Joanna decided she really needed to know.

He was at the door, pulling it open.

"Trevor?" Joanna called out softly behind him. She walked toward him, stopping as Trevor paused. He turned his head to watch her approach. She felt no hesitation at all. No doubt. "Stay with me tonight."

Trevor closed his eyes briefly and sighed, as if her request was too hard, too painful to bear. "You know what will happen if I stay."

Joanna stepped even closer to him, looking up poignantly into his face. "I hope so," she whispered boldly.

Trevor only hesitated a moment longer. He uttered a sound deep in his throat like relief or surprise. Or pleasure. He reached for her and pulled her into his arms with a kind of slow purposeful intensity, as if he were letting himself go. Giving up control.

"Jo," he groaned as he hugged her tightly.

As she gasped in surprise, Trevor lowered his head and covered her mouth, his tongue already seeking entry. The kiss was demanding, and Joanna welcomed it, wrapping her arms around Trevor's neck and standing on tiptoe to accommodate his height. Trevor tightened his hold around Joanna and lifted her clear from the floor. He never released her mouth, continuing to kiss her as he started to walk forward again, heading unerringly for the open bedroom door.

Eight

In the bedroom Trevor slowly lowered Joanna until her feet touched the floor. But he didn't let her go. He kept kissing her with a kind of urgency that was hypnotic. He didn't want to stop. He was enjoying the willing response from her because he hoped it meant not only desire for him, but trust. His lips held hers, drawing on the passion that was growing between them, and he let it stir his senses. He didn't want to rush through the sex to satisfaction, but wanted to experience genuine caring and affection. Something Trevor wasn't sure he'd ever had before.

Joanna liked the pressure of Trevor's mouth on hers. With her eyes closed she let herself go with the sensual stimulation of their fused lips. This felt so natural and pleasurable. Trevor held her against his body, and she was aware of the level of his arousal. She leaned into him, and he grew more rigid. There was something about knowing that she was desired by Trevor that held a primal excitement for Joanna. He hadn't been expecting this any more than she had. It had come as a surprise. It wasn't going to be predictable.

Trevor rode both of his hands caressingly up Joanna's back. And with the pressure of his hands, he gently pushed her away, his mouth reluctantly releasing hers.

He stared down into her face and still couldn't believe that Joanna wanted him.

She opened her eyes, blinked at him, and lifted a hand to stroke his jaw. The gentle touch made Trevor feel vulnerable and overwhelmed by her capacity to forgive. His thumb gently brushed over the slight discoloration on the side of her nose. Trevor felt a surge of anger that she'd been hurt and an unexpected fear that it could have been so much worse.

He sighed and shook his head, bewildered. "I've never met anyone like you before," he confessed in a gravelly voice.

"I'm afraid to ask you what that means," she said shyly.

"It means I'm sorry I didn't tell you everything at the beginning. I wasn't straight with you."

She pursed her lips into a smile and placed her hand over his mouth. "I know you'll tell me everything."

He kissed her fingertips, then pulled her hand away. "Yeah. But not right now."

She helped him as he shrugged out of his coat, his head again bending to kiss her expertly. He then pulled his sweater and T-shirt over his head. Joanna stared at the wide expanse of his chest. She was surprised by the tightly curled black hair that was generously sprinkled across Trevor's brown skin. Mesmerized, Joanna let her hand brush over his chest and the hard nubs of his nipples. She looked into his eyes and saw a raw need and desire which made her feel more like a woman than she ever had.

Joanna turned away from the intensity of Trevor's dark eyes and the incredible heat of his body. She began to undress, excited and tremulous by the prospect of making love with him. She heard movements behind her as he finished undressing. She felt the gentle touch of his lips on her bare shoulder as he slid her unbuttoned blouse down her arms. Joanna let it drop carelessly to the floor. His hands stroked her shoulders and arms before searching for the front clasp on her bra. Joanna held her breath in anticipation as he quickly opened it and pulled the silk and lace aside. And then she felt his arms around her, his hands covering her breasts and slowly massaging and rubbing her flesh. His hands slid beneath to cup them, and Trevor stepped closer until Joanna was leaning back against his chest. She reached back with her hands and found him naked.

She swallowed and her heart began to race. Trevor's thighs were tightly muscled. He pressed his hips forward against her, and she gasped quietly as her flesh felt his hardened masculinity. Joanna's eyes drifted closed, and she tried to breathe through her slightly parted lips, anticipating Trevor's touch and his intentions. His strong long fingers were sure and knowing over her sensitized nipples, hardening them in turn, and she felt the curling of need in the pit of her stomach.

Trevor continued to stroke her breast with one hand, but let the other hand travel down her rib cage to her stomach. Her muscles contracted involuntarily. She held her breath. His fingers slipped easily under the elastic band of her panties, his hand searching lower. Joanna's knees weakened, and she moaned.

"Trevor . . ." she whispered at his bold invasion.

He kissed her ear, the side of her neck. "Shhhh . . ." His hand continued to explore.

Joanna's breathing became labored. She felt dizzy and let her weight rest entirely against Trevor. After a moment he turned her around, back into his arms, and found her mouth again. Trevor began to maneuver her panties down her hips until they were both bare and their heated flesh pressed together.

He gently pushed Joanna backward onto the bed. They didn't bother pulling down the comforter but lay together kissing urgently. Trevor's hands held Joanna's bottom, and he provocatively undulated his hips against her until the buildup of their desire was an intense pleasurable pain. Joanna moaned his name again. Trevor turned out the bedside lamp and suddenly got off the bed. Joanna heard him rustling among his clothing and things, heard the telltale ripping of foil packaging and watched the shadowed application of protection before Trevor returned to the bed.

He didn't prolong the foreplay. Trevor could feel Joanna's hot breath against his shoulder and neck as he lay on her. Her knees came up and her arms circled his back as he settled between her legs. She was trembling, but Joanna's innate trust of him in this most intimate moment only made Trevor more excited. And more grateful. They were both ready. He whispered endearments, kissing her face, rotating his hips and searching until he found her sensitive opening. Gently pushing, he then thrust smoothly forward until he was sheathed within Joanna's soft body.

Trevor rested in her and groaned deeply. He never had had the experience before of making love and feeling like he was safely and securely home. That's the way Joanna made him feel—that he belonged. That he mattered and she wanted him.

But finally, Trevor began a slow cadence of in and out movement. Joanna lifted her hips, tilted her pelvis to meet him. Her hands were restless as she caressed his shoulder, feeling the play of sinew, the reassurance that Trevor was going to hold her and not let her get lost in the magic of the moment. There was something wanton and erotic about the single-minded desire to satisfy a curiosity, gain a knowledge, and fulfill a need, as if there weren't enough time and they had to get it right the first time. As if this was the only time.

She loved the way she felt with Trevor. They had not expressed their emotions to each other, but now words seemed anticlimactic. Their bodies rode in beautiful rhythm, straining toward a repletion that made it hard for either of them to think clearly.

Joanna felt the sudden tautening of Trevor's thighs and legs. A moan came from deep in his chest, and she felt the spasms of his release. Trevor then slowly relaxed. He lifted his head to kiss her, to plunge his tongue into her mouth. A hand rubbed a turgid nipple and sent her over the edge of her own climax while Trevor rhythmically rotated his hips against hers. She succumbed to the melting sensation that seemed to start at the center of her body and flow in a wavelike motion outward. A mewling sound of helplessness whispered past her lips, and she let out a long satiated sigh.

For a long silent moment they lay with their bodies joined. Joanna could feel the steady pumping of Trevor's heart as it slowed to normal. She enjoyed the weight of his body, the hard firmness of him on top of her. It made her feel protected. And she liked that he seemed not to want to move. To hurry and be done with it. Joanna stroked his back.

"Do you want me to get up?" Trevor mumbled, his words lost in the curve of her neck.

His breath tickled. Joanna shook her head. "No."

He let out a deep breath. "Are you sorry?"

Her hand massaged his nape. "No."

"You should be," he said in a tone of annoyance.

Joanna smiled dreamily to herself. "Sorry to disappoint you."

Trevor levered himself up on his elbows. He looked down into Joanna's face but couldn't see details in the dark. He didn't want to turn the light on and break the spell that had woven around them with their lovemaking. But he knew where her mouth was. He kissed it slowly. "I'm not. You make me feel like I'm a good person. You make me feel so strong."

"That's because you are," Joanna said softly.

He chuckled silently. "Where were you ten years ago?"

"Too young to know a thing," Joanna said wryly, and lifted her chin as Trevor began to plant kisses along her throat. He was starting to rock his hips and thighs against her. He was growing hard within her. "You wouldn't have wanted me then . . ."

Trevor grunted, falling back into the easy dance with her body, filling her with his. "I want you now, Jo."

Joanna arched her back as a delightful surge of pleasure made her breath catch in her throat. She held tightly to Trevor. "Yes . . ." she managed to get out before the ecstasy left her speechless.

"Are you awake?" Joanna whispered into the dark. She tilted her head back against Trevor's arm which she was using as a pillow.

"Hummmm."

Joanna sighed and let her hand play idly across his hard chest. She closed her eyes and felt the ridges and planes of muscles, the wiry texture of his hair. "What are we going to do?"

"About what?" Trevor asked, pretending not to know.

"About us."

Trevor remained still and silent. Then he rolled on his side to face Joanna, draping an arm across her waist. "What I'd like to do is make love to you again. What I'm going to do is get up in a while, get dressed, and leave."

"Trevor . . ."

"What you are going to do, Joanna," he overrode her interruption, "is to forget about me. I'm not the right kind of man for you."

"You keep saying that, and I don't believe it. I know what kind of man you are. I trust my feelings."

"Until last night you were sure there was a Santa Claus, too."

"You don't understand. Philip and I . . . there were problems. Philip enjoys being a celebrity. He likes being treated as if he's special."

"You mean by women."

"Yes. Women."

"Okay, so he was a fool. He still has more to offer you than I can."

"What Philip offered I've decided I don't want. He's not ready to be serious and committed in a relationship. He doesn't want to settle down with me. Right now he's having a good time. And that's okay. But I wasn't having fun. I don't think we were going in the same direction."

"What has that got to do with me?" Trevor asked carefully.

She thought for a long moment and began absently rubbing a foot along Trevor's leg. "You're thoughtful and considerate. You seem strong and centered. Sure about yourself."

"Hey, don't start any rumors," Trevor murmured, amused. "Someone might believe that stuff."

"Don't joke about it, Trevor. I believe it. Something is happening between us. Why can't we just see what it is?" Joanna said, reaching out to lay her hand along his hard jaw.

"Jo . . . you don't know. You don't understand."

"Then tell me," she coaxed quietly. "What is your story? Who are you?"

After a moment Trevor sighed deeply and shifted his position on the bed. He lay flat again, his arms circling Joanna so that she curled against his side and chest. She looped a leg over his thigh while her hand rested over his heart.

"I was never married to Sheila James. But I knew her. Sheila was married to my brother."

Joanna made a small sound of surprise. "Your brother? Then why are you here? What happened to him?"

Trevor sighed. "He died. He was killed in Desert Storm."

"Did . . . Sheila leave him while he was away?"

"She did more than that. They were having problems before Troy went overseas. He was stationed in Texas for a while but Sheila didn't want to move there. She stayed in California, and he supported her until he learned that she was not exactly acting like a wife. She cleaned him out. And she used his name and position to get hold of money and other benefits, and left a mess of debts for Troy to straighten out.

"It made life difficult for him with his superiors. Then he went to Kuwait, Sheila disappeared, and Troy never came home."

"I'm sorry, Trevor. If Sheila hadn't died, too, what were you going to do when you found her?"

"Try to recoup some of the money, if I could. There are still a lot of people and places that are waiting to get paid back. I'm trying to clear my brother's name. He was a kid. He didn't know any better. He thought Sheila was foxy and hot. Tough combination for any man to resist, I guess," Trevor finished wryly.

"You did."

"Not at first. She was beautiful. She seemed helpless, made men want to take care of her. Worked with Troy. Like I said, Sheila wasn't really mean. But she used people and never thought about them afterward.

"He was my kid brother. I tried to watch out for him, because I didn't want him to be like me.

"Troy started out as an infantry soldier. He worked his way up the ranks. He was an officer. What Sheila did tore him up."

"Well, that explains your brother and Sheila. What about you?"

Trevor sighed. "I'm not as good as my brother."

"But I never knew your brother."

"I'm a criminal, Jo. You heard Philip."

Joanna remained silent. She couldn't ignore that. "Did you ever hurt anyone?" she asked in a small voice, waiting stiffly for his answer.

"Only myself," Trevor muttered.

"What did you do?"

He rolled his head on the pillow in her direction. In

the dark Joanna could see the blackness of his eyes and the way he stared openly at her.

"I robbed people. I stole cars. I broke into stores . . ."

Joanna gasped softly. She couldn't help it. She *was* shocked. "Trevor . . ." she murmured, incredulous.

"I've been arrested, I've been in jail." He turned his head to stare up at the ceiling. "I tried to warn you. I told you you wouldn't like what you heard."

Joanna felt confused. She couldn't sort out her feelings or what the information meant. She only knew that she wasn't afraid of Trevor Jackson. "You watched out for your brother. You tried to take care of him. Even now you're trying to save and protect his honor and memory. I'm sorry, but that doesn't sound like something a criminal would care about."

Suddenly Trevor turned on her. He came up on his elbow and bent over her. Joanna blinked at him in surprise, a frisson of apprehension making her wonder at his mood.

"Leave it alone, Joanna," he said abruptly, almost angrily.

Trevor threw back the bed linens and swung his legs over the bed's edge to sit up. Joanna reached forward and put her arms around him. Trevor didn't try to break away, but she could feel the tautness in his body, as if he were poised to run.

"No, don't. What you're telling me doesn't make any sense. The person you're describing isn't the man I know. He's not the man I made love with."

He was shaking his head. "I shouldn't have done it."

"We did it."

"I should have stuck to what I had to do in the first place."

"What do you mean?"

"Find Sheila. See if there was any money left from what she took from Troy. Get out of Philly and back where I belong."

"Then why did you come looking for me?"

"You weren't what I was expecting," Trevor said impatiently. "I thought you'd be like Sheila. I thought you'd be a friend who knew a lot about her. I thought I could play you to get the information I needed."

Joanna stiffened. She let go of Trevor as if she'd been burned. "So . . . I was just part of your plan?"

"That's how it started out. But then everything went wrong. I should have given up when I found out that Sheila was dead."

"So why didn't you?" Joanna asked quietly.

Trevor turned to glance at her over his shoulder. He touched her face. "Because I realized you were for real, and I liked being with you. But I have no business liking someone like you. I don't want to hurt you."

Joanna listened, but then she caught something else in Trevor's voice. A different tone and sound that she'd not heard from him before. It was a surprising revelation. Joanna tried to smile at him but knew it was lost in the dark. She reached up with her arms and placed them around Trevor's neck. She leaned forward and kissed him on his mouth. He was perfectly still and didn't respond. She kissed him again, using gentle pressure to lure him. It worked. Trevor automatically opened his mouth to kiss her in return. Joanna pressed forward until he was forced to face her, and her breasts were rubbing against his chest. There was a guttural sound of pleasure from deep in his throat.

"Joanna . . ." he said.

She heard it again.

Joanna began to slowly lower herself backward onto the mattress. Her hold around Trevor's neck brought him down on top of her. Her tongue was teasing him, playing with his. Suddenly, he lifted his head to look questioningly at her. Already his breathing was rushed, and his erection grew harder between their bodies.

"Didn't you hear anything I just told you?"

"Yes, I heard. You're big and bad and dangerous. You love 'em and leave 'em." Joanna brushed her tongue and lips across his mouth. She rubbed her cheek against his. "So why are you so afraid of me?" she asked in a whisper. But she didn't expect an answer.

Instead, Trevor settled himself carefully, more comfortably on her slender frame, nestling between her legs and returning the caresses with gentle enthusiasm.

"I'm not anything like Philip," he confessed.

Joanna sighed, closed her eyes, and let his hand massage her breast until the nipple was stiff and sensitive. "I know that. What . . . what else haven't you told me?"

Trevor lowered his head, his mouth licking her nipple. She moaned. "I was born in Detroit. My mother died when I was thirteen. My grandmother raised me and Troy. I gave her a hard time."

"What else?"

He moved away from her for a moment, put on a fresh condom, then repositioned himself, seeking an entry into her waiting and willing body. "I like Fort Lewis. It keeps me out of trouble."

Joanna felt her chest heaving, felt Trevor pushing slowly at her. "What . . . else?"

He held tightly to Joanna as his body slid smoothly home. "I could fall in love with you."

Joanna made a sound halfway between a giggle and a groan. "This is . . . a very good . . . *aaaahh* . . . start," she whispered.

Joanna lay alone in the bed. She stared at the space next to her, felt the odd loneliness as she listened to the quiet sounds of Trevor getting dressed. He had taken his things into the living room. Just a half-hour ago, they had both been asleep. Trevor behind her, an arm holding her as his thighs touched the backs of hers. She hadn't been aware when he'd gotten out of bed, but the shower running in the bathroom had finally awakened her.

She didn't know whether to stay in bed and pretend to be asleep, or to get up and watch Trevor as he was about to leave. She didn't know whether to act as if this were normal and he was just going off for the day . . . or to cry because they'd had so little time together. Joanna didn't know how to make it easier for both of them. What she did understand was that Trevor was right. He had to leave.

Joanna lay on her side with her legs drawn up under the covers. She closed her eyes and indulged in a mental recall of the night before. She relived every wonderful, tender moment of her and Trevor together. The surprise of how caring and loving he was. The satisfaction that he was not a selfish lover, nor an inexperienced one. The awareness that Trevor could be endearingly vulnerable. She was going to miss him.

But she knew he had to leave.

They'd already agreed, whispering together and cuddling under the blankets, that what had happened between them was too quick, too impetuous, and under bizarre circumstances. They needed time and space to sort things out. They needed a reality check. They agreed not to make any promises. And in truth, Joanna couldn't deny that what she had done was totally out of character for her. She kept thinking about Trevor's troubled past. And she kept thinking about how her parents might feel about him. At the moment, however, it only mattered what she and Trevor felt.

Joanna sat up and pushed aside the covers. She got out of the bed and retrieved her robe. Still knotting the belt, she walked barefoot into the living room and found Trevor seated on the sofa. He was bent over the fastenings on his heavy boots. Joanna stood watching him silently for a moment, feeling oddly that Trevor didn't seem out of place even though they'd only spent one night together. It felt normal for him to be there, for them to be together.

"You weren't going to leave without saying goodbye, were you?" she asked quietly.

Trevor stood up and faced Joanna. He couldn't respond immediately because the thought had crossed his mind. He felt a tightening in his chest at the sight of her. With her kimono on, Joanna appeared smaller and more delicate. And there was something so familiar about the sleepy look on her face, the slightly mussed hair from the pillow . . . and their lovemaking . . . that made him feel like he might really belong here. With Joanna standing before him first thing in the morning, Trevor felt as if the past twenty-four hours had been a fantasy, and he'd do better to commit it to memory than to wish for the impossible.

"I was going to leave you a note," he confessed. "I didn't want to wake you up."

Joanna noticed right away that Trevor's protective formality was back in place. He had already placed her at arm's length. Did that make saying goodbye easier for him? She walked toward him noticing that his outer clothing was neatly folded over the back of one of her chairs. "You were very quiet, but I was awake the moment you got out of bed."

"Sorry . . ." he said, sitting to pull on his other boot.

Joanna stood awkwardly in front of him. "Do you . . . have time for some coffee?"

Trevor looked up at Joanna, and his heart turned over. He realized that all he had was time. Right now it loomed ahead of him empty and lonely. He shrugged. "Sure."

Joanna nodded with a brief smile and headed for the kitchen. She quickly got the coffee maker started, and then looked in her refrigerator to see if there was any orange juice. Before long Joanna also had eggs and English muffins on the counter, and she found herself making a complete breakfast.

"You didn't have to go to all this trouble."

"I don't mind. Unless you don't normally eat breakfast."

"I'm not used to having someone fix it for me."

Joanna split the muffins, but she was aware of Trevor standing behind her in the small space of the kitchen. If she reached behind her, she could touch him. "What? No family? No friends? No . . ."

"No one," Trevor answered emphatically. He leaned against the door frame, his hands in his trouser pockets. "Did you make breakfast for Santa Claus?"

A small smile played at her mouth. She turned to look quickly at Trevor, and saw a frown of consternation furrow his brow. "Do you care?"

"Just curious."

"You can do me a favor," Joanna said easily.

"What?"

"Set the coffee table so we can eat."

Joanna pointed out to Trevor the cabinet with the plates and glasses. He searched out the flatware and paper napkins. There was a comfortable coziness to the way they functioned easily around each other that she was alert to. Joanna wondered if Trevor had noticed as well.

What Trevor had noticed was that he didn't want to leave. He'd felt the reluctance when he'd gotten up to shower. He'd felt it when Joanna had come quietly from the bedroom, her sweetly tousled appearance evident of the night they'd spent together. As he waited for Joanna to come in from the kitchen, Trevor suddenly wondered why he was trying to be so noble. Was Joanna right, and he was just afraid?

Yes.

Joanna had everything on a tray, which she placed in the center of her coffee table. She sat on the sofa and Trevor pulled up a side chair. The smell of coffee and eggs filled the air. For a moment, Trevor just sat and looked at everything, looked at Joanna and shook his head, bemused.

"What?" she asked, noticing his pensive expression.

"So, is this what it's like when people are married?"

"I wouldn't know. I've never been married," Joanna murmured, keeping her gaze averted as she spread a napkin over her lap and poured milk into her coffee.

"Me either."

"How come?" she asked carefully.

He shrugged. "Usual reason. Never thought much

about it. Never found the right person." He bit into the muffin.

"Why are you thinking about it now?"

Trevor shifted restlessly. "I'm not," he prevaricated. "Maybe I'm just getting old."

"Maybe you're ready," Joanna said quietly, sipping from the coffee but still not looking directly at him.

Trevor looked at her, then met Joanna's steady regard. He wanted to go with a sudden gut feeling, but then he thought about his past and got stymied. "Joanna, I . . ."

Her telephone began to ring. It made her jump. Joanna looked at Trevor, uncertain.

"You'd better get that," he said.

Joanna put her cup down and reached for the phone. "Hello?" she asked cautiously.

"I'm just checking to see if you've calmed down any."

Joanna swallowed and felt the nervous tension flow quickly through her. "I'm fine. You didn't have to call."

"Jo, I know you were upset last night, but think about it. You found some strange man in Sheila's apartment, the police were all over the place. That Jackson character was hanging around . . . it wasn't a good time to try and talk."

"I still don't think there's anything to talk about," Joanna said, acutely aware that Trevor sat listening to every word, watching her closely.

"So you want to just toss out the three years we've had."

"I thought you'd be happy. Now you can do what you want—and with whomever you want. I just don't want to be a part of it."

"Hey! How do you think I felt seeing that guy around

you all week? Why didn't you tell him to find someone else to help him?"

Joanna hazarded a confused and bewildering glance at Trevor. He finished his coffee and stood up. He lifted the tray and carried it back into the kitchen. Joanna followed his movement. "Philip, it doesn't matter anymore. Trevor Jackson is leaving Philly, and you're free to do whatever you want. I have to go."

"Okay, if that's how you feel. But you can't say I didn't try to work things out."

"It's because of you that there's anything to work out," Joanna said wearily. "What happened didn't just happen. Apparently it's been going on for a while."

"You're not going to forgive me?"

Joanna looked up as Trevor slowly appeared from the kitchen. "It's too late for that. I wish you well, Philip. Bye . . ." She hung up, still looking at Trevor.

"I think it's time for me to leave."

Joanna stood up and approached him. "Yes, I know."

"It's been one hell of a week," Trevor said dryly, letting his eyes take in every detail of her. He reached for his coat and shrugged into it. He pulled the brimmed cap from the pocket. "I didn't mean to mess things up for you, Joanna."

Joanna smiled tentatively and reached out to take Trevor's hand. She was surprised at the hard firm grip of his fingers . . . like he didn't want to let go. "If you mean Philip, you had nothing to do with that. If you mean for me, it was my decision to help you as much as I could. I don't regret that. If you mean anything else . . . I'm glad we had last night, Trevor."

"You probably won't still feel that way in the morning."

She laughed lightly. "It *is* morning." She let go of his hand. "So, did you get all the information you needed about your brother and Sheila?"

"Pretty much. I can put it to rest, clear Troy's name."

"And the police might know who's involved with her death."

He hesitated, remembering that he still had some letters and papers to go through that he hadn't given to the police. "Looks like it." He turned and headed toward the door. He didn't want to look too long at Joanna.

"Trevor?"

He stopped at the tremulous note in her voice even though Joanna seemed composed and calm. She was twisting her hands together.

"You have to tell me. What . . . what's going to happen now? Will I ever see you again?"

The sound of her uncertainty tore at him. He wanted to gather Joanna into his arms and promise anything . . . *anything* . . . as long as he could stay with her forever. He'd never felt like this before. He'd never wanted anyone else in his life like this before. With Joanna, Trevor realized he could have a second chance, be forgiven for the past, earn a future and love. But what did he have to offer her?

"When you have time to think about last night . . . about me and what you know, you may be glad that I had to leave." Against his will, Trevor reached for her. He pulled Joanna toward him, looking hard into her face. "Last week was like a glitch in time. Things will go back to normal, and you could start to see things more clearly."

"I know what I feel," Joanna whispered, afraid now

that she was going to start crying. She didn't want to do that in front of Trevor.

"Give it a month. Let's make a date for February fourteenth."

"That's very romantic," Joanna said quietly.

"Send me a card if you still feel the same."

"And what are you going to do if I send one?"

"Be on the next flight to Philadelphia," Trevor growled, pulling Joanna into his arms and holding her tightly.

Then he began kissing her face, her eyes, and the tears that dampened her cheeks. Her parted lips waited for him to assuage her pain. He slowly explored her mouth, wanting to remember the way her tongue darted and retreated from his shyly, and the way she leaned her body into his, as if she couldn't get close enough.

Trevor finally tore his mouth from Joanna's and hurried to the door. He got it open. He wasn't going to look back, but did anyway. Joanna stood with her hands clasped together and pressed to her trembling mouth. Tears rolled down her cheek.

Joanna's vision was too blurred to see what was in Trevor's eyes as he walked through the door, closing it behind him. The sudden silence was devastating. She cried even harder. She made her way into the kitchen with the intentions of getting a napkin or paper towel for her face. She found a folded piece of notepaper under the edge of the coffee maker. It had her name written in Trevor's handwriting.

Joanna snatched the note up and opened it quickly. There were only a few words written in a hasty but clean scrawl.

Thank you. Sincerely, T

Nine

Joanna waited anxiously as her father finished looking over the page she'd given him. He removed his glasses and looked thoughtfully at her.

"Who did you say this man was?"

"Someone I met a few weeks ago. He knew the woman who lived next door to me. You remember. The one who was found dead in her apartment."

"Yeah, I remember. How did you come to meet him?" Samuel Mitchell asked alertly.

Joanna grimaced. She wondered how little she could get away with telling her father about Trevor Jackson. The fact was, she realized that she knew very little and was hoping her father and his professional contacts could supply the rest.

"I met him at the funeral services for Sheila. He was hoping I could tell him what might have happened to her."

"Could you?" her father asked.

Joanna shook her head. "Not about how she died. We found out a lot about the kind of life she led and who she knew."

"Ummmm," Mr. Mitchell said, staring at his daughter and scratching his chin with the arm of his glasses.

"Why was that so important for him to know? How come you want to know about him now?"

She shrugged, trying to keep her features bland and hoping that her father wouldn't do what he'd always been able to do, which was to read her mind. "I'm not totally sure about his motives. And I'd heard some things about him. I want to find out if they're true."

Her father meticulously folded the paper and absently tapped it on his knee. "Would this Trevor Jackson have anything to do with the fact that Philip doesn't come around anymore?"

"No, he doesn't."

Mr. Mitchell sighed patiently. "You know, I promised your mother I wouldn't pry and ask a lot of questions. Sooner or later you'll tell us what happened between you and Philip. But if you want me to help get information about Trevor Jackson and where he came from, I want to know what's going on."

"Can't you just do me this favor and not ask how come?" Joanna inquired hesitantly.

Mr. Mitchell beamed complacently. "I could. But I won't."

"Daddy, that's blackmail."

"That's negotiation. Come to a lawyer, that's what you get." He leaned forward suddenly, looking earnestly at her. "Look, you're my daughter. I want to know if there's a problem that involves your safety and well-being. I want to know if you're in some sort of trouble. I want to know what this Trevor Jackson has to do with you, and what is going on with you and Philip."

She sighed, crossing her legs at the knees to keep them from shaking. "Philip and I broke up."

"Your mother and I figured that much out," he said dryly.

"It was my decision. I can't give you the details, Daddy. I don't want to bad-mouth Philip. Let's just say he's not really interested in a relationship, and he isn't the man I thought he was."

"Is there any chance for a conciliation?"

Joanna recalled the phone calls from Philip recently, a clever attempt on his part to shift the blame for the breakup to her for expecting too much and for not being forgiving. She had stopped taking the calls and disconnected the answering machine. "I don't think so," she answered.

Her father frowned. "I'm sorry to hear that. We had expectations . . ."

"I know."

"Trevor Jackson," he repeated slowly, as if testing out the name to see if he liked it. "Jo, you're asking questions that involve me going to the police, district attorneys, and judges in another jurisdiction to pry into someone's possible criminal background. You're asking me to investigate a man's life to find out if he's wanted and dangerous. And you can't tell me why?"

Joanna blinked at her father. "You won't be very happy if I tell you . . . I think I'm in love with him."

Her father, to his credit, never batted an eyelash. But he did stare long and hard at her, trying to read through the stiff body language, the furtive glances, and careful information. "You're right about that," he finished softly.

"I think he's a better man than what I've been told. I couldn't love anyone who wasn't kind and thoughtful, smart and sincere. I want to find out if I'm right. If your report comes back that Trevor Jackson is trouble, I'll forget him and I'll never mention him again. But if it comes back clean, I'm going to do everything I can to persuade him we belong together."

Her father's brows shot up. "Does he need persuading?"

"Yes," Joanna nodded.

Her father sat back in his chair. He rubbed his chin, unfolded and stared at the list again. He sighed and shook his head. "I'll give him two points for that. The chances are slim to none that the report is going to come back in favor of him. I haven't seen too many success stories of the younger brothers who manage to survive a bad start in life. But I'm glad you haven't done anything foolish, Jo. I'm not very happy about what I've heard so far but . . . I have to trust that you know how you feel. I'm glad you came to me first."

Joanna blushed. She hoped her father couldn't read in her expression the joyous memory she had of that one night with Trevor Jackson. "How long will it take?"

Mr. Mitchell stood up and held out his hand to his daughter as she rose from the sofa. "Oh . . . about a week or so. I'll call you as soon as I hear anything."

"Bye, Jo. Thanks for everything."

"You're welcome, Robby. You were a good assistant," Joanna said as the tall lanky youth released her from a bearhug.

The staff party for Robby had ended a half-hour earlier, and just the two of them were together in the film library as he gathered his possessions and prepared to leave. He looked around the crowded, cramped space. "I can't believe I'm really going to miss it here."

"That's easy to say because you're leaving. I bet if you knew you had to work here until June you wouldn't feel so sentimental," Joanna said sagely.

He shrugged. "Yeah, you're probably right."

She walked him out of the room, and they headed down the corridor in the direction of his uncle's office. Station staff called out further goodbyes as the two of them passed open offices.

"Thanks for leaving a number where I can reach you, just in case I can't find a tape or get in trouble with one of the units."

"No problem," he said.

"And I guess I should thank you for going to Mr. Kincaid on my behalf."

"Well, you should take the offer. You'd be a great field reporter. You're as good as anybody out there for the station," he said, smiling.

"I'm not sure I want to be in the public eye all the time."

"Yeah, but why should someone else get the credit for the information you find. Nobody thought to check with the police about what's going on with Nathan Mac-Cauley until you mentioned it. Nobody even knew he was on the list of people that had anything to do with that woman, Sheila James."

Joanna shrugged. She hardly thought her own curiosity was a reason for a reward. She'd thought for sure that an alert reporter would have wondered why MacCauley had been questioned by the police in regards to a videotape found in the woman's apartment. "Why should I get credit for that?"

"Because it was a breaking story and *we* got to it

first. I told Uncle Bernie you were sharp and he should give you a big raise or something."

"Robby!" Joanna chuckled and shook her head, incredulous. "It's a good thing you're leaving. I'm afraid to think of what you'll tell people next."

"Well . . . I sort of said that if they didn't give you some kind of reward for the great job you did two weeks ago filling in for Ann Marie, you were going to accept that offer from ABC in New York."

Joanna stopped walking and her mouth dropped open as she stared at the tall youth. "Robby . . . you didn't! There wasn't any offer . . ."

He laughed and kissed her on the cheek. "See ya," he waved, and loped off toward his uncle's office.

Joanna was still standing flabbergasted when she heard Linda calling out her name. She turned her head to find Linda beckoning to her.

"Hurry up," Linda urged, waving with her hand. "There's something on the news . . ."

Joanna entered the office just in time to see a clip of Nathan MacCauley entering City Hall pursued by reporters shouting questions. The reporter voice-over repeated what had been ignored when Sheila James was first found dead: that she was pregnant.

". . . additional evidence has been submitted to the police investigating the case that suggests MacCauley and the dead woman might have been involved. The police are asking for MacCauley to cooperate by submitting a sample of his blood for DNA testing to determine if he was the father of the child . . ."

The clip then showed MacCauley smoothly and calmly submitting to questioning by several persistent reporters. Joanna observed that, like any good politician, he knew exactly how to field and dodge to avoid answering directly.

"Did you know about him?" Linda asked Joanna, titillated by the breath of scandal so close to someone she knew.

Joanna slowly shook her head. "No, I didn't." She thought of the video she'd watched with MacCauley and Sheila together.

"I can't believe he would kill her just because she was pregnant," Linda voiced in disgust.

"Maybe the child wasn't his. Maybe that wasn't the reason. Maybe she was blackmailing him because of his position," Joanna speculated.

"Or maybe someone else is responsible and is setting him up."

Joanna turned away. "I can't imagine who else there is that the police wouldn't know about by now."

"Well, I think it was MacCauley. Men in power always think they can do what they want and get away with it. It's always the guys who look so great on the outside that turn out to be liars and cheaters. *You* know what I mean," Linda said significantly.

Joanna frowned at her. "No, I don't know what you mean."

"Look, I know you and Philip have called it a day, so I'm not telling secrets out of school. I just figured you finally found out about what he had going on the side . . . or rather, behind your back."

Joanna felt a odd sinking in her stomach. "You mean I was the last one to know?"

Linda nodded. "Something like that. I'm sorry, but I couldn't say anything. You wouldn't have believed me and you needed to see for yourself. Philip wasn't right for you. He's a great reporter, but poor husband material."

"Like you said, it's over," Joanna said indifferently.

"So that leaves Trevor with a clear field."

"I don't know what you mean," Joanna murmured.

Linda sighed. "I thought the man was *it*. But unfortunately he wasn't interested in me. He wanted you. I don't know if anything was said before he left, but don't put him out of the game yet."

Joanna hadn't. But she also had not heard from Trevor. At least, she didn't think she had. A bouquet of flowers had been delivered to her office the Friday after he'd left. There had been no note attached. Joanna had chosen to believe, excitedly, that that had been Trevor's silent and secret way of sending her a message. He hadn't forgotten. Neither had she.

But it had been all that she'd had to go on. That and the growing realization that her feelings had not been misplaced with Trevor Jackson. She'd had a dream about him. She'd relived their lovemaking. Joanna had to admit that she was falling more deeply in love with a man whom she'd only known a week, but whose nature and being she'd recognized her whole life. She was going to hold Trevor to his February deadline.

Joanna also had not heard anything from her father about Trevor's background. She'd given him so little to go on. Trevor said he was originally from Detroit. That his mother, at least, was dead. That he'd had a brother. That he now lived in Fort Lewis, Washington, and worked in a hospital. It seemed like a lot, but it wasn't.

Joanna also held out hope that her instincts about the inherent character and personality of Trevor were right on target. It helped that Preston Canin had had the same feelings, as had Linda and even Mrs. Thatcher, who'd had only passing conversations with him. Could all of them have been so wrong?

And two other things kept returning to her mind over and over again. On the morning he was leaving, as he'd gotten out of bed, Trevor had carefully kissed her, a simple brushing of his mouth over hers. Joanna had been half-asleep, but she recalled the utter tenderness of the touch, the thoughtfulness of it. And the other thing had been the note. Men who hit and run don't leave notes. Men who leave don't say thank you. Men who want to remember, do.

Joanna was with Preston the night it was reported that although early lab reports indicated that Nathan Mac-Cauley was, in all likelihood, the father of Sheila James's unborn child, he had been eliminated as a suspect in her death. However, one of MacCauley's associates was being questioned about a break-in in the James apartment several weeks ago, during which time incriminating letters from MacCauley to Sheila had been removed.

"Well, I'm glad to hear that," Preston muttered as he finished the dinner Joanna had prepared for him.

Joanna just sat staring at the screen. She wasn't sure that she was so glad. Now she was totally confused. If the police were certain that Nathan MacCauley had nothing to do with Sheila's death . . . then who did?

"Why are you so glad?" she asked absently.

"Well, the man may be a jerk and a womanizer, but he didn't do it. I told you before. The police are looking for a killer, and they aren't going to find one."

Joanna sighed. "Preston, sometimes I don't understand you."

Preston suddenly gave Joanna a sage, complacent grin.

"You have to listen more carefully, Jo. I know what I'm talking about. I was the one who told you Philip was a passing fancy. I was the one who told you Trevor Jackson was a gentleman. A man of honor."

Joanna got up to remove his dinner tray, but stood with her hands braced on her hips, looking down on her neighbor with a slight shake of her head. She spoke gently. "You also keep telling me that 'What's My Line' is the best show on TV, and Hannah forgot to refill your medication."

Preston blinked at Joanna, and then pouted. "Okay, so I get confused sometimes . . ."

Joanna chuckled and patted his shoulder. She lifted the tray to take into the kitchen. Preston called out behind her, "Listen, when they find out, you be sure to let me know right away."

Joanna frowned. "When who finds out what?"

"About Sheila. You let me know."

She returned to the living room and stood next to Preston's wheelchair. "Maybe the police will never find out."

"No," he sighed. "It all has to come out sometime."

"Well, if the case gets solved, I promise to let you know."

"Good, good. And Joanna . . ."

She glanced quizzically at him. "Yes?"

"You know I like Trevor. He's the one for you."

"How come you feel so strongly about him?"

"I talked with him a long time on the phone."

Joanna looked sharply at Preston. "You talked to him? When?"

"He called to ask me some questions about Sheila.

He didn't lie to you, you know. He just didn't tell you everything that was going on."

Joanna felt funny and couldn't respond at first. She was disappointed and curious about Trevor having called Preston, of all people, and not herself. "There's a very slim difference, Preston."

"Only if you don't trust your heart, or him."

"Well . . . enough Philosophy and Psychic Reading 101 for the night. What else can I do before I head upstairs?"

Preston furrowed his brow and stared long and consideringly at Joanna. He wheeled his chair over to her and looked up into her face. "You could do me a big favor. Could you talk to Danny? Tell him I need him to change one of the inner tires on my chair."

"Sure," she said, heading for the door. "I'll talk to him on my way out in the morning."

"No, no. Wait until tomorrow night when he's in his apartment. He's all over the building during the day."

"I've never been to his apartment," Joanna shrugged. "It's so eerie down in the basement."

"That's where people keep their secrets," Preston said cryptically in a theatrical whisper. "Remember the two cases you found belonging to Sheila?"

"Yes, but Danny doesn't have any secrets. He's one of the most harmless people I know."

"He can be hurt just like everybody else. You have to be kind and patient with Danny."

Joanna grinned. "I hope that being asked to change a tire wheel won't scare him to death."

"I'm serious, Joanna. You be careful when you talk to him."

Her good humor slowly faded. "Why?"

"Because he *is* scared."

Joanna frowned at Preston and stood half in and half out of his apartment as she tried to decipher the conversation. "Preston, are you trying to tell me something?"

He sighed and shook his head tiredly. "Nothing that you won't find out eventually. Just promise you won't forget what I said about Danny."

She shrugged nonchalantly as she left. "Okay. I promise."

But given Preston Canin's habit toward flights of fancy Joanna put his gloomy theorizing out of her mind as she waited for the elevator back to the fourth floor and her own apartment. For one thing, it had always been difficult to know if Danny was particularly happy or sad about anything. He operated on the most basic emotional level, like a child. Things were either good or bad. There were people he either liked or didn't like.

For another, it was hard for Joanna to concentrate on Preston's musings or Danny's sensitivity while she was acutely aware that there was less than ten days left to the agreement she and Trevor had made just before he'd left Philadelphia. Joanna only wanted to know if she was ever going to see him again. She was desperate to know if there was any reason to hope that she hadn't misread her own feelings or the silent signals from Trevor. So that when the call came in late that night from her father, Joanna's relief was profound.

"The good news is that Trevor Jackson never hurt anyone, was never convicted of a crime, nor did any time in jail."

"He said he had done time," Joanna frowned.

"Juvenile detention. There's a big difference," Mr. Mitchell corrected.

"And the bad news?" Joanna asked in a thin voice. She was unaware that her hand had a death grip on the telephone and her heart was thudding in her chest.

Her father sighed deeply. "Well . . . he was a difficult kid. Did a lot of acting out in anger. Probably because he lost his mother young. I'd say the scenario is pretty typical. You know, middle class black family falls apart when father drops out and something happens to the mother. Trevor Jackson was apparently incorrigible."

"Ooohh," Joanna couldn't help moaning, feeling pain deep within her.

"Now take it easy. I'm not finished yet. He got into a lot of trouble . . . but nothing I'd call serious."

She heard her father turning pages.

"He was smart and managed to stay out of gangs and other typical inner city mine fields. Not easy for a young black teen with no one to guide him."

Joanna nodded absently to herself. She wasn't feeling outrage or even disappointment. Just empathy and a sense of waste. *Almost* waste. The Trevor Jackson she knew was still a man she could love.

"Now the most important thing is, no one is ever going to know about his record."

"How come?"

"Because all of Trevor Jackson's ripping and roaring happened before he was seventeen. The records are permanently sealed."

She sighed. "Thank goodness. That means no one can hold it against him."

"Obviously you're not going to," Mr. Mitchell murmured wryly. "So none of this makes any difference in how you feel about this man?"

Joanna took a long moment to think about it. She also

thought about Philip Lee and the impressive credentials he'd built up for himself, the benefits of an attentive family, good education, ambition, and drive. He had all the elements to be a shining example of accomplished black manhood . . . except for two things. Maturity and sincerity.

Joanna didn't even know if there was a chance for her and Trevor to form a relationship, let alone to plan any kind of future. But now she understood clearly why he'd tried so hard to convince her that he was not the right man for her. Joanna smiled peacefully to herself and shook her head.

"No, it makes no difference at all."

"I gotta tell you, Jo, your mother and I aren't convinced yet. I'd like to meet the man. But I can tell you why I'm feeling a lot better than I did when you dropped this bombshell into my lap last Sunday after dinner."

"Okay . . ."

"Trevor Jackson came to his senses. He got the attention of a sympathetic police sergeant and a family court judge. He pulled himself together," more turning of pages, "he finished high school, did a year at a private prep school, courtesy of the sergeant, and then he joined the Army."

Joanna blinked. She wasn't sure she'd heard right. "The . . . what?"

"Military. Army."

"The Army." Joanna tried to process the information. But she couldn't see it. She didn't understand how. Trevor said he worked in a hospital. He'd said . . . "Daddy, Trevor said he was from Fort Lewis, Washington."

"That's right. That's an Army base. Didn't he tell you any of this?"

"No. I think he wanted me to know as little as possible. And he told me all the bad things."

"He gets two more points." Samuel Mitchell chuckled dryly. "Your Trevor Jackson is beginning to look better and better. Now your mother and I still don't think you should be so quick to scrap Philip, but Sergeant Major Trevor S. Jackson, S for Steven, of the U.S. Army Medical Corps, might do just fine."

Slowly Joanna began to relax. And to sigh deeply. And to grin foolishly from ear to ear.

Trevor slowly read over the note. Then he read it again. He lifted his pen, intending to scratch out a word that he'd written, thinking that it made him sound too ridiculous. Trevor frowned over the phrasing and the message. That was the problem. He couldn't seem to get the message right. In frustration, he ruthlessly crushed the paper and tossed it into the wastebasket. He got up abruptly from his dining table and began pacing the room.

This is crazy, he thought, as the entire realm of mixed emotions he had since returning from Philadelphia began once again tumbling around in his brain. He thought it was going to be so easy to walk away from that one week . . . that one night. He thought that with distance between them, there would be no problem forgetting about Joanna Mitchell and remembering that they were worlds apart. But Trevor hadn't counted on the constant memories or the unexpected images of Joanna, and the sound of her voice and laughter. He hadn't counted on the erotic dreams of longing. And he still had a lot of trouble believing that she would want anything to do with him. But what if Joanna really meant it?

So what was he going to do?

Trevor sighed and walked into his kitchen to pour a cup of coffee. He checked his watch. He had a class in new emergency techniques in an hour, and then a division meeting. He might go to the gym later or put in some hours at the library. But then there would be the rest of the night. Alone with Joanna's essence as a nightly guest.

Trevor brought his coffee back into the living room, frowning over what he should do. When he'd gotten back to Fort Lewis, the idea came to him to send Joanna flowers. He'd never sent flowers to a woman before. But he'd read some of those dozens of letters to Sheila from various men, and they'd obviously shown their feelings for her in gifts and attention. He'd attempted a letter, but the results had always ended up in the garbage.

Trevor sighed deeply. "Damn . . ." he muttered softly. What if Joanna was actually glad that he'd left? No. He didn't believe that. He'd seen the tears in her eyes as he'd walked out the door. One thing he'd learned about Joanna Mitchell. She wasn't capable of faking her feelings.

Trevor wondered if maybe he should just throw caution and his protective instincts to the wind and call her. What was the worst thing that could happen? She'd blow him off or say she'd come to her senses. Or Joanna could actually say she missed him and wanted to see him again. Trevor stared at his telephone. Then he shook his head to clear it, his insecurity discarding the idea.

He sipped at the black coffee and considered the stack of letters and cards that he had tossed onto the coffee table. He'd given the bulk of the items from the chest and suitcases to the police. He'd only kept some of the correspondence out of curiosity. He wanted to read what men wrote to women. What did they put in love letters and cards that they wouldn't say in person?

Besides MacCauley there had been at least two other men involved with Sheila. But Trevor had also found cards or notes to Sheila from Preston Canin and Danny. Christmas cards and thank-you notes from Preston. Childish "I like you a lot" cards from Danny.

Trevor frowned and continued to stare at the pile. At the library several days ago, he'd asked to see a copy of the *Philadelphia Enquirer,* one of a number of major newspapers the library kept stocked from across the country. There had been a small item about MacCauley's involvement with Sheila James. But it also said that the police had eliminated him as a suspect in her death.

Trevor narrowed his gaze and his frowning consideration deepened. He slowly approached the table and stared down at the papers. He'd spoken openly to the detective on the case, since he could prove that Sheila had been his sister-in-law. And he'd been impressed that they actually knew quite a lot about Sheila's life and times. So if the police have cleared MacCauley as a suspect . . .

Trevor put his coffee cup down and picked up a handful of the cards and letters. He began scanning through the names and signatures. He stopped abruptly as a powerful realization gripped him, and Trevor, in surprise, let out a rush of air through his nostrils.

He closed his eyes tightly to think. And the longer he stood there, the more Trevor's idea focused and took shape . . . and made perfect sense. He dropped the letters he held and went to his telephone. He picked up and began dialing, but glanced at his watch again and hung up. It would only be five o'clock in the morning in Philadelphia. Joanna would still be asleep.

After his class, Trevor tried calling Joanna. There was no answer, and her answering machine didn't kick in to take the call. It was Saturday. He reasoned that Joanna could be out doing errands. She could be with Preston Canin or visiting her parents. But not knowing for sure was making Trevor very nervous.

He tried again later. And later.

Trevor called his superior and requested a leave of absence.

"You just got back from one, Jackson."

"I know, sir, but I have the time."

"Is there a problem you want to talk about?"

"No, sir. I can handle it."

"Another family emergency?"

Trevor hesitated. "You might say so . . ."

Joanna pushed the button for the basement and watched the door close smoothly before her. She sighed as she glanced at her watch. She didn't have much time. She and Linda had plans to meet for church and, afterward, lunch, and Linda would be calling her soon.

Joanna hoped that this time Danny was somewhere around. She'd only caught a glimpse of him on Friday as she'd left for work. He was piling up the recycling from the basement through a side door. On Saturday she hadn't seen him at all.

The elevator door opened and Joanna stepped out. She checked the laundry and utility rooms and found them both empty. She turned in the opposite direction, toward

the storage and equipment rooms. But as she neared
Danny's apartment, Joanna realized that the door was
slightly ajar and there was a light coming from inside.

"Danny?" she called out and waited. But there was
no response. Joanna repeated his name.

When there was still no answer, Joanna felt mild impatience and knew she couldn't hang around any longer.
She was about to turn away, having decided to try later
when she returned home, when she hesitated and stared
at the open door.

Joanna lifted her hand and knocked loudly on the
door. "Danny," she fairly shouted. And then, knowing
that she was about to do something that was not appro-
priate, probably illegal, and an invasion of privacy,
Joanna slowly pushed the apartment door open and
peeked inside.

Danny was not inside, but he couldn't be very far
away since the TV was on, a half-eaten doughnut and a
container of orange juice were on a cluttered small table.
Joanna leaned out the door and listened intently for a
few seconds. Hearing no evidence of Danny's return, she
took a few steps into the apartment and looked around.

It was an L-shaped space, with a tiny bathroom just
off the entrance, which probably shared plumbing with
the laundry room. The space didn't have much furniture,
and what there was had obviously been gathered piece-
meal. Probably some of it was tenant discards, Joanna
speculated. There was a book unit against one wall,
crowded with a haphazard collection of odds and ends,
junk and treasures. There was a single bed, just visible
around the corner of the apartment, neatly made.

Mesmerized, Joanna walked farther into the room.
Now she could see the bed clearly. There was a teddy

bear propped on the floor in the corner next to it. She pivoted slowly around, trying to take in everything. A rod stretched between a short alcove, which created an open closet. An impossibly tiny kitchenette and a huge Nautilus outfit took up the remaining space. Joanna nearly tripped over a number of barbells on the floor, and several of them rolled and clanked noisily together. She inadvertently bumped into an unseen wall shelf between the door and the Nautilus unit. It was stacked with a few small weights. And, peculiarly out of place, was a glass-covered dish. Joanna leaned forward to see it better. It was a candy dish, filled with butterscotch candy. It was the dish that used to belong to Sheila.

A strange frisson of clarity shot through Joanna, and she experienced a jolt of surprise. She stepped back into the center of the floor. She looked swiftly around again, trying to see if there was anything else that didn't belong. Of course the teddy bear came to mind. She was tempted to pull open one of the bureau drawers or to search quickly through one of several open cartons on the floor behind a big easy chair. But she knew there wasn't time. She had to get out of there.

Joanna suddenly felt panic. She was in the basement all alone, and no one knew where she was. Her imagination began to create worst-case scenarios that made her heart race, and she felt a sweat break out under her knit jersey dress, and she was stifling hot under the winter coat. Stumbling through the door into the corridor, the cool sublevel temperature immediately calmed her down. Still, Joanna felt an urgent need to get back aboveground. She rushed to the elevator.

When the door opened, Danny was standing there. Joanna couldn't help gasping, and quickly covered her mouth with her hand as she stared wide-eyed at him. But it was clear that she'd startled Danny, too.

"H-hi, Danny," Joanna croaked, staring at him as if she expected to be attacked. He grinned agreeably at her.

"Hi, Miz Mitchell." He blinked at her and his grin vanished.

Danny stepped off the elevator and looked down the corridor in the direction of his apartment. Joanna's heart began to race faster. Thinking quickly, she reached into the coat pocket.

"I . . . I left . . . this . . . this in the dryer." Joanna held up a wrinkled handkerchief. "I thought I'd lost it."

Danny turned to stare at it. "Oh," he nodded, convinced.

"I was looking for you, too."

"I was helping the lady in 6D. A box in the top of her closet. She couldn't reach it."

Joanna breathed out. "Preston would like you to change a tire in his wheelchair. Can you do that?"

"Okay," he shrugged.

"Maybe later tomorrow afternoon. He's at physical therapy in the morning."

She stepped into the elevator and pushed a button. Wrong one. She pushed another, noting that her hand was shaking slightly.

"Bye, Miz Mitchell . . ."

The door closed, and Joanna collapsed against the wall. She closed her eyes, wondering what was she going to do about Danny . . . and the candy dish.

Ten

Joanna stood tapping her foot impatiently in front of Preston, her arms crossed as she glared at the older man. He pouted and refused to meet her gaze.

"I'm waiting, Preston."

"I got nothing to tell you."

"You've been *trying* to tell me for weeks that the police don't know what they're doing. You said they're looking for a killer and there is no killer. You kept telling me that you heard or smelled or saw something the day Sheila died. I want to know what. Or *who*," Joanna said emphatically.

"Why do you want to know now? Why do you believe me now?"

Joanna sighed and looked poignantly on Preston. She was sorry it had taken her so long to see what he was getting at. It had taken her only a moment to realize why he had been so careful . . . and who he was protecting. It was so like Preston, Joanna thought. He always had a cause. He cared about people. Especially those who couldn't care about themselves.

"Because now I know why you couldn't say anything, why you were afraid to."

Preston gave her a furtive, speculative glance. His

pout turned into a frown. "I always told you you were a smart woman," he murmured.

Joanna pulled up a chair next to his wheelchair and sat facing him. "Look, I want to help. I don't know how yet, but there must be something I can do. I understand now why you didn't want to say anything to the police, but you must know we have to tell them sooner or later."

"I know, I know . . ."

She reached out and took hold of Preston's bony hand. It was hard and ice cold. He held tightly to her.

"I finally figured out that Sheila hadn't been murdered. Whatever happened was probably an accident. You said there was no killer. Danny kept saying she wasn't suppose to die. Why, Preston? What do you know?"

Preston sagged in his chair, looking older than Joanna had ever seen him. He was getting old and suffering from forgetfulness now and then, but he had one of the sharpest, funniest, most intuitive minds of anyone she knew. Now, trying to piece together the events of January 1, Joanna knew that Preston Canin had not lost a single one of those faculties. He had been using them all along.

"Danny gave Sheila his Christmas money."

"You mean the money the tenants gathered for him? He was supposed to use it to get winter boots and clothing."

"That's right. But Sheila must have said something to him. Persuaded Danny to . . . *lend* her the money. She wanted to buy a dress for New Year's Eve.

"I was very angry when I found out. Danny told me. When I next saw Sheila, I told her she had to give the money back, and she had to stop teasing Danny. Stop leading him on. She thought she was being friendly and

making Danny feel special. But it was only confusing
him and making him believe things that weren't true.
That *couldn't* be true."

Joanna thought for a moment. "I asked Danny why
he never bought the boots. He never said he'd given the
money away."

"No. Maybe he thought you'd get mad at Sheila. I
don't know."

"Preston, when Sheila was found, she was wearing a
fancy blue party dress. Was that the one she bought with
Danny's money?"

He frowned and nodded. "I think so. When she came
to see me that morning, she had the dress so I could
see it."

Joanna got up suddenly and began pacing Preston's
living room. She felt the excitement that comes with
having figured out a problem, having gotten answers to
questions. She didn't know everything yet, but it was all
falling into place. Joanna immediately considered calling
Trevor with the information as it was unfolding. He'd
want to know. And she'd have an excuse to contact him.
Joanna knew that the very sound of his voice would let
her know if he had been thinking about her; if he was
still interested. But Joanna kept a tight rein on her fervor.
There were still pieces missing from the puzzle.

She looked at Preston. "You said that you heard something. Smelled something."

Preston scratched his chin and shook his head.
"Well . . . not exactly. I sort of knew that something
was up when Sheila called me later in the day and said
Danny was mad at her. She said he slammed out of her
apartment. I thought I heard the door. When Danny came
to tell me that Sheila was dead and the police were in

her apartment, I thought I smelled perfume on him. A *lot* of it. And he was crying."

Joanna frowned. "So what? What does that all mean?"

"Sheila said she'd hurt his feelings. And I . . . I told her she had to apologize."

She waited. "And? What else?"

Preston sighed and clasped his hands together. "That's all I know. I don't know what happened after that. I never saw Sheila again. I don't know what happened."

Joanna leaned toward him. "Preston, what do you *think* happened?"

He slowly lifted his face to look at Joanna, his pale eyes watery and sad. "It was an accident, Jo. I know it. Danny would never have hurt Sheila. I bet he thought Sheila loved him. I was going to go and talk to him, but I couldn't get the damned chair through the door by myself. And then afterward, when Sheila was taken away, I asked him if there was anything he wanted to tell me . . . but he wouldn't. He just kept saying that Sheila wasn't supposed to die.

"I told him I would help him. I wouldn't let anyone do anything to him. But he wouldn't tell me anything."

Joanna gnawed her lip, remembering the inside of Danny's apartment from the day before. "I saw a candy dish in Danny's apartment, Preston. I'm pretty sure it belonged to Sheila. It was filled with your butterscotch candies."

He shrugged. "She could have given it to him."

She sighed in disappointment. "You're right. But you and I both know that there is a connection here. For one thing, Danny doesn't like butterscotch."

"I thought of calling the police. But I was so afraid of what Danny might do if he saw them. If he thought they were coming to get him. I kept telling him I could help. I still know a lot of people at ACLU."

"Well, I think we can still help Danny."

"We?"

"That's right. No one knows Danny better than we do. No one cares about him as much. Maybe I can get him to tell me what happened."

"Now look, don't you go trying to handle this yourself. I don't know what happened with Sheila, but she *did* end up dead. Be careful."

"I will," Joanna said, getting up and smiling reassuringly at her neighbor. She got ready to leave, kissing Preston on the cheek before she headed for the door. "The first thing I'm going to do is call Trevor."

"Good idea," Preston said enthusiastically. "He'll talk some sense into you. He'll tell you what to do."

Joanna searched out a telephone number from the information her father had given her. She had no idea if it was for his home, someone else's home, an office, what. Trevor had said he wasn't married and had no children. He'd indicated that he had no family to speak of. But that didn't mean he wasn't already involved with someone—and might not live alone.

The sudden thought occurred to Joanna once she got back to her apartment and began dialing the number. For a moment uncertainty and insecurity made her hesitate. Joanna recalled all the times Trevor had tried to convince her that he was all wrong for her. That she would be better to forget about him. Had he been trying to tell her that someone else was in his life?

Joanna didn't believe it as she finally finished the West Coast number. She didn't believe that she wouldn't have been able to tell if Trevor, who had loved her so thoroughly, so tenderly, so convincingly, wasn't being honest. And sincere.

A man answered the phone.

Joanna was so surprised she missed everything else he said after identifying himself by name.

"H-hi. I'm . . . trying to reach Trevor Jackson. Is this the right number?"

"The sergeant isn't here," the voice answered briskly. "Can I take a message?"

"I . . . was hoping to speak with him. This is a . . . personal call."

"I'm sorry, but he's on leave."

"Oh. Well, is it possible for me to get his home number?"

"Can't do that, ma'am. It's confidential."

"All right. Thank you," Joanna said, hanging up in disappointment.

It had never occurred to her that she wouldn't be able to contact Trevor. She had counted on his telling her what to do. She had counted on hearing his voice. Joanna had decided that she needed Trevor's strength and his cool, calm ability to reason. But not being able to talk with Trevor wasn't going to stop her. She knew there was still something important that had to be done. She had her own ideas and plans. And it couldn't wait until Trevor got in touch with her.

"I think you should wait a little longer," Preston said in agitation.

"I can't," Joanna said, shaking her head as she stood up and looked at her watch. She wiped her hands nervously down the front of her slacks. "It's already been an hour. I'm afraid something's going to go wrong and Danny will get scared. If he gets scared, he might do something foolish and get himself hurt."

"Or you could get hurt. Give it a little longer."

She shook her head. "No. Don't worry. I'll be okay. I'll be very careful. I . . . I know Danny wouldn't deliberately hurt me."

"You can't take the chance, Jo. I'm telling you, don't do it alone."

She smiled crookedly at Preston. "What are you going to do? Call the police?" He made an impatient sound and scowled at her. Joanna patted his cheek. "Everything's going to be fine."

Preston protested as she left his apartment. Joanna had left her apartment keys with him and had nothing else on her. Her heart began to race once she got on the elevator. Her hands weren't sweaty anymore. They were cold. And they were trembling. Joanna balled them into fists to try and control them. She took a deep breath but couldn't stop the painful beating of her heart.

When the elevator stopped on the second floor, her heart lurched. Two chatty teenage boys got on. Involved in their own conversation about the merits of the latest Sylvester Stallone movie, they ignored Joanna. They got off on the first floor. The elevator continued its descent to the lower level. But the minor delay only added to Joanna's tension. When she got off the elevator, she could feel her whole body begin to shake.

Walking slowly, she approached Danny's apartment. Joanna stood outside the door, listening to sounds from within. She could hear the TV. She could hear the rhythmic sound of metal against metal, and Danny's grunting, and she decided he must be working on the Nautilus equipment. Taking a deep breath, Joanna knocked on the door. She had to knock a second time when the Nautilus continued, but then it stopped and there was only the sound of the TV for a long moment.

"Yeah?" came Danny's voice. It was clear but cautious.

"Danny, it . . . it's Joanna Mitchell from apartment 4A. Can I talk with you for a moment?"

"Miz Mitchell?" he asked blankly.

"Yes. Do you have a moment?"

Joanna heard the scurrying inside, and in a moment the locks on the door were being turned. The door opened and Danny stood dressed in a sweaty and stained T-shirt and workout shorts. He wore socks, but had no shoes on.

Joanna smiled at him. "Hi. I'm sorry to bother you, but I, uh, wanted to talk to you. About . . . Sheila."

The moment the name was spoken, Joanna could see suspicion cloud Danny's eyes. He closed the door several inches.

"I don't want to talk about her. She's gone."

"But I think you know what happened," Joanna rushed ahead quietly. She was afraid that he'd suddenly slam the door in her face. She put her hand on the door and eased her foot into the frame of the opening. "Preston and I want to help you, Danny. We know that whatever happened was an accident."

"No." He shook his head vigorously. He gritted his teeth. "No!" he said forcefully.

Joanna felt fear shoot through her. "Danny . . ."

Joanna heard sounds down the corridor and didn't know whether to be glad or more scared. Several male voices called out authoritative orders. Joanna turned to the door that Danny was now trying to close. She pushed at it firmly.

"Danny, let me in. I'm trying to help you."

Behind her in the corridor, a number of men came through in a careful pattern. They had shields and bulletproof vests . . . and weapons. Detective Schultz was in the middle.

Joanna paid no attention to what was being said. She only saw the detective. She made frantic eye contact and lifted one hand. "Please, give me a minute. Don't do anything. Don't come . . ."

Joanna didn't have a chance to finish. Danny was trying to close the door on her. Joanna contorted her body and squeezed quickly into the apartment through the narrow space. The door slammed shut behind her. She faced Danny, who had backed away into his apartment, a look of sheer terror and confusion stretched across his face.

"Police! Open the door!"

Joanna turned and fumbled for the lock. She got one of the three shut in place. "Please . . . please wait," she shouted through the door. Her breathing was ragged.

"Miss Mitchell, it's Detective Schultz. I got your call. Will you open the door, please?"

There was no nonsense in his tone, and it was exactly that tone, that imperative, that Joanna was trying to avoid. If Danny got scared, she didn't know what he would do . . . or what the police would do to him if he panicked.

"Detective Schultz, please wait. I want to talk to Danny. He's . . . scared."

"This is not the movies, Miss Mitchell," the detective said angrily. "We don't want either one of you to get hurt. Open the door and let us in. We'll take care of this."

"Don't let them in, don't let them in!" Danny pleaded.

Joanna turned and flattened her back against the door. She felt as if her heart was going to jump right out of her chest. She shook her head. "I won't. Not yet. But you *have* to tell me what happened with Sheila. And then I'll tell the police and everything will be all right. They'll know it was just an accident. Right, Danny? You didn't mean to hurt her."

Boom, boom, boom, the officers pounded on the door. "Miss Mitchell. Open the door. He could be dangerous."

Danny stared wild-eyed at her. His chest was heaving in agitation, and sweat was running down his reddened face. He backed up, bumping into his own exercise machine. He reached out and picked up a barbell, holding it protectively in front of his chest.

Joanna kept her full attention on Danny. She wondered if she was indeed in real danger. Would he use the exercise bar on her? Had he used that on Sheila? "I just want to talk to you. I want you to tell me what happened with Sheila. How did she get hurt?"

"Are they going to take me away?"

"Not right away. And they're not going to hurt you. Preston and I won't let them."

Danny began to quietly cry, his mouth pulled in anguish. Like a child. "I thought Sheila liked me. But she laughed at me. She laughed . . ."

Joanna swallowed, suddenly overwhelmed by the pain of Danny's circumstances. "I'm sure she didn't mean to, Danny," she said in a soft voice.

"She said she was sorry, but I didn't believe her. I . . . I pushed her away. And she fell. I didn't hurt her. She wasn't supposed to die. She wasn't supposed to."

Joanna kept staring at him. But her own vision blurred

because of the tears which slowly spilled forth. "I know, Danny. I believe you . . ."

Trevor stood staring at the closed and locked door in frustration. He hadn't expected there not to be an answer at Joanna's apartment. As he stood and considered what to do next, he unzipped his winter coat, his anxiety making him feel overly warm. All the way in from the airport all he could think was that something was wrong. Trevor hadn't been able to reach Joanna by phone before leaving the base that morning, either at her apartment or the studio. He'd tried once more before boarding his flight in Olympia. He was anxious to see her, but he tried not to be too concerned. She could be at the studio right now, although it was already after eight o'clock. She could be out to dinner or shopping. She could be with Preston Canin.

Trevor pivoted on his heels and headed for the stairs. He reached Preston's apartment on the third floor and rang the bell, holding it longer than was necessary. He wanted to make sure that Preston heard it.

"Joanna?"

Trevor heard the voice from beyond the door. "It's Trevor Jackson," he responded, already wondering why the man had called out Joanna's name.

After a moment Trevor heard Preston opening the door. The older man wheeled his chair back as Trevor came through the door.

"Trevor," Preston exclaimed in surprise. "How did you get here? Have you seen Joanna?"

"I just got in from the airport. Joanna's not home. I thought she might be here with you."

"No, she's in the basement."

Trevor frowned. "The basement? Why?"

"Well, we talked. She and I think that Danny might know something about what happened to Sheila. We think—"

"He might have had something to do with it."

It was not a question but a statement, and Trevor watched as Preston slowly nodded, an expression of worry spreading over his wrinkled face. Trevor braced his hands on his hips and exhaled deeply. "Is she with Danny now?"

Preston nodded. "The police should be there, too. We called them . . ."

Trevor didn't wait for any more. He turned and rushed out of Preston's apartment. He bounded down the stairs, two, three at a time, fear propelling him forward. He cursed himself for not having thought to call the detective who was on the case. And if the police were already on the premises, anything could happen.

When he reached the basement, there were already two officers in the door. They turned when they heard him coming down the stairs. Trevor came down the last flight with his hands up and clearly empty.

"Sir, there's police action here. Will you please go back upstairs?"

"I know," Trevor nodded as calmly as he could. "Who's the officer in charge?"

"He's busy right now. If you'll please . . ."

"I know Joanna Mitchell. Maybe there's something I can do to help."

"What's going on?" an annoyed voice came from the corridor.

Detective Schultz appeared in front of Trevor. He

quickly recognized him and nodded to his officers to back off. "This is turning into a convention," he muttered darkly. "What are you doing here?"

"I was worried about Joanna. I figured the maintenance man was somehow involved with Sheila, and I got concerned."

"Well, you had a right to be. Miss Mitchell has locked herself in the apartment with the potential perpetrator. I don't want to force an entry. I don't know if he's armed or holding her against her will."

"Can I talk to her?"

The detective was already shaking his head. "No. I got enough problems and enough amateurs mixed up in this."

"If Joanna knows I'm here, I might be able to talk her into coming out. I don't think Danny's going to hurt her."

"I'm not willing to take that chance with her life."

"Neither am I," Trevor said smoothly. "Do you have another idea besides waiting?"

With a jerk of his head, the detective indicated that Trevor was to follow him. Together, the two men walked cautiously and quietly through the center of half a dozen prepared and alert police officers positioned and ready for orders. Outside Danny's door, Detective Schultz leaned to whisper to Trevor, "Say whatever you have to to get one of them to open the door. I'll keep my men back and out of sight."

Trevor nodded and knocked quietly on the door. He listened but could only hear a TV playing on the other side.

"Joanna? It's me, Trevor. Are you okay?"

Joanna wasn't sure she'd heard correctly. But when the voice identified itself, relief washed quickly through her and made her feel limp and boneless. But she didn't answer. She was afraid of distracting Danny, and for the moment, Joanna knew she had his attention.

She'd moved away from the door and stood within five feet of Danny. She was standing next to the Nautilus machine but had decided not to move any closer. Danny was still holding the barbell, and Joanna wasn't one hundred percent sure that in panic he wouldn't use it . . . even if he didn't mean to.

"How did Sheila get hurt?" she persisted, although the previous two times she'd asked Danny he'd only say that she fell. "Tell me how it happened."

Danny shook his head. "I didn't do it."

"Danny, did you get mad at Sheila? Was it because she laughed at you?" After a long silence, Danny nodded. "Why did she laugh?"

"She wanted to go out to a nice party. And that guy who was going to take her, he wasn't going to come. I would take her out. I would take her anyplace she wanted to. But she laughed. And she wouldn't stop."

Joanna nodded and murmured soothingly, "Is that when you got mad?"

He nodded, looking hurt and dejected. "Sheila made fun of me."

"I'm sorry she hurt your feelings. She probably didn't mean to."

"She wanted to apologize, but I didn't believe her."

"What did you do?"

Danny looked stricken again. He shook his head and stammered. "All . . . I . . . I did was . . . push her. She fell. She fell by herself."

"Where?"

Danny pointed.

Joanna swiveled her head around, looking. But she

didn't know what Danny was indicating. There was a wall, the metal book unit, the stacks of workout equipment, and the Nautilus. "Here?" Joanna asked, but she didn't really know where "here" was. She looked closely all around the area.

And then she noticed spots on the floor. Joanna moved closer to examine the stains and finally decided it was dried blood. She jumped back. She looked again at everything and tried to visually piece together what might have happened. She couldn't, and also decided that it wasn't her job to figure it all out. She'd only wanted to confront Danny and try to coax some answers out of him. If she could persuade Danny to talk to the police, Joanna knew the full details and story would come out.

Joanna would guess, in any case, that however Sheila had gotten hurt while she was with Danny, he'd panicked and taken her back up to her apartment and left her there, unconscious and bleeding internally.

She turned back to Danny and gently smiled at him. "You're absolutely right. It was an accident. Sheila must have fallen and hurt herself, right? You just took her back upstairs." She nodded at him to encourage a response.

Danny slowly nodded in return.

Joanna walked over to him and gently pulled the barbell from his hands. Danny just stared at her and didn't resist. She put the weight on the floor and took Danny's hand in her own.

"What happened to the shoe?"

Danny blinked at Joanna. "The shoe?"

"Yes, one of Sheila's shoes was missing the day she was found. Do you know where it is?"

Danny averted his eyes and silently nodded.

"Where did you put it?" Joanna coaxed quietly.

"Behind the teddy bear." Suddenly his eyes widened. "I didn't take the bear. Sheila gave it to me."

"Come on. I'm going to help you get this all straightened out. Preston's going to help, too. Even my friend Trevor is here. And you know Philip."

"Philip's your boyfriend," Danny said agreeably, allowing Joanna to lead him to the door.

"Philip's going to write a story about you and put it on TV. And the story will say that what happened to Sheila was an accident."

"That's right," Danny declared in a firmer voice, now that his secret was out. "It was an accident."

When they heard the lock turn from the inside, all the men in the corridor became instantly alert. Detective Schultz stood on one side of the door, and Trevor stood just behind him.

"We're coming out," Joanna said quietly. "Don't do anything to scare him. We're coming out."

The door slowly opened and Joanna, her gaze sweeping quickly around the hallway, stepped outside holding onto Danny's hand. The detective signaled for his men not to move. He stood in front of Joanna, and her eyes pleaded silently with him. The detective looked at the stocky young white man cowering behind the slender young black woman.

"Hi, Danny. I'm Detective Schultz. It would be really helpful if you could tell us about the accident. Do you think you could do that for me?"

Danny looked at Joanna for guidance. She smiled. "It's okay. Everyone is here to help you."

"Why don't we go back inside and have a talk . . ."

Danny reluctantly did as he was told after Joanna gave him more reassurances. Several of the officers followed.

"Jo?"

Joanna whipped around, her eyes widening at the sight of Trevor. She couldn't move. She couldn't say anything. She just drank in the sight of him in his heavy coat, the khaki shirt and pants visible underneath. Her entire body reacted to Trevor being there, and his presence released all the emotions that had built up in the past twenty-four hours.

Joanna thought she'd never see him again. But the look in his eyes told her at once that the lack of contact had been equally hard for him. His lean face and brown skin was etched with tension, and his jaw was tight.

"You just took ten years off my life," he muttered gruffly.

Then he opened his arms, and Joanna walked right into them.

As soon as the door was closed and locked behind them, Trevor reached for Joanna and pulled her into his arms. His mouth descended to capture hers, and the kiss said everything that words couldn't. The embrace was not frenzied or hurried, but slow and deliberate because it was going to take a long time to appease the hunger and need, and even longer to express the joy. Probably all night. Maybe forever.

Joanna opened her mouth to give Trevor full access. She thoroughly enjoyed the way he'd chosen to express his relief that nothing had happened to her and that they could be together again. She loved the way his large hands pressed her against his body and the way the forward tilt of his hips demonstrated so eloquently his response to her. Nothing had changed. Except that they obviously wanted each other more than ever.

They'd spent nearly three hours at the precinct with Danny and Detective Schultz. He was booked on charges of involuntary manslaughter, but no one believed there would be a conviction. Joanna had promised Danny that Preston was going to find a lawyer to help him and that Mr. Tillman was not going to fire him. Joanna hoped that she would be forgiven for that last line. She had no idea if Mr. Tillman would be sympathetic or not.

And just to make sure that Danny's story would be heard, Joanna had also called her station and asked for a crew to meet them at the precinct. Once again, WDRK would have the first opportunity to report on late developments in the ongoing investigation into the tragic death of Sheila James.

"You'd make one hell of a detective," Detective Schultz had complimented Joanna as she and Trevor were about to leave. "Maybe you should go into law enforcement."

Joanna had accepted the compliment graciously, but declined emphatically. There was only one thing she wanted. And only one person—one man—who could give it to her. The very moment she and Trevor reached her apartment, Joanna knew the long wait was over.

Trevor cupped his hands around her face and slowly withdrew his lips from hers. But his eyes were slumberous with desire and sparkling with something much deeper and more significant than mere passion. Joanna smiled peacefully at him. She'd never been so happy.

"I'm in love with you," Trevor murmured in a gravelly voice.

"You don't have to be afraid to say it," Joanna said softly, hugging him around his waist. She stood on tiptoe to briefly kiss him again. "If it makes you feel any better, I love you, too."

Trevor gave her a whimsical grin as he rubbed his chin and jaw against her soft skin. His mouth brushed slow lazy kisses across her face. "This is crazy. You know that, don't you? We've only known each other a month."

"My father might agree with you, but I don't think so."

He frowned. "Your father?"

She nodded. "I told him how we met, how I feel about you."

Trevor groaned and rested his forehead against hers. "Did you tell him everything?"

She giggled. "No. Not everything."

"So what did he say? How does he feel about me? Is he coming after me with a shotgun?"

"He says he'll reserve judgment until he meets you. I'll take you home on Sunday for dinner. That is, if you can stay."

Trevor shook his head and chuckled silently. He gazed lovingly into Joanna's dark eyes and let his hand gently stroke her face. "Home . . . I guess I'd better if I'm going to do this the right way."

"It's not my father you have to be afraid of. It's my brother."

He raised his brows and his frown deepened. "I didn't even know you had a brother."

Joanna touched her fingertips to his mouth. "All we

need to know for now is that we love each other. Everything else will come in time."

He kissed her fingers. "What happens now?"

"I hope you're going to take me to bed and make love to me," she whispered.

Trevor blinked at her, almost disbelieving. But when he lowered his head to kiss her again, her response told him everything he needed to know.

They left their coats on the living-room sofa and hand in hand headed for Joanna's bedroom. There, they began a tantalizingly slow disrobing. It took a long time because it was punctuated with kissing and touching.

"I've . . . never made love to a man in uniform before," Joanna said somewhat breathlessly as Trevor unbuttoned the khaki shirt and she began on his belt and the zipper of his trousers.

Trevor drew in his breath at Joanna's sudden boldness. Her hands were small and slender. Light and gentle on his skin. The feel was erotic and stimulating, and he wasn't sure if she was fully aware of the effect.

"I thought you'd be put off. Most of the guys I know joined the service to run away from something."

Joanna murmured something sympathetic. She looked warmly at Trevor, shaking her head. She put her arms around his neck and began to plant hot little kisses on his bare chest, where the shirt now hung open. "What about you?"

Trevor groaned as she pressed her body against his. He grabbed her hips and slowly ground himself against her. He wanted Joanna to feel what she was doing to him. "I was trying to save my life . . ."

And as the words left his mouth, Trevor covered Joanna's parted lips with his own. His tongue foraged inside to reclaim her. To stamp himself on her senses so that there was no question that they belonged to one another. He felt Joanna's light touch as her hand trailed down his chest and his stomach. She pushed down the unzippered pants which sat on his hips. And then her hand searched out and found his rigid manhood. She gently stroked and squeezed him.

With a soft grunt, Trevor bent and lifted Joanna from the floor. Their mouths still fused, he carried her to the bed and laid her on the coverlet. Trevor finally released Joanna's mouth and heard her gasp. But he only transferred his attention to her breasts. He gently captured one jutting nipple between his lips and let his tongue flick and torture the stiffened bud. Joanna squirmed beneath him, succeeding in making Trevor even harder. He pressed her into the mattress. Her hands restlessly stroked his shoulders and his neck.

"Trevor . . ." Joanna pleaded, barely able to speak.

He gave his attention to the other breast and felt the way Joanna arched her back and opened her legs. She was ready for him to join them together.

Trevor was enjoying the way Joanna was willingly and wantonly responding to him. But he couldn't last any longer. He put on a condom, and with a deep sigh of supreme satisfaction, Trevor settled between her legs and heard Joanna moan. He began to kiss her again, absorbing her sounds of pleasure. He slid his hands beneath her, under her bottom, and held her for his entry. Joanna held her breath.

Joanna had never known anything like this. She felt complete. Full. Needed. Loved. She curled her toes and melted, and let the sensation of floating transport her to a state of euphoria. She held tightly to Trevor and let the magical ride spin them around until she was dizzy. The release, when it came, felt like a hot wave of sunlight had washed over her.

When Trevor finally moved, it was only to lie next to Joanna, satisfied and exhausted. He pulled her into his arms, and she nestled with her head tucked into his shoulder.

"Your family might not approve of me," Trevor suddenly drawled out in a lazy, sated voice.

"Are you trying to back out now that you've had your way with me?" Joanna murmured sleepily.

"God, no. I've had more chances than anyone has a right to expect. But I don't want to lose you, Jo."

"You won't. I love you. So what if it happened last month or last night. It doesn't change anything. I just want us to have a life together."

His hand began to slide slowly and caressingly over Joanna's side and thigh. He massaged a breast, rubbed his thumb back and forth over the already sensitized nipple. He bent to pull a light kiss from her swollen lips. She began to respond, letting Trevor again stimulate and arouse her as his hands freely explored every erogenous inch of her body.

"I'm in the medical corps. I'm thinking of leaving the service and trying for medical school."

"That's . . . wonderful . . ."

He kissed her breast, rolled his body on top of hers. "It could be years before I'm finished."

Joanna groaned and stroked her hands down his back, feeling the taut, contracting muscles in his behind. "I'm . . . in no hurry."

"How do you feel about kids?" he asked, sliding stiffly into her warm body.

Joanna groaned and undulated her hips to meet him. "Two . . . or three . . . would be nice . . ."

But she didn't have the voice to ask Trevor if he would deliver them.

"Oooh," she moaned in delight. Life was good.